PATH
OF THE
RAVEN

RECURRENCE VOL I

DEVON
MANNING

 FriesenPress

One Printers Way
Altona, MB R0G 0B0
Canada

www.friesenpress.com

Map Design by Matt Smithman
Illustrations by Vita Kotova

ISBN
978-1-03-914705-8 (Hardcover)
978-1-03-914704-1 (Paperback)
978-1-03-914706-5 (eBook)

1. FICTION, FANTASY, ACTION & ADVENTURE

Distributed to the trade by The Ingram Book Company

For Tyler, Kayla, Deanna, and Dakota
Without you, there would be no Meridia
Ladies and Gentlemen, roll for initiative

Table of Contents

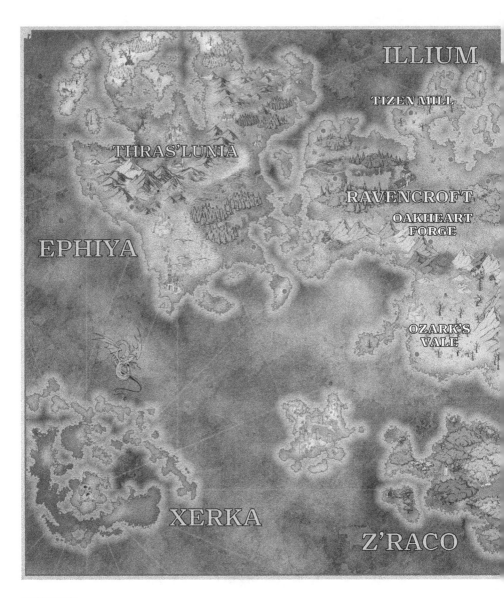

LEGEND

LANDMASSES / COUNTRIES

CAPITAL CITIES

LOCALS OF INTEREST

PROLOGUE

———

It wasn't supposed to be like this, the man thought, looking at a world on fire. His left arm barely worked and the sword it held had dropped long ago, but he raised his mangled hand to his face and touched the chasm where his eye had been. The other eye was full of blood from a wound on his head. He coughed, a red mist spraying out, and he thought that the wet sound in his lungs was *not* a good sign.

"I'm dying," he whispered, looking at the carnage all around him.

His companions were falling left and right, the horde of skeletons and rotting corpses crashing into them in waves. These men who had pledged their allegiance to the cause, were being torn apart like paper cranes. On the horizon, he saw the cause of it all, the madman responsible for this chaos—bathed in a luminous green glow. His magic was the cause of all this destruction.

The man looked down at the shafts of two arrows sticking out of his stomach and let out a groan as another arrow flew through the air and struck him in the chest.

How could we think we were going to win? His thoughts were jumbled, but he pressed forward, swinging the other sword in his right hand in a wide arc, decapitating a skeleton. Two more surged forward to take its place.

We can't win this war, but if we fall, there's no one else to stop him. This is it. He grunted aloud as a corpse jumped onto his back, biting into his neck, and driving him to one knee.

It wasn't supposed to be like this, he thought again, and fell under the weight. As the darkness clouded his vision, his regret surged, but in the blackness he saw a green flash and heard a wondrous sound—many voices layered atop one another, like a choir of angels.

A voice slammed into him like the waves of the ocean. "How was it supposed to be?"

"I wasn't supposed to die like this—we were betrayed! We never got the support we requested. I never got to tell her why I left!" he called into the abyss hopelessly.

"What would you give for another chance?" the voice called out, challenging.

"Anything!" His certainty startled him. After a life full of split decisions, he was surprised at his own venomous intent.

"Then you shall have a chance, my champion."

The green light swallowed him and the wind rushing past his head sounded like the wings of a million birds. He flew into the light and knew no more.

THE SLAVE

CHAPTER 1

THE DRAGONBORN SLAVE

Day 0 – Somulous Experiment: I'm starting this journal for my fellow researchers—in the hopes I can inspire my colleagues with this experiment. As you well know, Xerkans are the master race, mainly due to our intrinsic abilities to reach others' thoughts and feelings. The hypothesis: By depriving myself of sleep, will I be able to enhance this ability, either via the range reached or the level of context? I will update this journal in a week's time. A.G.

Valex rubbed a scaly arm across his horned forehead. Being cold blooded had its advantages, but it was hard not to swelter this far beneath the surface.

For a broodling, Valex cut an imposing figure. He was dragonborn, meaning that somewhere in his heritage was dragonblood, and this caused his physical features to mimic those of his ancient ancestors. Valex had never met either of his parents; his first memories were of being handed a pick and being put to work in the mines of Gallowspire. But at the age of ten, his horns had finally just started to grow in, a fact he was very proud of, and their dull-brown colour accented the brassy tones of his scales nicely. If it hadn't been for the dirty grey singlet he wore every day and the heavy iron manacle around his ankle, he could easily have been mistaken for one of the monsters they sometimes encountered down in the tunnels.

Valex used his powerful talons to crush the remaining slate away, revealing a raw, glistening, blue gemstone. Inspecting the chunk of stone, he felt sure that this piece of rock contained the azurite ore that would guarantee his supper.

Satisfied, he had turned to deliver his good fortune to the depot, when a hand covered in tacky gold rings slammed into the side of his head. Valex crashed to the floor, and before he could process what had happened, the stone was ripped from his grasp.

Looking up above the distended belly of the thief, Valex glared into the face of the mine's overseer, Malek. From the other slaves, he had heard that Malek had once been just like them, chained and broken, but his cruelty and willingness to serve had made him a valuable asset to the shadowy figures who operated the mines.

Malek's greed and pride were evident in his choice of finery, as he opted for garish silk fabrics and obnoxious gold jewellery, as if to mock the other residents of the mine. Although he was almost a head shorter than the much younger slave, Malek's rotund belly made him seem very large indeed. Clasped on his waist was his prize possession, a knife that had been gifted to him by the mine's mysterious owners. Dragonborn had retractable talons they could use to smash through stone, but the scales of a dragon seemed impervious to them whereas this knife had no such trouble. Valex had seen many of his fellow inmates receive grievous wounds from the wicked-looking blade.

"Well, well, what have we here, whelpling? Trying to pocket one of the master's gems?" Malek sneered down his snout at Valex, lying prone in the dirt.

"No," Valex said. "I was just on my way to the depot to..."

Malek ignored him, "Now, why don't I take this over to the depot, and you can return to your post, and we can keep this our little secret. I'm sure if you dig fast, you'll be able to find a gem before the dinner bell rings."

Valex's indignation flared, and the words flew from his mouth before he could think them through. "Listen here, you fat fuck!" ("Fuck" was a word that his friend, the blacksmith Garm, had taught him, and Valex was very fond of "fuck.") "I dug all morning to find that, and it's mine. I've already earned my dinner! Maybe you should try doing the same thing, instead of stealing what isn't yours!"

Malek stared at Valex for a moment and then began to unfurl a long, spiked whip from his belt. His mouth peeled back into an imitation of a smile. "It's clear to me that you'll have to spend a week in solitude to teach you some manners. But I think I'll start your lesson right now. I'm going to enjoy this, you little runt."

Malek's arm cocked back, and Valex had just enough time to bring his arms up over his face before the whip came slashing down. White-hot pain flared through him, and as the whip came down again and again and again, his mind faded into blackness.

A week later, Valex limped into the mess hall and scanned the tables. His eyes had been blackened, but after a moment's search, he spotted who he was looking for. A great, green dragonborn, Garm Selvascale, was waving his massive arms back and forth. With a smile, Valex made his way across the room to him.

Garm was quite a bit older than Valex, and although brass dragonborn made up the bulk of the workforce, dragonborn of other colors we're not unheard of. Garm had told the tale many times of how he had been a travelling blacksmith's apprentice, but bandits had attacked their camp, killing his master and taking him hostage. After a few very disorienting nights, he had wound up here, in the place they called "The Underdark." Fortunately for him, the skills he'd learned from his master had kept him from the back-breaking labour the rest of them endured. Every single anklet manacle in the mine bore Garm's signature, but it was a fact he was bitterly resentful of.

"There he is!" Garm crowed. "How was your stay in Hotel Malek? Did you get the five-star treatment?" Garm too had been subjected to a few bouts of solitary under the cruel taskmaster, and his voice dripped sarcasm.

Valex couldn't help but chuckle. "Very funny, greenbean. But I swear, one day, I'll pay that bastard back ten-fold."

"Well, that day might be much closer than you think, mijo." Garm occasionally peppered his speech with bits of a southern dialect he'd picked up while on the road. "Now, put your hands out, but be smooth about this. I've got something for you."

Casting a furtive glance around the room before he did, Valex did as instructed and felt two iron implements pressed into his palms.

"Now, you're going to hide those in your singlet, and don't get curious and look at them before you're back in your cell," Garm said.

Valex stowed the instruments stealthily, letting them sit just above the narrow strip of cord that was tied at his waist. He shot Garm a quizzical look. "What are they supposed to do, help me mine for them faster?"

"Keep your bleeding voice down, whelp," Garm hissed, casting suspicious glances around. "*These* are the answers to your prayers. I've thought long and hard about this, and I've come to the conclusion that your heart is too good and your temper is too short for you to survive down here long." He stopped to give Valex an appraising look. "What I've given you just now is a chance, nothing more, nothing less. The first tool is a lockpick and should do a fine job of busting the chain on your anklet. The second was a little more tricky to get my hands on, but it's a wizard's focus. I've wrapped a spell scroll around it to break the tracking curse they placed on you when they brought you here. You might not realise it, but if anyone tampers with these manacles, Malek is able to check a special map in his office to see where the disturbance came from."

Valex stared slack jawed at his friend, who wore a smug smile. "Garm, what are you saying?"

"Blazes, whelp, I knew you were born during the day, I just didn't think it was yesterday. I'm saying with those two things, half an ounce of brains, and a fair amount of luck, you're going to get out of this place!" Garm spoke the last bit quietly, as a sentry was walking past their table.

"Garm," Valex stammered. "If you were able to make these things, why are you giving them to me, and not escaping yourself?"

Garm rubbed a talon on the scars that criss-crossed his neck. "I'm not a boy anymore, Valex. They broke me a long time ago and my fate is here, helping kids like you survive. And like I've told you before, I've taken a shine to you, but your temper is liable to get you killed."

"I...I don't know what to say." Valex looked into his lap. "Where will I go? I've never been outside of the mines"

"When you get outside, the vastness of Meridia is going to frighten you, but look to the horizon. This mine is deep beneath the grand city of Gallowspire, but one that won't serve to gain you freedom—too many of Malek's ilk. The exit I'd recommend will lead you out north, onto the face of the mountain. Head straight down the cliffside until you get to the road, then head west. Eventually, you'll see signposts that read, 'Grand Covus.' I've been there before, and our kind isn't persecuted there."

Garm looked up. Most of the other slaves had finished eating and were returning to their cells. "We're out of time. I'd recommend you make your escape tomorrow at first light. Just make sure you break the manacle *before* you use the focus. The curse is tied directly to Malek, so he'll know as soon as it's broken. Once you're unchained, just follow your nose and get free." Garm took a long look at Valex, before continuing in a hushed voice. "I'm going to miss you mijo. Remember what I taught you at the forge; a big fellow like you will have no problem building a new life."

Valex looked up at his friend and was shocked to see tears in his eyes.

"Good luck, Valex. May Leviathan protect you." Garm stood abruptly, grabbed his tray, and left Valex with his thoughts.

Valex returned to his cell, but sleep was the last thing on his mind. Garm's words were running in circles in his head. Escape? Outside? These ideas were almost foreign to him, but he knew that Garm was risking more than a beating and some time in solitary to give him this chance, and he wasn't about to waste it.

After inspecting the items his friend had given him, Valex was confident about the first tool. It was a long, serrated piece of iron, and the end looked similar to the keys Malek let jangle on his enormous belt. But the other item was more confusing. It seemed to be a plain golden rod with runes inscribed on it, wrapped in a piece of parchment, but when Valex clenched it in his fist, he felt a rush of power surge up his arm.

The paper was covered in strange markings, and the only thing Valex could make out was a word in the centre: "Shatter." He figured this must be the command Garm had spoken of and was careful not to say it aloud in his cell. Simple as it was, he tried to run the plan over and over in his head, and as he finally drifted off to sleep, the tools clutched in his hands, he was confident. Tomorrow was the first day of the rest of his life.

Valex looked around one more time. He'd taken great pains to situate himself farther up the tunnels where most of the ore had already been stripped, so he had the passage to himself, but he'd never felt so high strung. He couldn't help jumping every time his shadow flickered against the wall in the torchlight.

Steeling his resolve, Valex pressed the key-shaped tool into his lock, twisted it to the side, and holding his breath, brought his talon down hard on the end. With a snap, he felt the pressure on his ankle ease for the first time. *Okay*, he thought, *one down, one to go.* The parchment in his left hand, he grabbed the golden rod in his right, closed his eyes, and spoke in a whisper: "Shatter."

The parchment erupted into purple light and abruptly went up in flames. Startled, Valex turned to run, but came crashing down to the ground as the chain around his ankle pulled taut. He cursed and looked down at his tangled feet. It looked like the blow with the pick had cracked his manacle, but not freed him completely.

"Shit! Come on! Come on!" Valex scanned the room, looking for where the lockpick had fallen in the commotion, and couldn't see it. From deep within the mine, he heard an alarm begin to bray and the sounds of commotion. He was running out of time. There! Half hidden under a barrel he saw the handle sticking out of the dirt floor. Crawling forward, he grabbed the tool and pressed it into the lock, beginning to work the pins. One... two...then, with a satisfying clunk, the iron bracelet he had worn his entire life dropped to the floor. His relief was short-lived, however, as he heard a greasy voice call out behind him, and his stomach dropped.

"Oh my, who would have thought our escapee was the whelp with the attitude?"

Valex stood stock still and felt Malek's rancid breath puffing onto the back of his neck. Careful to keep his back to Malek, he slid the manacle forward with his foot, obscuring it from view. He kept his voice calm, terrified that any agitation would reveal his plan. "Malek, I wasn't trying to escape. I think there is a problem with my bracelet—can you take a look?"

"Boy, you've gotten yourself into deeper shit than you can imagine. Even the bosses are headed down…"

Quick as a flash, Valex whirled around and snatched the long, curved blade from the sheath of Malek's belt. He gripped the handle with both hands and drew it diagonally across the overseer's face, from jowl to horn. The flesh parted easily and Malek collapsed to the ground and began to shriek. Valex was tempted to revel in his victory, but the sounds coming from farther down the tunnel told him it was time to go.

Malek's words were slurred, obscured by his cut lips. "My face! My beautiful face! I'll get you, boy, if it's the last thing I do! You'll never walk again when I'm through with you!"

Valex dropped the knife and began to run the other direction, following his friend's advice and trusting his nose. Malek's wails followed him as he ran through the tunnel, but he felt no remorse. That animal had gotten what was coming to him.

He ran for what felt like hours, taking lefts and rights as the airflow directed, until he finally saw a bright-red glow ahead of him. Exhausted, Valex put on one more burst of speed and emerged into sunlight, for the first time in his life.

He was standing on a rocky cliffside surrounded by trees. In the distance, a blood-red orb hung over an enormous, blue body of water.

He had never seen anything so spectacular in his life, but the sounds coming out of the tunnel snapped him from his wonder. He hurled himself down the cliff, sliding in the shale, snapping through branches, and not looking back. He was running away, away from the underdark, away from the beaten faces of his kin, and towards a new future. A smile touched his lips as he breathed deeply and thought, *My first breath as a free man.*

After a few tense hours, Valex lost his pursuers and feeling confident, he picked a direction and began to walk. Eventually the sun fell completely, and he was forced to try to rest.

The hunger was the worst part. No, the thirst, or maybe it was how tired he was.

He laid down, alert at first, but the day's excitement had exhausted him, and he fell into a restless doze almost immediately.

He woke at first light, covered in a light dew, and freezing. Taking a look around, he realised he had no clue where he was, let alone where he was heading, and he began to walk in what he hoped was the right direction.

So began the struggle. For once, his bulky frame proved to be problematic. Any game he tried to catch escaped him with ease, and he was forced to scavenge the forest floor. He tried to eat a few fruits and mushrooms he found, but the effect they had on his stomach was awful and he became wary of eating anything else.

Adding to his misery, a storm came in and icy rain pelted him for several days. Valex's spirit was breaking. A part of him almost yearned for the mine. It hadn't been a good life but he'd never felt this cold or this alone, and part of him cursed Garm for giving him this idea.

He didn't know how many days it had been when he took a step, lost his footing, and crashed onto his face on the mossy forest floor. Trying to lift himself up, he found he couldn't muster the energy, and he settled back down as blackness began to creep into his vision.

"I'm sorry, Garm," he said to no one in particular. "Looks like you wasted your chance." He tried valiantly to keep his eyes open and as his consciousness faded, he saw something peculiar.

A pair of curled boots stepped into his view, and a strange voice spoke aloud. "What do we have here?"

The next few days were hard to quantify. Valex remembered snippets of things: looking up at the stars and hearing the heavy breathing of an animal, the smell of a crackling fire, a gentle hand pushing a spoonful of salty broth into his mouth, and a voice reciting strange words by his ear.

Valex opened his eyes in a warm room and felt that he was in his right mind. His first thought was that he must have been taken back to the mine. He rolled to the right and with a *thump*, fell a few feet onto a wooden floor.

From the next room, an elderly voice spoke out. "Ah, my new friend, you're finally awake." At the sound of approaching footsteps, Valex drew his talons and prepared for whatever was going to walk in.

Through a door on the other end of the room walked the last thing Valex had expected. It was a human man with charcoal-colored hair, a neat beard, and an outlandish, purple travelling jacket. He had a pleasant smile on his weathered face. Valex looked him up and down and saw the same curled boots he had seen before he passed out.

"Now, let's see if you can tell me…" Seeing Valex curled into a defensive position, talons bared, the man stopped abruptly. He cleared his throat and continued with his hands up. "Look, you don't know me, son, but I can assure you, you're safe. I've seen your scars, and I'm sure whatever brought you into those woods has you spooked, but you don't have to be afraid. My name is Callum Brightspire. I'm a retired court magician to the King of Grand Covus."

Valex retracted his talons but didn't move from his place on the floor.

"Let's see if you can tell me your name."

Grand Covus? This was the city Garm had mentioned. Valex got to his feet carefully, towering above the smaller man. "The name given to me was Valex," he growled.

"Valex, a fine name, a fine name indeed. Do you have a clan name? Most dragonborn I've met have always introduced themselves that way."

Valex knew of the custom, but the slaves in the mine were broken down, taught to be less than their captors. On a whim, he thought of his friend and the key to his freedom. "Shatterscale. I have no other clanmates, but…" He finished, not sure why he felt the need to explain it to the old man.

"Alright, Valex Shatterscale, it is a pleasure to make your acquaintance," Callum said. Keeping his eyes on Valex, he dropped into a comfortable armchair and gestured for Valex to do the same opposite him.

After a moment's consideration, Valex stepped forward and gingerly eased himself into the chair, which groaned in protest.

"I imagine you must have a million thoughts rushing through your head, but I've been living here alone for some time and I must say, I've been looking forward to the company. I don't know what your plans are, but I'm happy to provide you with room and board for the time being, in exchange for some help with some of the more laborious tasks around this old place. I've gotten a little long in the tooth for such things."

Callum spoke in a way Valex found very charming, even if he didn't understand all the words. He appraised the old man, and after a moment's hesitation made his decision. "I think that would work for me," he said.

Callum reached out a gnarled hand, which Valex looked at, perplexed. With a laugh, Callum grabbed Valex's talon and gave it a brisk shake. "It's a deal then." The old man beamed.

Valex found life with Callum to be very strange. He was never woken by a bucket of cold water being tossed on his head, he was able to relieve himself outside without asking for permission, and Callum never failed to make sure he was fed, whether he had worked hard that day or not.

One day, after helping Callum move a few books into his library, Valex grabbed one of the books and began to flip its pages absently, squinting at the strange symbols held within.

"Would you like to borrow that one? It's quite an interesting tale," Callum said, settling into his armchair.

"Oh, I'm sure it is…It's just…" Valex faltered and looked down, embarrassed.

Callum cocked his head at Valex. "Can't you read, boy?"

"Well…Only a little. They really only taught us a few words here and there in the mines—how to read the signs so we didn't get lost. My friend, Garm, taught me a few…" Valex stopped, his throat burning at the thought of his friend.

"Then that particular volume might be a little difficult, but grab that one there," Callum pointed to a skinny brown volume on the shelf behind Valex, "and we can work on learning the rest."

"Oh, I don't want to be any trouble, you've already done so much for me." Valex replaced the book and began to hurry from the room, but Callum's voice called out from behind him. "Nonsense. If you can't read, it's going to make it very difficult to make you my apprentice. Now, grab that bottle and a glass on your way back." He pointed at a small cart that held several clear bottles of liquid as well as a dusty selection of glassware.

Valex did as instructed, not daring to trust what he had just heard, and claiming the thin brown book from the shelf on his way.

Callum poured an amber liquid from the bottle into a glass, took a deep sniff, and poured the contents into his mouth. He grimaced, then smiled at Valex. "That's the stuff."

"Your…apprentice?" Valex asked, settling into the chair opposite the wizard. "What does that mean?"

"It means, Valex, that before I was an old man in the woods, I used to be one of the most powerful wizards in all of Illium. Retirement suits me—I've done enough for this realm, but it would be a shame if I were to die in these peaceful woods without teaching someone all the mysteries of the world that I've learned. It would be quite a waste, wouldn't it?" Watching Valex closely, Callum swirled the second shot of liquid in his glass. "We'll have to test your potential, of course, but dragonborn almost always have an aptitude for it. What do you say? Might be a more interesting way to pass the time than trimming the hedges or dusting my library."

Valex couldn't believe his good fortune. A month ago, his entire life had been spent believing he was only a tool, a chisel to pry precious stones from the earth, and now there was someone willing to take him under his wing. He was at a loss on how to respond.

"Well, boy? Speak up," Callum said, cutting through his thoughts.

Valex made his choice. "Yes, yes! If you're willing, I'll become your apprentice. I won't let you down!"

"Exceptional." Callum's grin was infectious, and Valex felt his own smile grow on his face.

"Then let's get to it," the old man said. "Open up that book and begin copying down all the letters you recognize, and we'll teach you the rest."

Valex was looking at the drink curiously. "Callum...may I have a glass of that, as well?"

Callum looked startled and then surprised him by laughing out loud. "Yes, you're a big fellow, so one shouldn't hurt. Just be careful you don't end up like me! Whiskey has a tendency to get its talons into you. Also, if you're going to be learning under me, I'd appreciate it if you called me Master Brightspire."

Valex poured himself a glass of the whiskey, taking careful effort to match the amount in Callum's glass, and then he repeated the sniff and sip manoeuvre he had just seen. The sting of the drink made Valex's stomach turn, but he imitated Callum's grimace and smile, and turned to the book.

Ending up like Master Brightspire sounded like a dream come true.

"Alright, boy, just like we practised! Hold the intention in your mind, speak the command word, and allow the mana to flow through you!" Callum had been asked to help a local village, where a tremor had caused a barn to collapse, trapping the animals inside. Always the believer in a practical lesson, he had brought Valex along and lent him his spellbook. Currently, he had summoned a large spectral hand, and was using it to sift through the debris and free the trapped animals.

Valex reread the notes in his master's untidy scrawl for the third time, then clapped the book closed and tried to empty his mind. He focused his intention, felt the magical forces within him, his "mana," as Callum had told him, began to swell and called out, "Mage hand!"

A cloud of blue energy materialised in front of him, taking the shape of a talon very much like his own. When he clenched his fist, the hand in front of him did as well, and he turned to Callum with pride written on his face. "Master! I did it!" he cried triumphantly.

"Great work, Valex, I knew you could. Before you celebrate, though, could you give me a hand?" He smiled at his own pun, but the sweat was beading on his forehead from the effort of moving several beams of timber with his spell.

"Oh, right, right!" Valex focused on a large block of stone, squinted, and moved the hand to pick it up. The strain of lifting it felt different, like a slight headache, and he groaned as he heaved the block of stone into the air. A panicked mooing spilled from the opening and a baby cow stumbled from the wreckage, followed by its mother. They galloped past Valex, and he dropped the load of stone to the side of the entrance, relieved.

The baby cow approached Valex and licked his outstretched palm, before running towards its mother in the field behind the barn. A warm feeling spread through Valex's chest, similar to the whiskey he and Callum shared as a nightly ritual, and he realised it was pride.

If I can do this with magic, what else can I do?

"It's important to remember, my apprentice, that while magic is a tool we use to help people, it can also be used as a powerful weapon. You must be careful in revealing what…Are you listening, Valex?" Callum said, frowning at his pupil.

"What? Oh yes, of course, Master." Valex spoke distantly, studying the shelves along the walls of the library. "I've been meaning to ask, do you have any books about Gallowspire?"

Callum sighed, snapping the book he had been using to teach Valex closed and heading towards his desk, which was covered in loose paper and books. "I figured you would want to know more about it one day, so I took the liberty of tracking down some information for you. Seems the ore that you mined down there was being collected for some cult, the…hold on, I know I wrote it down somewhere." He pushed a stack of books off the desk and retrieved a scrap of parchment. "The Servants of Bahamut."

"What's a Bahamut?" Valex asked, his attention fully reclaimed.

"A dragon—the worst of them all, I'd wager. The stories about him say that his ultimate goal was the subjugation of all 'inferior humanoid races.'" Callum rolled his eyes at this. "His own offspring notwithstanding. I have a few books about it on the fifth shelf, there."

Valex stretched up and grabbed the three books, bringing them to the table at the centre of the library where he opened the first one. He raised his empty glass to Callum, "Could you top me up, please, Master?"

"Boy, I don't know where you put all the whiskey you drink, but I'm going to have to increase our order!" His tone was scolding, but he filled the glass regardless.

"That's fine, Master, take it out of my pay from helping the townsfolk. I really enjoy our ritual." Valex took a seat at one of the library tables, cracked the spine on the first tome and began to work his way through the dusty volumes. Page after page of atrocities this "Bahamut" had committed, all in the name of empowering dragon kind, burned into his mind. The bile rose in his throat. Not only did Bahamut believe that humans, elves, and the rest of humanity were only worthy of subservience, this being believed that dragonborn were half breeds, no better than animals, and his followers held the same belief. In another of the large books, he discovered that the mines under Gallowspire had existed for hundreds of years. The sheer audacity of it startled Valex. Not only had his generation been born into slavery, but the generation before his, and the generation before that. The other unsettling thing he uncovered was that as big as the Underdark was, it appeared there were reports of many more mines across Meridia, with Bahamut and his cult of followers managing every one.

Valex had seen first hand the kindness of the people of Meridia, and he knew that Bahamut was working to extinguish it. For the first time in his life, Valex knew his purpose: he had to find a way to stop this monster from doing as it pleased.

Ten years, master and apprentice worked alongside one another, Valex honing his craft, and Callum giving what knowledge he could to his young progeny. Valex had allowed the subject of Bahamut to fade into the background when he spoke with Callum, but whenever he was given free time, he returned to the same books and allowed his rage to grow.

On a summer afternoon, Valex and Callum were sitting in the library, each reading a book, when Valex posed a question he had been waiting a long time to ask. "Master, is there a weapon, or a spell, powerful enough to kill a god?"

Callum choked on his tea, composed himself, and looked side-eyed at Valex. "So my apprentice learns a little thaumaturgy and suddenly thinks he can bring down the great Alexander?" He chuckled.

Valex had spent some time learning about the pantheon of Gods in society and what they ruled, Alexander being the god of light. "Not Alexander, no. I'm not even sure it's right to call it a god, but…" He studied his book, not daring to meet Callum's eye.

After a moment's pause, Callum slammed his tome shut and left the room. He returned a few moments later with a package, wrapped in brown paper and tied with twine. "My boy, I've been anticipating this day for some time. As wizards, we seek to understand the mysteries of the world and how to bend them to our will. I do not hold all the answers in my tower, try as I might, and the answer to your question will likely be found outside these walls. It's time that you leave this place and seek your answers."

Callum handed the parcel to Valex, who began to unwrap it. Tearing away the paper, he saw a dazzling blue book, bound with gold, and locked with a clasp. "My own spellbook?" he gasped. He had been using a tattered, old hand-me-down of Callum's, and had been saving his silver to eventually purchase his own, but at the rate he spent his coin, that day had seemed very far away.

Undoing the clasp, Valex saw the first few pages were filled with Callum's tidy scrawl, edge to edge filled with the incantations and instructions required to do the magic he'd learned at his master's side. After these, the rest of the book was blank.

"I've taken the liberty of transcribing the stuff you've already learned in the front—the rest is clear for your future research."

With alarm, Valex realised that Callum's voice was cracking, and that he was on the verge of tears.

"Valex, I never told you this, but I had a daughter. She was right around the age you were when I first met you, but she was taken from me, and I retired from the king's court when I realised how bitter and broken I was. I found you in the woods, and it felt like Alexander was giving me another chance—a chance to be a father again. I…I just…" His voice broke, and he felt for the handkerchief he usually kept in his pocket.

Valex grabbed it from the table and handed it over. "Callum, stop," he said, grabbing Callum's hand in both of his. "I feel the same way. I spent my whole life trapped in those mines. My only parents were the whip and the dark, but you showed me kindness when I needed it, and you showed me there was more to life than survival. I'm happy you were the man who could teach me that."

Callum's face broke into a grin and after wiping his eyes, he reached under the table and pulled out a bottle of whiskey. "Enough weeping like old maids, you're going to set out tomorrow, and it's time for a toast!"

"Now you're talking." Valex grinned. Callum was still very fond of the drink, a habit that Valex had absorbed easily, even though he could drink almost four times as much as the man nowadays.

"To the beginning of a legend: The all-powerful, god-killing wizard, Valex Shatterscale. May your name ring throughout Meridia when the people speak of your deeds!" Callum cried out as they brought their glasses together. He grabbed his staff, and shot purple fireworks from the end, lighting up the room.

"I'll settle for enough gold to keep my glass full and a roof over my head for now," Valex said.

"Well," Callum smirked. "I can help with the first part tonight."

Morning came and Valex shouldered his few possessions and set out into the world. The weeks passed, and although he was able to use his talents to scrape by, Valex was no closer to any sort of magical knowledge, let alone learning how to kill a god. Honestly, he was beginning to get discouraged. Where was all the magic in the world?

But on a sunny day, as he walked down the road towards the next small town, where he would hopefully be able to charm an innkeeper into a room and a few ales, he came across a raven, perched high atop a signpost at a fork in the road.

Valex stopped to look at the bird, which appeared to be watching him just as intently. He cocked his head to the side and laughed when the bird did the same. Suddenly, the bird's beak opened up and a gravelly voice rolled out, surprising Valex. "Yes, you'll do. I've been keeping an eye on you, and I believe that I may be able to help solve your god problem. If you follow my raven, it will bring you to a tavern where we may talk in person. I hope to see you soon."

The bird flapped its wings and took flight. Valex watched it rise up before soaring out to the northwest. He tightened the straps on his pack and began to walk in the same direction. It was, after all, the most magical thing he'd seen so far.

THE ORPHAN

CHAPTER 2
THE INVISIBLE ORPHAN

Day 9 – Somulous Experiment: After making it through the week (after many herbal remedies designed to heighten my awareness) I've begun to notice a small uptick in my ability to read my coworkers' feelings. I am very tired, so it might be a placebo effect, but I will endeavour to continue my research. A.G.

Not yet...Not yet...There! The girl, waiting patiently, leaned against the fountain in the middle of the square, with a black cloak pulled up to hide her white-blond hair. She had been standing there for hours, unnaturally still, until the rest of the market had become accustomed to her presence, rendering her almost invisible. Her purpose here today was to wait for her brother, Vincent, to pick a fight with one of the merchants, and an hour later than they had agreed upon, he finally sauntered into the busy square.

She scowled, checked the silver pocket watch she wore chained to her corset one last time, and began to weave her way through the crowd, catlike and silent. She watched as Vincent picked up an expensive-looking necklace and waved the heavyset shopkeeper over. Being careful to keep her presence masked, the girl got close enough to overhear their conversation.

"Well, I've gotta say, bruv," Vincent had perfected the northerner's lazy drawl, "that I'm surprised that such a reputable establishment as this would try to pass off such a flimsy trinket as a pure silver necklace!"

"I assure you, sir!" The shopkeeper's eyes cast about, hoping no one was paying attention to this outburst. "I don't know what you're implying, but this necklace is fine Z'racian silver. I purchased it there myself!"

Vincent closed one eye and appraised the necklace closer. "Well, it sure looks real, but you see these marks here?" he said, as he thrust the piece into the man's face, obscuring his view.

The girl's carefully constructed grimace broke a bit. Vincent wasn't the largest man, but he sure knew how to throw his weight around. Keeping a wary eye out, she began to weave around the stall, stowing baubles and trinkets in the many pouches attached to the criss-crossed belts she wore. The coup-de-grace was coming up soon, and she wanted to make sure she maximised their take.

"Sir, again, I've had these appraised by the king's own jewellers…"

Vincent's tone suddenly became icy, and his hands dropped to clenched fists at his sides. "Are you calling me a liar, guv? He stepped forward so their faces were inches apart and cocked his head. "I've half a mind to report this preposterous behaviour to the King's Guard, or I could just teach you a lesson right here in the mud."

The girl's scowl returned. What was he thinking? She'd barely had enough time to scout the stall and start pilfering, and he was already moving onto the big score. With a sigh, she moved into position behind the shopkeeper, unnoticed, and readied a small blade in her right hand. She nodded at her brother and got ready.

Vincent grabbed a handful of the poor man's shirt and dropped the necklace in the dirt. Faster than the eye could see, the girl used the blade to cleanly sever the tie holding the merchant's coin-purse to his belt, palmed the purse, and sidled past the man. Grabbing the necklace from the ground, she rounded on Vincent. "Now Marcel!" she whined at him in a nasally voice very unlike her own. "You promised that if Father took us to market, you wouldn't cause any ruckus! He's already had to pay the guard off three times this month! Father will be furious!" She turned to the shopkeeper, and pushed her hood back, revealing striking features and a pair of pale grey eyes, like a stormy ocean.

"My good sir," she batted her eyelashes at the flustered man, "I hope my brother has behaved himself, and I believe this beautiful necklace belongs to you!" Delicately, she took the man's hand in her own and pressed the necklace into his palm, her eyes never leaving his.

"I…well, it's fine, madam. Your brother was just voicing his concern about my craftsmanship." You could almost see the smoke coming out of his ears, as he tried to recompose himself in front of this new woman.

"Marcel!!" She rounded on Vincent and hit him in the arm several times. "You buffoon! You wouldn't know craftsmanship if it slapped you in the face!" Turning back to the shopkeeper, she ran a hand across her brow. "I would like to buy the necklace, to apologise for all the trouble caused." She looked at him demurely. "How much would you charge for such a beautiful thing?"

"For you?" The shopkeeper blushed crimson, his focus so intense that he didn't see Vincent roll his eyes. "Normally, I'd charge fifteen, maybe twenty silver pieces…but I think it belongs around your neck. I'll let you take it for five silvers." "Oh, but sir, I couldn't," she protested. "It's worth so much more!"

"I insist. Here, turn around and I'll clasp it on for you."

The girl turned, lifting the braid from her neck as the man stepped forward to secure the clasp. Vincent looked at her, blocking the man's view, and silently mimicked the shopkeeper's words. She shot him a look that could have frozen the fountain in the square, and he settled down with a sigh.

"Why, I feel like a princess!" She pulled the shopkeeper's grimy coin purse from her belt and counted out six silver pieces. "Five for the necklace, and one for you for being so sweet. Thank you, Father will be so excited about my first deal at the market! Come now Marcel, we shouldn't keep him waiting!" Pulling Vincent by the arm, she vanished into the crowded streets.

The shopkeeper shook his head, rubbed his hand along his stubble, and turned back to his stall. "Nobles, always so strange." He reached for the purse on his belt to deposit the girl's coins and fumbled at the empty air. "What the bloody hell?! I've been robbed!"

Vincent and the girl navigated the crowded alleys with ease, twisting and turning their way through the city's underbelly until they finally arrived at their hideout in the aptly named "Hawker's Alley."

"Vel, why did you buy the necklace? We could have just beaten him and…"

She whirled around, grabbed Vincent by the shirt, and pushed him against the wall, cutting off his words. "Listen Vince, you were sloppy today. You were an hour late, you rushed the whole job, and worst of all you called attention to us. We won't be able to hit that market again. You also forced me to rush the job, so I wasn't able to get nearly as much product as I could have."

"Oh alright. I'm sorry Vel," he whined.

She hated the sarcastic tone she heard in his voice.

"I was just having a few drinks with Balthazar's boys—now I know you don't like them, but the jobs they were telling me about could be our big ticket!"

Vel's expression darkened at the mention of Balthazar, but she released her brother and took a second to compose herself.

"Vincent, what big ticket? I thought the bank heist was our big ticket, but that money's been spent. The kidnapping scheme was the big ticket, wasn't it? But you let yourself get talked into buying a magic set of armour—what an investment! Only it was a regular piece of armour, and the vendor was gone the next morning. I keep trying to get us out of this horrible place, and you keep bringing us right back here, pissing our savings away on booze and get-rich quick schemes!" She panted, out of breath from the outburst.

"I know you don't understand it, Vel. We've just had some really bad luck lately. But the Scarlet Immortals could be the answer to all our problems. You've seen them around town; they live like kings!"

"You need to remember our promise. I owe you a lot—you've taken care of me for a long time, but the reason the Immortals live like kings is because they are contract killers. That's the line we can't cross." She crossed her arms across her chest. "Promise me. I mean it."

"Yeah…yeah, okay. Look, ease up a little bit will you? We got away with the grift today, we must have gotten, what, fifty gold pieces worth of stuff? Let's get a couple ales and celebrate." Vincent put on a large grin and held out his arms wide.

"More like twenty-five after we put it all through our fence." She tried to stay stern, but it was impossible to stay mad at him. "Come on, let's go. First rounds on me."

"That's the ticket! How about the first two rounds?" He threw an arm around her, and they made their way to the local haunt, The Castle and Rose.

In the early hours of the morning, Vel Valdove carried her very drunk brother through the dark streets, back to their hideout. She dumped him on the straw mat that served as his bedding, and looking down at his snoring face, felt her heart surge with affection.

They were not actually brother and sister, but he was the only person she had known her entire life. The first memory she had was of lying on the ground in a ball, as punches and kicks rained down on her. She was crying but she heard the sound of several shouts and blows, and when she dared to open her eyes, she saw a boy not much older than her with blood on his face and on his knuckles.

"That'll teach you assholes!" the boy shouted, shaking a fist at the fleeing attackers. "It's a lot harder when you're not fighting a little girl three on one!" He looked down at the fragile form of Vel, shook his head, cleared his throat, and spat a glob of blood into the dirt.

Wiping his hand across his mouth grimly, he crouched down beside her, and cocked his head. "You okay? Those guys have always annoyed me, chasing after dogs with rocks and beating up little kids… but I've got things to do, so you're on your own now. Good luck, kid!" Getting to his feet, he walked into a nearby alley, but after ten or so steps he stopped, and the little blond girl crashed into his back.

He turned around and looked at her, annoyed. "What did I say? Shoo! It's hard enough to look after myself, let alone some shrimpy girl. Where are your parents? Where do you live?"

Silent, she shook her head, and he realised that she must be an orphan just like him. Exasperated, he grabbed both sides of her head and looked her in the eyes. "What are you, deaf?"

Without taking her eyes off him, she shook her head again.

He shook his own head, realising he had made a real mess here. "Do you have a name at least?"

"...Vel," she said.

Her voice was barely a whisper, but he figured anything was better than the silence. He put his hands on his hips, surveying her. "Well, if you're going to run with me, you'll have to join my gang. My name is Vincent Valdove, so you'll be Vel Valdove, okay?" He spoke with the air of a king, and he saw Vel's eyes dazzle with delight.

"Valdove. So, you're my new brother?" She pulled the protesting boy into a hug.

"No, no! Now I didn't say anything about being your brother, you're just joining my gang!"

Vel stuck to him like a shadow, and after a while he noticed something peculiar about her. Every so often, she would seem to disappear, and Vincent would look everywhere for her. Once he realised he wasn't going to be able to find her, he called her name and she appeared at his elbow, scaring him to death.

He quickly learned how to make this talent profitable. He had always been an adequate fighter, but that was a hard way to make a living, unless you entered the fighting pits. But, if he could cause a ruckus, Vel could slip in and rob everyone blind, and then disappear before anyone knew what had happened. They made one hell of a team.

Vel smiled at the memory, but it quickly soured the longer she thought about it. They had done very well for a couple of street kids and had actually earned respect in the slums for their work, but a long time ago Vincent had told her that his dream was to make enough money to escape the life. He wanted to get a little piece of land outside the city, raise some animals, and relax. Vel loved the idea, she knew that as tough as Vincent acted, his heart was too big for this way of living.

But every time they pulled off a job, instead of being happy, or setting the money aside, Vincent would get moody and upset, complaining about how their talents were so much more valuable than the "tiny jobs," as he liked to call them, could pay. Often, he would take their entire score from a job, only to get swindled out of it by a con artist, and then the cycle would repeat, but of course, it was never *his* fault. The ideas were perfect, or the swindlers promised to return in a few weeks with triple the original investment, and he believed them every time.

Vel always tried to talk sense into him, but Vincent had big dreams and refused to see sense. Plus, she really did feel that she owed him her life, so she had to keep trying to help him achieve his dreams, even if he was the one keeping them from coming true.

The only thing she'd stood her ground on was they could do whatever it took to get the money they needed, except for on the contract hits from the Scarlet Immortals, the biggest gang in Grand Covus. Every time she thought about these lucrative offers, her chest froze up and she felt like she couldn't breathe. She imagined it must have something to do with the past she couldn't remember, but she'd rationalised it to her brother that they were world-class thieves, not some common killers.

Listening to the sounds of his snores across the room, Vel frowned. Lately, something had been different with Vincent. They used to stay up all night, talking about their dreams—about what they were going to buy first when they were free of Grand Covus and its endless streets full of violence and mayhem. Recently, though, he had been going out at all hours of the night, and when they were alone he was surly and withdrawn. She knew he had been spending more and more time at Balthazar Greenjaw's bar, The River's Mouth.

Balthazar was a local legend in the Alley. An enormous, half-crocodile lizardman, he ruled the Scarlet Immortals with an iron claw, and if rumours were to be believed, routinely ate the victims of his gang's cruel acts while they were still breathing. The River's Mouth served as a haven to the worst of the worst, and Vel took great pains to avoid it.

Oh well, she thought, *he must just have a lot on his mind. I'm sure he will tell me when he is good and ready.* She took off her cloak and hung it from a dagger that had been plunged into the rotten wood by the door.

Vel was, by conventional standards, an incredibly beautiful woman. At twenty-five, her trim build gave her a striking figure, but years on the street and meticulous training had coiled her frame with muscle, making her more like a cobra ready to strike than a lady. Her white-blond hair was the same as it had been all those years ago when she'd met Vincent, and she wore it in a tight set of braids, because when she wore it down, it was much too easy to identify her.

But she was home and safe, so she pulled out a few pins and her waist-length hair came tumbling down her back. She placed her hands on her lower back and stretched, grimacing at the cracking noise, and decided to check on Vincent one more time before going to bed. It would not do to have him choke on his vomit in the middle of the night. Besides, he really shouldn't sleep in his jacket and boots.

Reaching down, she had begun to pull his arms out of his sleeves, when a flash of colour on his bedside table caught her eye. Inspecting this, she saw a small red paper poking out of Vincent's personal lockbox. She didn't like the look of that. A red envelope in this city meant one thing. Money had changed hands, and someone had been scheduled to die.

"Damn it. Well now I know why you've been so squirrely lately." She sighed, looking at her brother. "Let's see what kind of trouble you've gotten us into this time. Maybe I can talk to the Immortals, get you off the hook."

She didn't like to disturb his privacy, but the envelope demanded an explanation that wouldn't wait for the dawn. She unclipped a set of tools from her belt and with very little effort, popped the small clasp holding the box shut. The contents were a little pitiful: bits of parchment with IOUs scribbled on them and a straw doll Vel had made him many years ago, an earring that belonged to an old flame, but at the centre of it all, as if mocking her, was a crimson envelope, emblazoned with the wax seal of Balthazar himself.

"Let's see who pissed off the 'crocodile king' enough for him to call a personal hit." She pulled the blade from its sheath and severed the wax seal. Unfolding the single paper, she began to read. "This contract is between Balthazar Greenjaw and Vincent Valdove. Payment shall be 5000 gold pieces." She let out a low whistle. Even for the Immortals this was a high ticket. "For the successful elimination of…"

Her breath caught in her throat and the world spun around her, as her vision started to blacken. She had to remind herself to breathe, but once she had herself under control, she tied her hair back, opened her own lockbox, and removed the contents. Throwing her coat over her shoulder, she took one last look at Vincent through her tear-filled eyes and left into the night.

The paper dropped to the floor beside Vincent, visible in the candlelight. The last line read, "For the successful elimination of Vel Valdove"

She took the routes she knew, and eventually found herself at the walls of the great city, on a deserted side street. Sitting against the wall, she made sure there was no one around to see, let loose the tears that had been threatening to appear the entire run over. Sobs shook her body, but she was still careful to stay quiet, not wanting to alert anyone to her presence.

The man who had saved her life, who had helped her grow into the weapon that she had become, had been designated to be her executioner. The ache in her heart felt like the blow of a hammer, but as the tears began to slow the ache was replaced with a pulsing rage. She didn't know why Balthazar had put out the contract, but he had known that Vincent wouldn't be able to say no to such a sum. Even after this revelation, she was saddened to find it did nothing to quell the feelings she had for her brother. Looking at the moon beginning to fade in the breaking of the morning, she made a vow. She would do whatever it took to find the money to free him from whatever this was and get him to his farm—or die trying.

After a few weeks, Vel was starting to get annoyed. It was definitely harder to make the kind of money she was used to outside the city. She had even been forced to resort to taking small jobs a few times, just to be able to afford a room at the inn. Sitting by her window, separating her money, she looked out into the night and saw a strange shape soaring through the night sky. Vel had spectacular eyesight, but with the lack of any sort of light out here, it was impossible to make out exactly what it was. A bat? No, it was much too large to be a bat, she thought, but what else would be flying around in the middle of the night?

But to her surprise the shape got closer and closer, until it landed on the windowsill beside her, startling her to her feet. She observed it warily as the beak opened up and a deep voice filled the room.

"I've seen you hustling in the small towns around here, working when you could, and stealing when you couldn't." The voice was unfamiliar, but Vel's eyes narrowed. She didn't like being observed, let alone by some strange bird. "But, I believe my enterprise could make use of your skill set, and I can promise you it won't require anything untoward. If you're interested in making more than a few copper pieces off some bumbling villagers, follow this raven. It will bring you to a place where we can talk."

The bird's beak closed, and it took wing without warning. Vel considered a moment, dropped from the second-story window landing nimbly on her feet, and took off at a trot to the west. She had never been much for honest work, anyway.

THE SAGE

CHAPTER 3
THE RELUCTANT SAGE

Day 45 – Somulous Experiment: I was forced to turn to more drastic drugs and chemicals in order to maintain my state of awareness. It's been quite difficult, but I'm a hundred percent certain that my abilities have increased in range and power. If I really concentrate, I can hear the thoughts in my department head's mind. I'm almost giddy with the potential of the experiment. A.G.

"Excellent work today Kaylessa." The red-headed elf applauded her student. "Your progress is impressive. In a few more years, you'll be ready to take my place!"

The pretty young elf smiled up at her mentor, Sariel, grateful for the praise. Sariel was the current Sage of Thras'lunia, the Elvish capital of Meridia, an impressive two tiered city. The magical dome that obscured the city from prying eyes was supported by an enormous oak tree, which Kaylessa's master had been blessed with the ability to communicate with. Blessed, as Kaylessa supposed she was, because every few centuries, an elf would be born with a connection to the great tree, and the tradition that their society followed was that before retiring, the previous sage would bestow the lessons required to commune onto the pupil.

As she sat through her lesson, Kaylessa began to stare out the open windows towards the gardens that surrounded Sariel's chambers, and her mind started to wander.

Kaylessa Siannodel was young by elvish standards, only a century and a half old, but she was loath to admit it. No one took her seriously when they found out how old she actually was. She had wide, sky-blue eyes that overflowed with kindness; her long, blond hair was held in braids above her pointed ears; and she was currently dressed in the purple ceremonial robes required for her lessons with Sariel.

Fortunately for her, she had been born into one of the twelve royal families that made up the city council. Long ago, the elves had turned away from monarchism in favour of a democracy, and thus the noble caste had been created. Kaylessa had never understood the need for the divide between the nobles and the common folk, something her parents told her she would understand when she was older.

But within the system was another component, that of the sage. Because the great tree was of immense importance to the city, the sage's ability was valued as highly as that of the council, and the Sage's influence could outweigh even the council's decision, if the tree believed that such a decision could threaten the city and its inhabitants.

When she was born, Kaylessa's aptitude was tested with all of the other children, and she had been found to possess the same magical signature of her mentor, much to the delight of her parents and the chagrin of her brothers. Almost from birth, she had been swept into special classes—lessons in the bardic arts to control her gifts, diplomacy and etiquette courses to prepare for relationships with other cities, and countless others, but while she was good at what she did, her heart yearned for a different life.

When her parents had insisted on language classes, Kaylessa had demanded archery lessons. They pushed her to read long, boring books about the city's relations with its neighbours, but as soon as they turned a blind eye, she would escape into the forest groves, running barefoot in the moss that surrounded the babbling brooks. Still, her position had its benefits. She was expected to spend long periods in isolation, contemplating the seriousness of the tasks that were to befall her. Often, she took this opportunity to put on a disguise and sneak through a break in the wall of the noble quarter to meet up with her commoner friends. Elves could live for centuries, and at only 150 years of age, Kaylessa was scarcely more than a teenager in Thras'Lunia society, and she found the other highborn elves her age to be quite boorish. The commoners in the city had a flair for life that the upper class seemed to lack.

In fact, this was what she had in mind for today. Another night of quiet contemplation was scheduled in the calendar that her parents had hung in their quarters, which meant she could finally slip down to the market and see her best friends, Rhagel and Falora. In the slums, they knew her by the name "Gilly," and they all would meet up frequently to play dice, or to practice shooting arrows down in the war quarter.

Her friends had no idea who she really was, and they could never find out. The nobles of Thras'lunia were forbidden from engaging with commoners, but Kaylessa had realised if she stayed here, she would have gone mad a long time ago. She was sick of the way everyone treated her, like some kind of fragile princess, and when she donned the cheap woollen clothes she kept hidden deep under the loose floorboard in her room, she was treated like the normal girl she yearned to be.

"Kaylessa, are you there? Hello?"

With a start, she realised that Sariel had cleared the blackboard in front of them, and was looking at her expectantly.

"Oh, sorry Sariel, I thought I heard the voice of the tree, and was straining to make out its words." This was a lie, but a small one. She often heard the voice of the tree intermingled with her thoughts, and Sariel had told her that was a large step towards taking her rightful place.

Sariel just smiled and closed the book in front of her. She looked out the window at the sunlight illuminating the garden and returned her gaze to Sariel. "I know the look of a girl who has had enough of her studies for one day. Why don't we call it early today? You can go spend some time with Erohir and Lucian before you head to your quarters."

Kaylessa nodded, but in her head she scoffed. Erohir was alright—he was only a few years older than her, but he was a bit of an oddball. Small, even for an elf, he had untidy brown hair and a very plain face. He'd never had many friends growing up, and he often resorted to spending his free time with Kaylessa, a fact that she hadn't minded when she was a little girl, but lately she'd found very tiring.

Lucian was another story. He was tall and had straight, black hair that he was very particular about styling *just right*. His lithe build was a result of his training in swordsmanship from the Royal Guard, a fact that Kaylessa had always been furious about. He was a century Kaylessa's senior, a fact he never failed to bring up around her, but he was a *man*, so he had been able to indulge in all of the rough and tumble activities she would have liked to be doing. Their relationship was tense at best, but she had known a long time ago that her brother was bitterly jealous of her future. As the eldest son of her parents, he had been set up to inherit their seat on the council and all the power that came with it, but as soon as Kaylessa had been born, everyone's attention, her parent's included, had shifted to her.

Lucian's ambition was very clear to Kaylessa, it flowed off him in waves whenever he was around, so she tended to avoid him. She didn't know how no one else could see it, but it was clear to her basically counting the days until their parents passed to the boughs of the great tree, a fact she found deplorable. As for his jealousy, she ignored it as best she could. She had never been interested in the pomp and circumstance of her new position.

With a start, she realised that Sariel had left the room while she was wool-gathering, and she kicked herself a little. Sariel was an amazing teacher, and she had learned much under her tutelage, but Kaylessa could tell she was getting frustrated with her indifference. It wasn't that Kaylessa didn't want to be the sage, because when she picked up her harp and sang the ancient songs, she felt the power that flowed from the tree into her, and she felt how right it was. She just believed, honestly, that she deserved to live her own life before she was conscripted into this one that had been chosen for her.

After she had gathered her things, she sped through the garden towards the Siannodel manor. Even if Sariel had given her more time than she thought, that just meant she would be able to surprise her friends and already be down at the range, firing shots before they arrived. Her head was already there, and in her daydream she didn't realise Erohir had been calling to her until she physically ran into him on the stairs leading up to their front door.

"Kaylessa! I was waving at you and you never noticed! Did Sariel let you finish up early today?" His eager brown eyes hinted at another afternoon of tailing her, and that wouldn't do today.

"She did, yes." Kaylessa sidestepped him, heading towards the door. "But I'm afraid that I've got plans tonight. Gilly will be seeing her friends."

Erohir was the only one who knew about her double life. She hadn't meant to tell anyone, but she had been so excited about making her new friends the realisation hit her that if she didn't tell someone, she was going to burst. Erohir was harmless enough anyway—no one paid him any mind.

"Oh. No, that's okay, I'm sure you'll have fun. I was going to invite you down to the river, but maybe tomorrow?" The hope in his voice vanished, and his crestfallen expression made Kaylessa feel like a bad sister, so she turned and sat on the step, slinging her arm around him.

"You know what, I've got the morning free tomorrow. Why don't we get some of Father's gear and go fishing early tomorrow? I'll take you to one of my secret spots, and we'll catch something so big, Mother can use it for dinner," she said.

"You mean it?" He lit up like a lantern, a big dopey grin spreading across his face. "Yeah, that sounds great!"

She patted him on the head and opened the front door. Cocking her head to the side, she could only hear the sounds of her father's laboured breathing from the room upstairs. The more she listened, the more worried she felt. Her father and mother had gotten very sick recently. Her mother was in better shape than her father and had returned to her duties on the council, but her father had recently taken a turn for the worse. Every day, he seemed to be weaker and weaker. The healers had been round to see him and had been baffled. All their usual tests, tonics, and tinctures had done nothing to ease the illness. They believed he would recover on his own, as elves rarely died from disease, but the sounds coming from upstairs had Kaylessa believing otherwise.

Fortunately, she didn't see Lucian's boots or his audacious purple cloak, meaning that he was out of the house. This was a relief, as she didn't feel up to answering any of his snide questions about her lessons, which he mockingly called "playtime." She didn't know exactly when things had gotten so bad between the two of them, but she spent most of her time avoiding the house just to keep from running into him. He'd been especially sharp and cruel lately, but she didn't have time to worry about him.

Kaylessa climbed the stairs and looked in on her father, her heart sinking. Once a strong man, full of life and humor, he had been reduced to a husk of his former self, barely filling out the blanket that covered him. Afraid to disturb him, she began to close the door quietly, until he called out to her, "Kaylessa, is that you?"

"Yes Father, I'm here." She rushed into the room as he began to cough, the sound deep in his lungs. Grabbing a pitcher of water from the table beside the bed, she poured him a glass, holding it to his mouth.

He managed a few sips before pushing it away and looked up at her with bloodshot eyes. "I hope you know exactly how proud of you your mother and I are. To think, our sweet tomboy daughter, chosen to be the great sage and lead her people! Are your lessons coming along?"

"Yes Father, I've been very diligent. Sariel even complimented me on my Dwarvish pronunciation today. She seems to think I'll be ready for the ceremony sooner than we thought."

"That's great news, my love." His eyes began to droop, and she knew that he was going to fall asleep again. The illness had robbed him of almost everything, and it broke her heart to sit by his bedside like this. "Make sure you take care of Erohir and Lucian, you know how they can be…" He trailed off on the last words and fell asleep.

Kaylessa wiped her eyes, and vacated her parents' room, the weight of her father's words hanging over her. But she had other plans today.

She dashed into her room, hanging the sign on the door, ("Contemplation and silence lead to solace") and locking the door. Shedding her ceremonial gown, she donned her brown linen slacks and white cotton shirt, sliding suspenders onto her shoulders to hold the slacks up. Fishing around in the hiding spot, she found the battered tan hat she wore to cover her hair and began to climb out the window.

She was halfway out when she looked at her hands and groaned. All of her rings were still on, including her Siannodel signet, which would have made her stick out like a sore thumb in the slums. She pulled the jewellery off and with a quick look up and down the street, scrambled down the side of the house. Cutting through a nearby alley, she found the spot she used to make her way from the Noble Quarter into the Winemakers' Terrace, fifty feet down the wall in the Commoners' Section. The ivy here was thick and strong, and it made an ideal ladder. After making sure all was quiet down below, she scaled the wall and made her way over to the meeting place with her friends.

The sun was beginning to set on the horizon, and she would soon see a beautiful harvest moon in the sky. The colours of the evening had taken the usually bustling terrace and turned it into the orange hues of fall, and the stillness had rendered it into a painting. With a smile, she knew tonight was going to be a good one. Heading down the street, she whistled a pretty song she'd learned in her lessons and wondered if Rhagel had finally gotten the new set of dice he'd been talking about for weeks.

Hours later, in the dead of night, Kaylessa climbed the lattice on the side of her home. It had turned out to be a bit of a boring evening. Rhagel hadn't managed to get his dice after all, so they'd resorted to playing stick and hoop with some of the neighbourhood kids and had all taken turns shooting Kaylessa's bow. Rhagel couldn't shoot worth a damn, and Falora had managed to hit the target a few times, but neither of them could hold a candle to Kaylessa. She'd almost managed to split one of her own arrows, after shooting a bullseye.

Once it had gotten dark enough, she'd left her friends and headed back to "Gilly's House", over in the Winemakers' Terrace. Only once she'd cleared sight of her friends, she scrambled up the wall quickly, afraid that she'd stayed out too late and had been missed. She climbed through her open window into her dark bedroom and was quietly closing the latch when she heard the sound of someone clearing their throat behind her. Whirling in surprise, she felt her stomach drop when her brother Lucian lit the lamp and revealed he was sitting in an armchair across the room.

"Lucian! I was just...you see..." She scrambled to find an excuse for her behaviour, as if climbing through her window in the middle of the night was a perfectly normal thing to do.

"Sister, what you do with your evenings has little interest to me." His nasally voice sounded perpetually bored, but she heard the contempt dripping off every word. "But I've been waiting here for an hour with some very grave news. At sunset today, our parents succumbed to their illness. Father passed first, and once Mother heard the news, she collapsed and was pronounced dead immediately. As of today, I am the inheritor of the Siannodel mantle."

Her stomach had turned to ice, and for a moment she was sure her brother must be lying to her, or playing a joke, but regardless of how he acted, she didn't believe he was cruel enough to lie about this.

"It would appear our all-powerful sage doesn't know everything." Lucian's face was a mask, but Kaylessa could have sworn there was the curl of a smile on his lips. "I'm told their passing was very painful, I'm sorry to say."

You sure don't look sorry, Kaylessa thought. *You look like you just got told you're getting two name-days this year.* But she composed herself and, holding back the tears that threatened to pour, looked her brother in the eyes.

"As the patriarch of the Siannodel family, I will have to sit down with you and Erohir tomorrow to discuss what this means for us. I suggest you get some sleep, tomorrow will be a very busy day, indeed." He turned on his heel, and with a flourish of his cape, he left the room like some monstrous bat.

Kaylessa wandered through the empty manor, towards her parent's bedroom, and stopped at the door to Erohir's room. She raised her hand to knock but faltered and let the closed fist hang. What could she say to him? Lucian had to have been as cold and unfeeling when he explained it to the boy, and Erohir was much more sensitive than she was. She pressed her ear to the door, and heard soft, broken sounding weeping. With a gentle knock, she entered her younger brother's room. He was sitting on his bed, the quiet tears running down his face, and she knew that regardless of how much this hurt her, it was hurting him more. She sat beside him, and placed a hand on his back. They sat together in silence for a moment.

"Kaylessa… What are we going to do?" His voice was thick with emotion, and almost too quiet to hear, but Kaylessa was at a loss for words.

"We're going to do what we've always done, we'll stick together," she said, aiming for a warm, sisterly tone.

But Erohir's response was cold. "You're going to be the sage. Lucian's going to be the head. I'll just be nothing."

The levy broke. Kaylessa cleared her throat, excused herself and sprinted to her room, almost colliding with a table in the hall from the tears that threatened to fall. Throwing the door to her room open, she slammed it behind her and she collapsed on her bed, her heart feeling like it was being torn in two. The tears came, and she wept for what felt like hours, until the sobs became hoarse, and it felt like she had no more tears to lose. She laid curled up into a ball until sleep took her.

Once the week of mourning had passed, and Lucian had performed the ceremony to take over their family crest, Kaylessa returned to her lessons with Sariel in a daze. Sariel was sympathetic to her trainee but seemed to think the best course of action was to carry on as normally as possible.

Kaylessa's mind kept returning to her conversation with Lucian. He'd said they would discuss the future of the Siannodel family the following morning, but when she and Erohir had descended the stairs, he had already left to attend court. They hadn't seen him at home at all during the day, and at night he went to his room and locked the door. She couldn't help but feel that no matter what he had in mind for her, it couldn't be good.

After a few pointless hours, Sariel let out a sigh, walked to Kaylessa, and pulled her into an embrace. Kaylessa fought against the tears that threatened to pour, she had cried enough this week, but Sariel was petting her hair and she felt the front of her robes begin to get damp.

"Hush now child, you of all people know that your parents have returned to the great tree. They watch over you now, protecting you," Sariel cooed into her hair.

Kaylessa felt a bubble of rage burst in her stomach. She pushed Sariel away from her, and Sariel looked taken aback.

"They haven't returned anywhere! They died, and we buried them in the ground, and now my brothers and I are alone. They left us! They got sick and left, and no stupid tree is going to make that okay!" she shouted.

She saw the naked hurt on her mentor's face, but Kaylessa turned on her heels and ran. She didn't look where she was going, pushing past startled ministers and traders, because she knew if she stopped she would collapse again. It wasn't Sariel's fault that her parents had died, but Kaylessa had never felt so hopeless and she didn't know how to contain the fire in her heart.

Suddenly, she knew what she had to do. Her friends, Rhagel and Falora, hadn't seen her since she had found out about her parents, and she craved their company like oxygen. Pulled from her trance, she turned on a dime to head towards her house, but she stumbled to the floor as Lucian side-stepped her.

"Kaylessa, I see that you're skipping out on your lessons. I should really teach you a lesson about responsibility, but perhaps this is for the best." He looked down on her with contempt, making no offer to help her to her feet.

For the best? Kaylessa thought, as she got up and dusted herself off, offering the traditional bow one gave to the family head. Just what was *that* supposed to mean?

"It's become clear to me that this 'Sage' nonsense has become problematic for you. You have neglected your studies constantly, and I believe that we've found another girl with the aptitude to take your place. I've spent the last few days reviewing our laws, to see how I could help you be free of this burden," Lucian said.

"I'm sorry Lucian, I think you're mistaken. I've every intention of becoming the Sage, and..."

"Silence, girl, your senior is talking. As I was saying, the laws are quite clear, and I've made the decision for you. If you are to wed before your 200th name day, you are considered to be unfit to become the Sage, and

I've had a few meetings with Osiyah Tremplain." At this, Lucian actually did smile, seeing the look of shock on his sister's face. "I can see you know where I'm going with this. You know Osiyah's wife died last year, and he has been searching for a pretty young bride. When I explained your situation, he offered us a sizable dowry for your hand, which I've graciously accepted on your behalf."

Kaylessa was stunned into silence, but revulsion began to turn her insides. Osiyah Tremplain, one of the heads of the noble families, had to be at least twelve hundred years old. He was grotesquely overweight, which was uncommon for elves, and seeing his heavy frame being supported by four of his nephews in an ostentatious sedan chair headed towards the winemaker's terrace early in the day was not an uncommon sight.

As the panic threatened to overwhelm her, her need to see her friends tripled. Without acknowledging what Lucian had said, she pushed past him and ran down the street towards their home, Lucian's cold laughter following her.

Once she had run out of sight, Lucian snapped his fingers, and a shadowy figure emerged from the hedges to his right. The figure knelt down and made a salute, and Lucian turned to address him. "I figured as much. The stupid girl has much to learn if she thinks that I'm going to let our family name be soiled by her activities. I want you to tail her and stay hidden until she meets up with her grimy little urchin friends. Once you've got a nice crowd, make a scene and bring her home. Maybe even have them all arrested—that would double as a good laugh and a reminder that she is a Siannodel, not some common street trash."

"At once, my lord." The figure vanished as quickly as he had come and Lucian walked towards the royal gardens.

Once she had returned to her room and locked the door, Kaylessa began to pack a leather travelling bag with her prized possessions and as many articles of clothing she could fit. She grabbed her harp, the journal she used in her lessons with Sariel, and she shouldered the shortbow her father had made for her, and slipped her Siannodel crest ring into her pocket. With one last look at the bedroom she had slept in for her entire life, she climbed out the window and down into the street.

Escape was the only option. The laws in Thras'lunia were clear; the head of the family had the right to decide the fate of its members, a law that her father had often laughed at openly. He had always believed that if Lucian, Erohir, or Kaylessa wished to be married, they would make it so and they didn't need him to hurry it along. That had been true, but she realised now that Lucian was not content to let her continue on her path towards a position of equal, if not greater, power.

She would have to find her friends and stay with them for the time being. She wouldn't have to explain everything, and she could buy herself some time to think. Plus, she needed their support right now. Just yesterday it seemed like she was living in a dream, and in the snap of her brother's spindly fingers, it had morphed into a nightmare.

She bolted through the Winemakers' Terrace, knowing that her friends would likely be at their usual place in the Traders' Market, and so she was unaware of the hooded man who was tailing her at a distance.

She skidded into the crowded square, the sounds of commerce flying around her: vendors hawking cheap jewellery, men smoking entire rounds of mysterious meat and selling it by the slice, dirty children running between the legs of the adults, laughing and grabbing at each other. The sight normally made her happy, as it was nothing like the prim and proper Nobles' Market, but today she only had eyes for two things: Rhagel and Falora.

She finally spotted them, sitting on a low cobblestone wall. Rhagel had a chunk of the meat and was tearing off pieces of it and feeding it to a stray dog beside him, while Falora laughed. Relief blossomed in Kaylessa's heart, and she made her way to her friends.

"Oh, Gilly!" Falora waved at her and saw the expression on her face. "My God, are you okay? You look terrible…"

Kaylessa felt the magic stir around her, even before she heard the command word spoken from right behind her. "*Reveal.*" She was frozen in place, horror-struck, as her carefully crafted disguise vanished, and was replaced with her usual day to day silk fabrics. The rings appeared on her fingers, and her carefully hidden hair cascaded down her back.

"Your Grace," a gruff voice called out behind her, "You know that it is against noble law for one of your lineage to be carousing with such people."

Turning, she saw the man who had trained Lucian in the art of the sword, arms crossed, cloak thrown back to reveal the Siannodel crest emblazoned on his chest. The people of the market took a single look at him and moved to create a wide berth, encircling Kaylessa and her friends.

"These lowborn creatures must have lured you here against your will," he barked out a laugh, and drew his long sword. The magic bestowed upon the City Guard's weapon caused the blade to glow with a purple light, illuminating the courtyard. "I'll have to arrest them for kidnapping, and I'll ensure you are given the proper escort to take you to your home."

Kaylessa turned to look at her friends. It felt like time was suddenly moving very slowly, as she saw the identical looks of horror on the faces of her best friends. Now she realised that she had been both naive and foolish to believe that Lucian wouldn't have found out about them and had been even more so to lead the captain right to them.

It was too late for her, but not too late for her friends. The fury she'd been grappling with since the news of her parents' death came bursting forth, and she whirled to face the captain, nocking an arrow into the shortbow as she turned. "I'm sorry!" she cried over her shoulder, "But you two need to run!"

Without a moment's hesitation, she fired the arrow at the captain, aiming for the soft spot in the shoulder of his armour. It found its mark, and the force knocked him off his feet. Kaylessa knew if she risked a look at her friends her nerve would break, so she bolted towards the Winemakers' Terrace again. She knew it was only a matter of time before her crime was discovered, and with the last of her courage she decided tonight was the night she left Thras'lunia, forever.

Darting towards the hedges that lined the exterior wall, she found the spot she was looking for. A few years back, she had been fooling around with her friends, and had found a spot in the stone wall that was cracked and allowed them to pass through. Her friends had dared her to try to step through, telling her about how the magic barrier would cook her before she could even put a leg through, but her noble upbringing afforded her the knowledge her friends didn't have; the barrier only served to keep outsiders from entering Thras'lunia, but the citizens could leave as they pleased. This information was kept from the commoners who flooded the crowded slums, and Kaylessa knew that crossing this barrier would have given too much away about who she was. So, she had simply let them make their jokes until they moved on, but she had never forgotten the spot in the wall. Finally, it was going to be of use to her, her means of escape.

She squeezed through the crevice and emerged in a dense forest where large trees towered over her. She looked back at where she had come from and saw that the towering tree that supported her city had vanished, replaced by even thicker overgrowth. She knew this was her last chance to say goodbye to the city, but it was too late. She cursed her brother, cursed her fate, and most of all cursed herself. If she had only been smarter, maybe this wouldn't have had to happen.

Faintly, as if underwater, she heard whistles and shouts coming from the direction she had come and was startled from her reprieve. Shouldering her bow again, she took off into the forest, darting left and right at random to throw off any pursuers. She ran for hours, until she could barely see the way in front of her, cloaked entirely in darkness that was only broken by snatches of moonlight breaking through the canopy.

She stopped to catch her breath and all at once the exhaustion hit her. Looking about, she spied a strong-looking elm tree, branches jutting out at all angles, and saw a spot in the crown of the tree that would support her. She scrambled up the tree and made herself as comfortable as she could.

Once again, she wept. This world was so unfair. Yesterday she had attended a lesson, eaten a magnificent dinner, and slept in an unbelievable bed. Today, she had lost her home, lost her friends, killed a man, and was sleeping in a tree. Feeling more lost than ever, aware of every sound in the wood around her, she realized she had never said goodbye to Erohir.

She woke to the sounds of birds singing. As the events of the last week came flooding back, she remembered the promise to her brother to go fishing, a promise that would never be kept. On opening her eyes, she was shocked to see a large, black raven perched on the branch across from her, only a few feet away.

"Mr. Bird, you startled me!" Kaylessa laughed when she had caught her breath. She often spoke to animals, as the Great Tree had told her that they could usually understand elves, even if they couldn't respond.

But to her surprise, the bird's beak opened and an unfamiliar voice flowed out. "It's not every day you find the daughter of a noble asleep in a tree. Are you in danger?"

"I don't think I am now," Kaylessa was sure this was a dream, and pinched herself in an attempt to wake up. It didn't work, and the bird continued to look at her. "But I will be if I don't get myself far away from Thra-these woods." She had almost slipped up and revealed the location of the Elvish capital, but the bird paid her no mind.

It hopped between the branches until it was perched in her lap. "I just may be able to provide help and refuge. If you follow this raven, it will lead you to a place where we'll be able to talk. I'll explain everything when you get here, but time is of the essence if you're to escape unnoticed." The bird's beak clamped shut, and it immediately took flight to the east.

Kaylessa considered her options, which were few and far between. East would take her away from Thras'lunia, and that was probably the most important factor to making her choice. *What could it hurt?* She thought, *I'm already at the worst I've ever been. Nowhere to go but up.*

THE BENEFACTOR

CHAPTER 4
THE DRAWING OF THE THREE

Day 60 – Somulous Experiment: I've maxed out what my body can tolerate for chemical stimulants, and I'm finding it difficult to stay focused. My perception of time has become hazy, and I've lost a few hours each day, but otherwise all results are positive. My ability to read thoughts has become much deeper. I can practically hear my colleagues' jealousy over the support I'm experiencing... but damn them, This is my discovery. A.G.

Twilight was on its last legs, as Valex finally saw the raven begin a slow descent into a sleepy little hamlet called Gilramore, just outside of Ozark's Vale. He was exhausted, as the raven had set a steady pace in its trip from the fork in the road, only stopping for a few hours at night so Valex could sleep. He had frequently lost sight of his guide, and it would double back to squawk at him. Valex couldn't be sure, but he thought the bird might be mocking his need for rest.

But at long last, the bird had turned a lazy spiral and descended towards the earth, and Valex was afforded time to catch his breath. This town looked like dozens of others he had passed through on his journey and just like the ones he had passed through at night. Most of the windows were dark, and he was the only soul on the road. In the distance, where the raven had dipped down, he could faintly make out loud voices, and the muffled sounds of music, which could only mean one thing: a tavern.

Excellent, he thought, *I've had to stay moving just to keep up for so long, that I haven't been able to stop for a drink these last few days.* He pushed his dry tongue around his mouth and realised *just* how thirsty he really was. Each morning, he had woken up with tremors and nausea, but he was sure this was because of how hard he was pushing his body to keep up with the bird.

The prospect of a cold ale before him, he made one more effort to quicken his pace. The narrow streets wound their way through the silent city, the distant commotion getting closer and closer. As he rounded the final corner, he groaned. Of course, he thought, *it's the only tavern in town, there was always going to be a line.*

The tavern was a two-story outfit and looked fairly scruffy amongst the other buildings in the area. It shone like a beacon, lights sparkling in every window. A small wooden sign out front proclaimed it was "The Angry Beaver." The entrance was two large, heavy doors, one closed, the other propped open and manned by a surly-looking half orc who stood around seven feet tall, with thick tusks protruding from his lips, was decked out in some very outlandish leather armour and had a vicious-looking black oak club on his back. He was currently frisking what appeared to be three gnomes standing on each other's shoulders in a long jacket.

Without warning, the orc seized the gnome on top in one hand and the one in the middle in the other, and turning them upside down, he began to shake vigorously. The gnomes cried out in shock, as various bottles, vials, and knives cascaded from their pockets and fell to the ground. Evidently satisfied, the brute laughed and tossed the first gnome into the bar, then the second. He turned his gaze on the final fellow, who was smiling sheepishly and emptying his pockets. The bouncer allowed his entry and after collecting the assorted trinkets on the cobblestones, placed them into a large chest behind him and motioned the next guest forward.

Valex waited and waited and waited some more. The thirst felt like a physical ailment; he could smell the ale inside but he held his place, not wanting to be turned upside down like the gnomes. Finally, he had reached the head of the line and the half-orc motioned him forward.

As Valex stepped out of the shadows, the doorman's eyes widened as he took in the size of the dragonborn. "A big one!" he grunted. "It been long time since Gog see Lizardman in The Vale!"

Valex grimaced, this guy was setting every stereotype he'd heard about half-orcs in stone. He stepped forward, hands outstretched so Gog could inspect his gear.

"Okay big lizard, you want to come in for drinks, you must give Gog all weapons."

"I'm not actually a Lizardman, you know," Valex unshouldered his quarterstaff, pulled the dagger from his belt, and began to undo the clasp on his spellbook but stopped short. Surely they wouldn't see many wizards in this part of the world, and he would feel more comfortable walking into this unfamiliar situation with an ace in the hole.

The half-orc gave him a long look, lingering on Valex's claws and talons, but eventually he cleared his throat. "Looks like you clean. Before you come into Angry Beaver, you need to know rule. The one rule here is no killing. If you fight, end quick, or I come end for you. Have fun!" The green-skinned man's tusks pulled to the side in an imitation of a smile, and he stepped aside to allow Valex access.

Valex stepped through the threshold, squinting at the light and noise that washed over him as soon as he entered. Looking about, he was surprised to see all manner of creatures sharing food and drink: from tiny gnomes sitting upon stacks of books to reach their tables, to childlike halflings, most of them barefoot and grinning honestly, to haughty elves, and even a few of the shadowy looking tieflings, all red skin and horns. At the end of the room, he saw a very attractive halfling bard, playing a harp and singing along, while a bewitched set of instruments followed suit, as if being played by spectres.

The thirst barked again, demanding his attention. Valex figured before he made heads or tails of the place, a drink (or three or four) couldn't hurt, and he approached the long, dark, wooden bar that ran the length of the left side of the room. He spied a tall, thin human, sporting a shining bald head and an extravagant wax moustache, cleaning a glass and with a distressed look watching a trio of dwarves at the end of the bar. Valex stood awkwardly for a while but eventually, after he'd cleared his throat several times, the barman addressed him.

"Alright, alright, keep your shirt on…" He finally turned his attention to Valex and his voice faltered. "Crickey, we're really getting all types tonight. First the bird man, then Nogret shows up, and now an honest-to-God dragonborn. What can I grab you, big fella?"

"Why don't you pour three ales," Valex had placed several silver coins on the bar. "Two for me and one for you, and maybe I could ask you a few questions?"

Quick as a shot, the coins vanished into the man's hands and with a furtive look left and right, he turned back to the taps. Returning with the ales, he raised a glass to Valex, who clinked his own against the barkeep's.

"The name's Tim, Tim Crenshaw. What can I help you with?" the barkeep said innocuously, sneaking large gulps anytime he felt the patrons weren't looking.

"Valex Shatterscale. You said something about a bird man. I was sent here to meet someone, and I believe that might be my guy. Where can I find him?" Valex spoke in between large gulps of ale, the first drink almost gone by the time he had finished talking.

The bartender's eyes darted to the back of the tavern, opposite the stage where the bard was performing. Valex followed his gaze and saw something interesting. The majority of the bar was bustling, people squeezing past each other to get to tables, but the table at the back of the room was deserted, except for three people. The other patrons seemed to be giving it a wide berth.

Two of the people at the table were facing Valex: one a fairly innocent-looking elf, the other hard to discern in a voluminous black cloak. The third was a hulking man, clad in plate mail armour, with a leathery blue hood pulled over his head. It was strange, because the only thing the man could see from where he was sitting was the wall; however, a raven was perched on a chair opposite him, and seemed to be looking directly at Valex with interest.

"The man there…" Tim spoke in a whisper that suggested conspiracy, "has come in every night this week. Sits at the same table, same chair, and always orders exactly one ale that he never touches. People come and go from the table, but you can tell that they have some business with him themselves, because you'll see money or paperwork change hands, and then they leave. He keeps the window open all night and those great black birds fly in and out—could swear he was talking to 'em. Most of my regulars are freaked out by the guy, and quite frankly, he gives me the willies, but he always pays his tab, plus tip. Doesn't start any trouble either, so I leave him be."Before Valex could ask any more questions, the dwarves at the end of the bar had begun shouting at Tim.

"Oy, you great useless lump," the dwarf sitting in the centre called. "We've had empty glasses for almost five minutes now, and that's unacceptable for such a 'fine establishment' as this."

Sarcasm dripped off every word, and the two dwarves sitting on either side of the speaker let out throaty chuckles at his wit. Valex gave him a side glance and almost started laughing. While the two dwarves flanking him were, well, exactly what you'd expect when you think of dwarves, all long hair and long beards, the one in the centre was as different as could be. With a bald head, trim beard, and a leather eyepatch that covered almost the entire left side of his face, he looked like a very small human. Valex's amusement came from the fact that the man was completely shirtless, sporting a pot belly, and smoking a noxious-smelling cigar.

"See something you like, scale brain?" The dwarf had turned his attention to Valex, his accent making the words difficult to make out. "I'd suggest you take your dumb ass elsewhere, this here is a private party."

"I'll be right over, Nogret." Tim rolled his eyes at Valex, mouthed an apology, and attended to the rowdy trio.

Valex walked away; he didn't want to start the evening with a brawl if he could help it, but before he did, he dropped another two silver coins on the bar. Callum had taught him the value of overpaying a bartender—they were worth their weight in gold in information.

Valex approached the table at the back of the room and as he drew near, the raven perched on the chair gave out a caw. The two figures looked up as he approached, and Valex saw the one in the black cloak was a human woman. They both wore identical expressions of surprise, but the man in the hood spoke up without turning his head.

"Ah, this must be our third adventurer." His voice was gruff, but warm. Valex didn't sense any malice in it, but felt it was wise to keep his guard up all the same. "I was worried that you had gotten lost."

"'Bout time." The cloaked girl put her boots up on the table, drawing a concealed dagger from her wrist and she began to spin it on the table.

How did she get that past the bouncer? Valex thought.

"I was about ready to leave and put this whole business behind me," said the girl.

Something in her accent reminded Valex of his old mentor, Callum, and he wondered if she hailed from the same city that he came from.

The girl on the other side of the table looked at him curiously but said nothing. From her slender build and pointed ears, Valex guessed she must be an elf and although it was hard to guess age with them (the forest folk lived damn near forever), Valex got the impression she was quite young.

"Sorry," he mumbled, setting his drink down and settling into a chair. "I've come quite a long way, you see."

The strange man spoke again, his head down, pressed against his knuckles. "This is very true. And Vel, I'd advise you to play nice. Valex is potentially your partner in our new enterprise."

"Yeah, an enterprise you've *still* told us nothing about," the cloaked woman, Vel, snarled. "We've been following your damn birds halfway across the…"

The elf spoke up, her words sounding almost musical. "I believe what she's trying to say is that we would all like to know what exactly it is that we're doing here."

Finally, the man raised his head from his hands and surveyed them, revealing a weather-worn visage. His size betrayed his age, but he had to be in his mid-sixties. Scars criss-crossed his cheeks, his nose had the crooked look of one too many breaks, and his beard had been trimmed into a neat salt and pepper goatee. Strangest of all, while his right eye was a piercing blue, the left was entirely black. He pressed two fingers to his temple and gave his head a shake, and the darkness faded from his eye like mist.

"My apologies."

Valex realised that this was the same voice that had spilled from the raven he had met on the road.

"I was tending to some far-off business while we waited for our friend." With a crack of his neck, he took a moment to look at each of them and with a deep breath, began to speak. "I've been keeping an eye on you three, in particular. The slave turned apprentice."

Valex jumped and spilled his ale.

"The royalty playing commoner."

The elf looked at him grimly.

"And the orphan thief."

Vel didn't meet his gaze and continued to spin her dagger on the table.

"For reasons I choose not to disclose at this time, I believe that the three of you have the potential to fulfil a greater destiny than you've been able to achieve thus far, and I am in a position to help you pursue the things you are after. Be it power, money, or knowledge, I believe you'll find that I'm a man with the connections to get you all three, in exchange for some work. I know the three of you have been toiling for some time, unsuccessfully, to make names for yourselves. I believe it's time for Meridia to know your names and fear or respect them, whichever you would prefer." The man spoke slowly, allowing his words to roll over them.

There was a moment of silence as he finished, while the three of them digested this information.

"What do these 'jobs' entail, then?" Vel spoke with the air of someone who had fielded this kind of request before.

"Nothing terribly untoward, I assure you," the man said. "Mostly what I'm in need of is a competent group to make contact with certain individuals, for various reasons. You'll be part messenger, part delivery people, the odd bodyguarding, and I can assure you that you will be compensated *handsomely*." Reaching into the folds of his cloak, he produced three identical cloth bags, which made a metallic clink as they hit the table.

"As a show of good faith, consider this an advance, whether you decide to accept the job or not." The man crossed his arms and leaned back in his chair.

"Fine by me." Vel pocketed the bag of coin and sheathed the dagger. "I'm no stranger to shady work."

"I'm afraid that I would need to know more before I accept." The elf looked at the bag of coin, as if she was afraid picking it up would bind her in contract.

"But that, my dear Kaylessa, is part of why I will be paying you as much as I am. I need people who can act and move without second guessing the reasoning. I promise that there will be very little that would break the laws of Thras'lunia," he said.

At the mention of her home, Kaylessa fell silent. She looked at the stranger and reached out with her senses, honed by her training with the sage, and was shocked at the amount of power that flowed from the man, in particular from the curved sword he wore on his back. It was a strange blade, thin and long, in a red and gold sheath. Kaylessa realised that, if push came to shove, this man was likely more powerful than Lucian, and she made her decision.

Valex pondered—he needed to learn more in order to complete the spellbook and to find the information he needed about taking his fight to Bahamut. It appeared that this man knew much and could be the key to Valex getting what he needed. Besides, it never hurt to make a little coin on the way.

"Good, it appears I've at least got your attention." The man turned in his chair, and looked towards the bar. "I'm in need of strong fighters, but I would like to ensure that my chosen people are also reasonably diplomatic. Do you see the dwarf at the bar? The one with the eyepatch?"

They all turned to look, and Valex felt a surge of annoyance as he realised it was the dwarf who had called him "scale brain." The three dwarves were surrounded by bottles and flagons, and it was clear that they were very drunk. The one in the centre grabbed his companion on the left by the beard and brought his head into his own with a resounding crack. The dwarf who had been grabbed looked stunned for a minute, then the three of them burst into laughter and began pouring their drinks down their throats.

"Charming," said Vel, rolling her eyes.

"Yes, I admit, he may not look like much. But once upon a time, he was a brilliant architect and stone mason, and the first job I'll have you do for me is to get him to come to my table and have a drink." The man's voice was even, but his face betrayed the humour he felt looking at the three of them.

Valex blinked at the man, trying to figure out if this was a joke. "Wait, what do you need us for? Just ask him yourself."

"Valex, that wouldn't be much of a test, now would it?" The man turned and shot another glance at the dwarf, who was pouring the last drops of a whisky bottle directly into his mouth. "Besides, I don't believe it will be that simple."

Vel looked closely at the man. "You said this would be our first job, I assume that there will be payment?"

"Of course. If you succeed, I will double the coin I've just given you, and we can move onto more…shall we say, profitable ventures."

"Oh for goodness' sake," Kaylessa spouted. "I'll just go talk to him." She pushed her chair back and approached the three men at the bar. The others all watched as she tapped the bald dwarf on the shoulder and exchanged a few words with him. Suddenly, the dwarf made a lewd gesture that was hard to misconstrue and Kaylessa turned *very* red. She returned to the table, walking fast with her head down, to a chorus of dwarvish laughter.

"You. Would. Not. BELIEVE. The nerve of him! The things he called me, suggested I do…I've never met such a…a foul…bastard!" She spat the last word out with a surprised look, as if she had never used the word before.

Chuckling, Valex surveyed the room. Considering his previous interaction with the dwarves, he could have told her that method wouldn't work. Callum had always taught him that he should use his mind before using his fists, and he was searching for a way to do just that. He did notice, however, that the dwarf was watching the halfling bard very closely as she sang, and when the singer dropped him a wink, he blushed and looked away.

"I've got an idea," Valex muttered to no one in particular, and as the bard was just settling into a break he slinked away to the stage.

Vel rose to her feet, cracked her knuckles, and drew the dagger from her belt. She had, of course, smuggled several into the Angry Beaver, knowing that bouncers couldn't check everywhere. "There is only one language scum like him understands, and fortunately I'm fluent in it," she told Kaylessa as she began to cross the room.

Dagger held loosely at her side, where no one would see it but her target, Vel tapped Nogret on a bare shoulder. "Now look here. You heard the girl. We need you to come over here."

"Oh lassie." Nogret's words were slurred, but he held her gaze steadily. "I highly advise you to stow your little toy and turn around, before I have to make a lesson out of you. Nogret Boulderspine doesn't *have* to do anything, and I'm having a grand old time right here. Why don't you head on back to your little girlfriend and try to enjoy your night."

"Enough. You're coming and that's final." She flipped the dagger up, meaning to draw it to his throat.

But with a mechanical clicking noise, Nogret pushed a button on the leather bracer he wore around his right wrist, and six inches of steel shot out of the hidden compartment. He swung the blade high and fast, disarming Vel. With the same click, the blade was suddenly gone from sight.

The dwarf slid off his stool, downed the last of the bottle he was working on, and with a crack of his neck turned to face Vel. "You're gonna wish you hadn't done that, love." His voice was razor thin as he brought the bottle over her head, and as it smashed down he tackled her to the ground.

"Oh for heaven's sake, not again!" Tim cried out, as he threw his towel on the bar and made for the door. All of the bar's patrons moved away, creating a rough circle around Vel and Nogret, where they all cheered as Nogret straddled the larger human, raining down blows.

Valex had just finished arranging for the bard to come talk with Nogret, for a regrettably large sum of gold, when he heard the bottle smash and the crowd start to cheer from the circle.

"Ugh, come on!" Valex sighed, but he barrelled through the crowd towards the scene. As he reached the edge of the circle and saw the dwarf sitting atop his new companion, he started forward to assist, but something hard slammed into the side of his head. Valex kicked the wooden mug aside and turning to the direction the projectile had come, he saw one of Nogret's dwarf companions standing atop the bar.

"Nah, your fight is with me, big boy!" the dwarf shouted, and he flung himself from the bar at Valex, elbow first. The two fell to the ground in a tumble of arms and legs. Kaylessa approached as well, and seeing the situation, grabbed the nearest chair and tossed it in a low arc at Nogret's exposed back. The momentum knocked Nogret off of Vel, who took the opportunity to flip onto all fours, and pounce onto the stocky dwarf. Where Nogret had been raining down haymakers, Vel was making targeted strikes to his midsection, and the bald dwarf was groaning in pain.

Before Kaylessa could celebrate her throw, the other dwarf watching drew inspiration, and brought a chair down onto her back, splinters of wood flying in all directions. She rolled off to the side, grabbing pieces of the shrapnel and lobbing it in the direction of her assailant, who was returning pieces in kind.

Valex got back on his feet and the dwarf he was fighting threw his arms around his neck, trying to choke him. Valex braced his feet, grabbed the dwarf's beard, and jerked him forward. The dwarf yelped as he was pulled in front of the dragonborn, who had decided to end this particular fight. Still gripping the dwarf's beard, he grabbed the front of his trousers, and with a mighty heave brought him over his head, face first into the bottle-strewn bar. The crowd let out a collective gasp at the sound, and the dwarf slid to the floor unconscious amidst a smattering of applause.

Valex looked at Vel, and seeing the situation was under control, moved to help Kaylessa, who was hiding behind a table as the dwarf she was fighting threw anything within reach at her, but was interrupted as the crowd was split by an enormous green figure, who was bellowing in rage. Gog, the bouncer, hurried into the circle, drew the large club from his back, and struck the dwarf attacking Kaylessa on the side of the head. The crowd let out a collective "Oooooh," but began to disperse as the half-orc's eyes looked around the circle, daring anyone else to step forward.

He started toward Valex, who held his hands out in a gesture of peace. Gog grunted at that and turned to where Vel was still raining down blows on Nogret like a prize fighter. Gog brought the heavy club down, cracking the hardwood floor, and bellowed at the two of them. "Dwarf! Girl! How many times I tell you! Drink, no fight! I will break you!" Spittle flew from his tusks and Vel sidled up to the bar, pulling her cloak up.

"Gog, calm down now, 'twas just a bit of fun between friends! Teaching the lovely lass how to throw a punch is all!" Nogret got shakily to his feet and held his hands up as the half orc sauntered up to him, club in hand.

"No, no fun! You break Tim's chairs! You pay Tim!" Gog brought the club down on the remains of one of the chairs, shattering it further. Tim moaned from behind the bar, and Valex thought to point out that now Gog had broken a chair but decided to keep it to himself.

Nogret slid a few gold coins onto the bar top. "Look, money where it's owed, no harm no foul, big green."

Gog grunted, returned the club to his back, and forked his fingers towards his eyes, then into Nogret's face, and walked toward the front.

Nogret touched his ribs and winced but turned to face Vel, who stood in a defensive stance. "Nah lass, I'm gassed. Hell of a punch you've got. You fight like a girl." He chuckled when Vel's face darkened. "But for dwarves, that's a compliment. You should see how me ex-wife was when she threw fists. If *she* had gotten in the ring with me, I would have retired on the spot."

Nogret let out a loud laugh, then grimaced and spat a wad of blood onto the floor. He looked at the shattered remains of the bottles on the bar, then looked hopefully at the table where the cloaked man still sat, facing the wall. "Shame, the fisticuffs seem to have sobered me up a mite, think this chap you want me ta speak with might have a bottle?" He limped over to the table, pulled out a chair, and slid the man's untouched ale over to himself.

Vel, Valex, and Kaylessa watched as the two talked, and then the mysterious man excused himself and came over with a smile on his face. "Splendid. Absolutely splendid. Not at all the way I would have handled it, but a job well done." He tossed them each a second bag of gold. "I've already booked rooms for the three of you upstairs. I'd recommend cleaning yourselves up." He looked at Vel (holding a kerchief to her split lip), then Kaylessa (pulling splinters of wood out of her forearm), to Valex, (plopped into a chair, drinking whisky out of the remains of a shattered bottle). "...And getting some rest. I've got another job for you in the morning."

With this, he returned to the table and spoke to the dwarf, who was nodding enthusiastically. The trio got the keys from Tim, who was looking morose over the state of his bar, and climbed the stairs, their bodies protesting each step. Valex crested the landing of the stairs with a sudden realisation.. All this madness, and they'd never even learned the name of their benefactor. What kind of trouble had he gotten himself into?

CHAPTER 5

OAKHEART FORGE

Day 110 – Somulous Experiment: I feel that I've been able to prove my hypothesis and have discontinued the stimulants but am alarmed to find that I am still unable to sleep. My loss of time has become marginally more pronounced, and I have been coming to my senses in strange places. The thoughts are coming in clearer and clearer, however, and today I even heard my department head weighing the pros and cons of promoting me to his position when he moves on. A.G.

Vel, Valex, and Kaylessa all woke around dawn, the sunlight streaming through the inn's windows mingling with the birdsong outside—but the groan that followed their waking was collective. All three of them sported injuries of various severity, but knew that there was work to be done, and they convened in the hallway, eyeing each other warily and not speaking.

They descended the stairs and were greeted by the sight of a clean tavern. It appeared that Tim and Gog had gone to work over the course of the night, tidying up the chaos from the previous evening. Valex caught Tim's eye and flagged him over, and Vel and Kaylessa walked away to survey the room.

"...Thank you." Vel's voice was very quiet, and Kaylessa almost didn't hear her. "For the assist, with the chair. I would have had him, but he surprised me with that blade."

"Sure, I'm not a big fan of dirty fighting, and personally I'm an even bigger fan of seeing that dwarf get hit with a chair," said Kaylessa.

Vel snorted and scanned the room, letting out a noise of surprise as her gaze settled on a familiar face in an unfamiliar setting. Sitting at a table by himself was a very large, green-skinned man, sporting round spectacles and reading a dense-looking tome. He was delicately spooning eggs onto a piece of toast, while perusing the book one handed.

"Gog, is that you?" Kaylessa walked over to the hulking figure, who looked up, bemused, and wiped the corners of his mouth with his napkin.

"Oh, I didn't realise you guys had stayed the night! I hope you slept well. Sorry about the ugliness last night, Nogret and his boys can get a little out of hand." His cheery grin was very different from the raging berserker they saw last night.

Vel smirked as she peeked over his shoulder at the book. "I must say, I'm a little surprised to find you reading, let alone such a complex-looking book. I had you pegged for the 'strong but dumb' type last night."

"Well, in truth, I'm studying to take the mages exam at the Mages College, in Grand Covus. Unfortunately, the tuition is pretty expensive, and as you can see," he gestured down at his muscular form, "given my disposition, it's easier to find work with my brawn, rather than my brains." He shrugged.

"Fair enough, I suppose," Kaylessa interjected. "But you'll have to excuse us, we've got a meeting with our new...colleague?" she finished, not sure what to call the man they'd met last night.

"You're going to be working for him?" Gog cast a look at the table at the back. "Nogret actually met with him at sunrise. They had a discussion and Nogret rode north with a satchel full of blueprints and a large satchel of gold. Also a pretty big smile, so I imagine the news was favourable.

I'm glad to see him go, if I'm being honest, he's always more trouble than he's worth."

Valex joined up with them, two ales clutched in his left talon and another in his right. He set the three drinks down as he joined the ladies, and Kaylessa cast a disappointed look in his direction.

"A bit too early for ale, don't you think?" Vel chimed in, eyebrows raised.

"Oh, shit, did you want an ale?" Valex had pounded the first drink down and was working on the second. "I can go back and get you one."

"I…no, that's fine. Let's go see what our new friend has in store for us." With a flip of her cloak, Vel led the way to the table at the back.

"Best of luck!" Gog called out as they left, returning to his book. "If you ever find yourselves at the Mage's College, look me up!"

They headed towards the same table from the previous evening and saw the man sitting in exactly the same spot, another untouched beer sitting flat, his head in his hands. The raven across from the man let out a caw, and the man's head tilted slightly at the sound. They took their seats, and the man raised his head. The blackness from last night was now obscuring both his eyes. With a shake of his head, it again cleared, and when he raised his face, his eyes were back to their piercing blue.

"I'm happy to see you all made it through the night." It was unclear if this was sarcastic, but his smile said it was. "Before we get down to business, I believe introductions are in order. My name is Wravien Leonhart, and this is one of my familiars, Anubis." The raven let out a happy noise and hopped in place. Valex let out a laugh at the behaviour.

"To my left, we have Kaylessa Siannodel, a powerful Sage-in-training from the noble elvish city of Thras'lunia. Her skills as a Sage are only rivalled by her skill with a bow."

"That's…that's correct." Kaylessa looked uncomfortable at the way this information had been revealed.

"And here, we have Vel Valdove. She is an accomplished con artist and great with a blade. You hail from…"

"That is quite enough," Vel interrupted, annoyance flashing across her face. "My personal business will stay just that, personal."

"Us 'cloak and dagger' types, always so secretive. No matter, I'm sure you'll get to know each other in due time. Finally, our large friend here goes by Valex Shatterscale. Despite his appearance, his greatest talents lie in the magical arts. He apprenticed under Callum Brightspire for many years."

"Aye." Valex let out a belch. "Guess you could say I'm a big lizard wizard." He laughed a little too loud at his own joke.

Vel looked at him sharply. She had written him off as a musclebound idiot, but his connection to Brightspire caught her off guard. Growing up in Grand Covus, it was impossible not to know the name of King Roland's right-hand man, who had mysteriously left the court when she was a teenager.

"With that out of the way..." Wravien began, but Valex interrupted, looking around wildly.

"Hey, is that nasty little dwarf going to be joining us? I wonder if he looks as bad as I feel!" he giggled. But Wravien caught his eye, and he deflated under the stern look.

Wravien allowed the silence to marinate for a second before continuing. "No questions regarding the venture—that was the deal, Valex. Why don't we proceed to your first official job in my employ?"

Wravien unrolled a weather-worn map of Meridia onto the table. He tapped a spot on the map, southeast of the town they were currently in. "Two days' ride from here, you'll find the ruins of the Oakheart Forge. In its heyday, it was the premiere facility for high-quality weapons and armour, and it was touted as the best in all of Illium. The original proprietor, Magnus Oakheart, and I go way back, and he owed me a few favours I intended to call in. Unfortunately, I've discovered that he passed away several years ago, and the forge fell into the hands of some...unsavoury characters." He rolled the map back up and hid it in the folds of his cloak.

"So that's the job?" Vel looked antsy, and was having trouble sitting still. "Shake up a few bookies, recover the deed?"

"No, I doubt you're powerful enough to take on the Scarlet Immortals just yet."

Vel started at the mention.

"But my friends have been keeping an eye on the place for me, and it looks like Magnus's son has been surveying the area. Magnus had spoken of his boy to me, I can't quite remember his name. I know he rolled with the Tempest Waves for a few years."

Valex had read about this organisation, an anti-piracy religion that worshipped the god of the sea, Leviathan. They were more commonly referred to as the Tempest Paladins.

"But I am in need of a skilled blacksmith," Wravien continued, "and if he inherited even a tenth of his old man's skills, he is the one we're going to need." He reached into a pouch on his belt and retrieved an envelope, sealed with a dollop of wax pressed into an elegant R and started to hand it to Valex, but he saw the empty flagon and the way Valex was swaying in his seat and instead handed the letter to Kaylessa.

"That letter should explain everything nicely, including that we're calling in all of the favours his father owes us. It also contains the location of where I'll need you to bring him, and if you can bring him to me, I'll have a very nice reward waiting for you. Any questions?"

Kaylessa's hand shot into the air and he nodded to her with a raised eyebrow.

"Excuse me, Mr. Leonhart." She spoke clearly, but stammered when she saw the look on his face. "You said two days' ride, but I believe we've all arrived here without mounts. How long is the journey on foot?"

Wravien sighed, leaned back in his chair, and lit a hand-rolled tobacco cigarette. "Just Wravien is fine, Kaylessa," he said, leaning back in his chair and blowing out a few smoke rings. "And if you're going to be working for me, I can't have you walking all over the place like peasants. I've already picked out something for each of you, and again, consider it a down payment for the good work you're about to do. Now, if you have no other questions, I suggest you get moving. There is no guarantee that the boy will stay at the forge indefinitely."

His tone implied dismissal, and as the three of them rose to leave, he stubbed out the smoke and said a single word in a strange language. His chin fell to his chest as his eyes clouded over, and Anubis took wing out the window.

Valex staggered across the bar and approached Tim, his arms outstretched. "Timothy! It appears we are taking our leave, and I don't know if we'll ever be back. I just wanted you to know you've been a fantastic bartender, and I'm sad to have to leave you." He clapped the much smaller man on the shoulder and licked his scaly beak. "Any chance you've got some portable options for a few days of ale?"

"Of course, and it's just Tim, thank you," He took a step back and leaned under the bar. After a few minutes of rustling, he emerged with a large wineskin, which he took to the taps. "But you know, you might be seeing me sooner than you think. Wravien has made me a fairly tempting offer!"

"That's nice to hear." Valex looked hypnotised by the golden liquid flowing into the skin, and then he removed a few coins from his pouch to pay the man. "Perhaps we'll meet again, then."

The trio stepped outside and heard the sounds of horses. To the right of the entrance were three fully equipped steeds, tethered to the hitching post out front. It looked like the horses had been handpicked for each of them, and they all approached the animals as they stamped and whinnied.

Vel petted the mane of a satin-black mare and looked at the equipment hitched to the saddle. There were rations, a bed roll, and the leather the saddle was made of actually matched the leather of her armour. She looked at her companions, who were inspecting their own steeds with awestruck faces. Kaylessa's horse was a milky white, the mane and tail braided, and Valex had an enormous palomino Clydesdale, which was happily chomping down on the hay in the trough.

Just who is this man, Vel thought, *and what kind of network does he have at his disposal?* Three purebred horses, plus all the equipment, would easily cost ten times what he had paid them for the work last night, and this was supposed to be a down payment? She wasn't sure that she trusted Wravien, but she believed he might be the answer to her brother's salvation. She mounted up with a practised ease, and they rode off to the southeast, a black bird soaring overhead.

After riding through the day, they found a spot in the woods to make camp. Kaylessa excused herself and grabbed her bow, intending to hunt some game for their dinner. Valex stacked tinder into a pyramid inside a circle of stones, and when he was satisfied with the structure, pulled the book from his belt, uttered the command word, "Ignite," and the fire roared to life with a flash.

Looking satisfied, he leaned back, removed the wineskin from his backpack, pulled the cork out with his beak, poured ale into his mouth, and sighed. He wiped his hand across his mouth and held out the skin to Vel, who was rolling loose tobacco into a paper.

She looked up, a little surprised, but took the skin and drew a long draught. "Thanks." Handing it back to him, she licked the edge of the parchment and deftly rolled it into a tight cylinder, which she lit on the fire. She pulled on it deeply, exhaled smoke, and held it out to Valex.

Valex had never smoked tobacco before in his life, but he didn't want to lose face in front of his terrifying new companion. Taking the cigarette, he put it in his mouth, breathed in, and collapsed into a fit of coughing.

Laughing, Vel took the smoke from his hands and clapped him on the back. Once the fit had passed, she settled down against a nearby tree and looked up at the stars. "Don't let it bother you, big fellah," she chuckled. "Everyone coughs the first time."

"No, I'm just not used to that particular type of tobacco." Valex's eyes were still streaming tears. "I smoke all kinds of things, all the time, just usually from a pipe." He wasn't sure why he was lying outright, but he didn't want this scary woman to think he was uncool. Abruptly, he changed the subject. "I was wondering, if we're going to be working together, we ought to know why we're going along with this crazy venture. What made you follow the raven?"

Vel spoke, after staring into the fire for a while. "... I need gold. I've got a problem that can only be solved with money. Seems like Wravien has more than enough to spare. What about you?"

"Hmm…" Valex mused, "The gold is nice, but to be honest, not my real reason for sticking around. I grew up pretty rough, and I've learned in the last couple years that the one responsible is a being called 'Bahamut.' I've read everything I can get my hands on, but haven't been able to find any references to something powerful enough to be able to fight it. I'm pretty sure I'll have to make the weapon myself, and I think our friend can get me the information I need."

"Bahamut, the dark dragon? That's a fairy tale. Mothers tell their children about it so they'll behave, nothing more." Vel ashed her cigarette into the fire.

"Well, I can assure you that regardless of its existence, there are people that swear their allegiance to it. And they have incomprehensible power and influence." He ran his talon down the side of his neck, feeling the raised scales from the many scars incurred by the whip. Seeing Vel watching him, he dropped his hand self-consciously.

She looked a moment longer, then pitched the end of the smoke into the fire. "Well, you've got your work cut out for you," she said.

Kaylessa emerged from the treeline at the edge of their camp, three rabbits slung over her shoulder. Vel rolled to her feet, took the game, and began to dress it down to roast over the fire.

Kaylessa watched her with amazement as she took her dagger and glided through the carcass with practised ease. "Wow," she gasped. "Where did you learn how to do that so fast? It would take me twice as long."

"When you grow up the way I did," Vel grunted, splitting the animal in two with the blade, "you pick up a few things here and there. Valex and I were just discussing our reasoning for joining this merry crusade—what about you, Princess? Can't imagine you're in it for the gold."

"I am *not* a princess," Kaylessa snapped, and then with a breath she composed herself and continued. "I do, however, have a great destiny within my people. Well…I had a great destiny. I'm not sure if that future has changed, but I know that I'm going to need great power in order to return to them, and this seems like the smartest way to acquire it."

"Sounds like we've all got our reasons to make sure this job goes smoothly," said Valex, handing the wineskin to Kaylessa. She sniffed at it, then took a small sip.

"Come on, let's eat and settle down to bed," he said. "We've got a long day's ride ahead of us tomorrow."

They ate and after dinner, Vel rolled another cigarette. She taught Valex how to smoke it properly, and after an hour or so he was trying and failing to blow smoke rings. At some point, Kaylessa had drawn a beautiful wooden harp from her things and begun to sing. Valex and Vel both felt it wash over them in waves, and as the relaxation settled in they drifted off to sleep.

The next day, they followed the signposts for the forge, many of which had broken or fallen into a serious state of disrepair.

"Kaylessa," Valex stretched his back while they rode, "did you do something to us last night, with your singing? I slept like a hatchling and I woke up feeling rejuvenated, not what one usually expects from a night on the road."

"Well, yes," Kaylessa said, a red flush creeping up her neck. "One of my duties as the sage was to learn the bardic arts, and that song was one of the first I was taught. It's designed to relieve stress and cure wounds."

"Interesting. I didn't realise there were other types of magic than the ones you learned from the tomes."

"Quiet, you two," Vel hissed. "Do you see that, up there?"

They all squinted down the road. For the last hour or two they had been following a winding canyon into the mountain range, and the forge had to be getting close.

Valex pulled his reins, bringing his Clydesdale to a halt. "Hold on, I'll scout ahead," he said, undoing the clasp on his spellbook.

Vel looked at Valex in exasperation. "Don't you think I should be the one to do that? You aren't exactly…inconspicuous, and you've been drinking all day."

"My dear, there is always more than one way to see," Valex retorted, with a slightly cockeyed stare. Flipping through the pages of his book, he reached into a small pouch he wore around his waist and pulled out several sticks of incense. Breaking them, he placed them on the open book, and muttered the command word. There was a blue flash of light, and something flew from the centre of his book, taking rise into the air. Upon closer inspection, it appeared to be a spectral blue owl.

"Now, while I'm looking through his eyes, I'm basically dead to the world. Don't let me fall off my horse, okay?" Valex said. His eyes rolled up until only the whites were visible, and the owl began to flap its wings, gaining height. It flew in a slow circle and Valex began to speak.

"Okay...Okay! Looks like the forge is only about a mile ahead, and there is a little courtyard out front, a few dilapidated buildings. Wow, this place has seen better days, I'll tell you what...Oh, I think I see our guy! There's a dwarf hiding in the ruins of the nearest building to the forge. He's got a big sword, but he looks kind of scared."

Valex was swaying in his saddle, dangerously close to falling, when his eyes snapped back. He blinked at his companions rather owlishly and adjusted the grip on his reins. "Shall we go say hello?" he said.

"Follow my lead," said Vel. She turned to Kaylessa and held out her hand. "Do you still have the letter?"

Kaylessa reached into her bag and removed the heavy envelope, handing it to her. Vel spurred her horse forward and cantered into the centre of the courtyard, allowing her mare to do a slow circle.

"Young Oakheart!" she called out, "A mutual friend sent us to come find you!"

A head popped up from behind a segment of ruined wall, then disappeared from view. A few moments later, a broad-shouldered dwarf in dark-blue chainmail stepped out into the clearing, his hand on the haft of an enormous great-sword he wore on his back. A noble face peered out of a bushy beard, worn in intricate braids, and a crown of chestnut hair flowed down his back.

"How do ye know who I am?" His voice was thick with the Dwarvish brogue, making it difficult to make out his words, but his eyes were darting between them, and he'd undone the clasp on his great blade, "An' who might this friend of ours be?"

"Calm yourself dwarf," said Vel.

Kornid's eyes narrowed as Vel reached into her cloak and the grip on his blade tightened for a moment before she pulled the letter out.

"We come on behalf of a friend of your father's, Wravien Leonhart. He bid us to give you this letter, and to ask you to come with us."

Slack jawed, the dwarf let his hand fall from the sword and walked towards the human.

Vel dismounted, aware that even though her horse was small, she could save the stocky fellow the embarrassment of reaching for it.

"Blimey, that's a name I've only heard in stories from my da." The dwarf drew a small dagger from his belt and slit the wax seal on the envelope. "He was always going on about a human sellsword he used to sail with, who apparently saved his life a few times. According to Da, the man was a devil with those blades of his, whirling around the deck of their ship like a hurricane."

The dwarf scanned the letter, nodded, and stowed it away before speaking again. "Ay, he is calling in my da's favour and I'm inclined to oblige. By the by, my name is Kornid, but I've got some business at the family forge and I canna' leave until it's settled." He turned to look at the decrepit entrance.

"Could we perhaps be of some assistance?" Kaylessa tied her mount to some rubble and joined her companion. "Wravien said that your presence was of paramount importance."

"You aren't wrong; I could use some help. But ye will think I'm mad when I tell you why." Kornid hesitated for a moment before saying, "I've seen a few things in there that defy logic."

Valex looked the dwarf up and down, noticing some scrapes on his face and gouges in his armour. Pulling the tome from his belt, he said the command word and a ball of fire appeared in his hand, pulsing gently. "Trust me," he smirked, "I'm no stranger to strange occurrences. Most phenomena can be explained, as long as you understand the rituals."

"A wizard, are ye? Aye, that could be just the ticket." Kornid put his hand on his chin, stroking his beard as he found the words. Then he continued, "So, as far as I know, the place is deserted. I did a quick sweep of the perimeter to see if Balthazar had placed any men to watch the place. See, after my da passed, I ended up with the deed to the place, but I also inherited all the debts attached to it. Pa was a great smith, but he didn't have much mind for business. Kept giving things away he should have been selling. At any rate, the deed got taken by some debt collectors from Grand Covus."

He walked towards the large, cavernous entrance. A sign, hung crooked by a single chain, the other snapped, proclaimed, "Oakheart Forge." Kornid looked up at it for a moment, then turned to face Vel, Valex, and Kaylessa.

"I donna care about the building—it's a lost cause. But I've been thinking of starting up my own smithy, and something inside told me I needed to get Pa's tools. I knew he hung them up in the back office so I went in to go retrieve them, but once I got to the shop, swords flew off the wall and started swinging at me as if they were possessed! I tried to grab ahold of them, but after a few slices, I retreated to come up with a plan, and then I ran into you lot."

Kaylessa, listening intently, realised that even though he was built like a man, this dwarf couldn't have been older than twenty. The experience had clearly shaken him badly, and she felt a surge of sympathy.

She rested a hand on his shoulder. "I know what it's like to lose someone and to have nothing to remember them by. We'll go in with you and we won't rest until we've reclaimed your heirloom. Right, you two?"

Valex nodded enthusiastically, but Vel frowned. "I understand being sentimental, but our job was to bring Kornid to Wravien, and I'm pretty sure we're not getting paid for a trip down memory lane."

"Well, never let it be said that an Oakheart took a favour unreturned." Kornid crossed his arms, looking up at Vel. "My father was a master craftsman, and I'm sure that the sharks who took the place over won't miss a few of his finer pieces. They wouldn't have had the eye for quality."

"Right, well, who would we be if we can't help our new friend!" Vel's previous attitude of indifference vanished, and her eyes were gleaming. "Valex, lead the way!" She gave him a gentle push towards the entrance, and he looked back at her in exasperation.

"Boy, you are a piece of work, hey?" He rolled his eyes but motioned for the others to follow him.

The entrance to the forge was a large, rough-hewn cave mouth. Crossing the threshold, Valex was struck by how dark it was, and he felt his mouth dry up. This felt just like The Underdark. Directly in front of him was a staircase going up into the darkness, the chamber lined by blackened sconces. Valex uttered a command word and a ball of brilliant white light flew from his open hand, rising a few feet above them and settling there. He began to climb, the ball of light following his progress.

"I guess you do have some uses," Vel said. "You know, beyond being enormous and able to drink at all hours."

"Indeed I do, but I've yet to see what you bring to the table." Valex's tone was sharp, the familiar, oppressive darkness setting him on edge.

"Oh, trust me, you'll see what I can do when something needs to be broken into, or someone needs to be filled with holes. " Vel pulled the cowl up over her head and placed a hand on the dagger she wore on her belt.

"Cut it out you two, we need to keep our eyes open." Kaylessa's irritation was evident, and they finished their climb in silence.

Cresting the top of the staircase, Valex's ball of light flew up to the top of a large, domed room, adorned with intricate carvings of dwarven heroes. Directly in front of them was a large archway, with the word "Shop" carved into the stone, but there were doors on either side of the room, each with a sign in a strange language mounted beside it.

"Er, does anyone read Dwarvish?" Valex wondered, and to his surprise, both Kaylessa and Kornid said yes at the same time.

Kornid looked at her in surprise and speaking in Dwarvish said, *"Where does an elven lass learn the mother tongue?"*

"It was part of my studies. I was required to learn the language of all the races of Ephiya, in case we were required to make diplomatic contact." Kaylessa's pronunciation was flawless, and Kornid looked pleased.

"We're all very impressed, but would you mind letting us know what the signs say, so that we can move on?" Vel was looking bored, but the lust for potential treasure still held its sway.

"Ah, of course." Kaylessa leaned in close to read the weathered sign. "The door on the left reads 'Armoury.'"

"An this un says, 'Storage,'" Kornid called from the other side of the room.

The armoury door had a large, rusted lock, but the door for the room marked storage was hanging ajar and Valex pushed it open. He stood for a second, then motioned for his companions to follow.

Upon entering the room, Valex flicked his wrist and the ball of light soared through the doorway, illuminating the area. Broken crates and chunks of ore were scattered all over, but strangest of all was a large, rough-cut hole in the centre of the floor.

Kornid approached the edge and let out a low whistle. "By Leviathan, that wasn't here before."

Valex pointed a finger at the ball of light, which split into two. One orb stayed suspended at the top of the room, and the other flew into the chasm. They watched its progress, dimming as it descended until it vanished from view completely, swallowed by the darkness.

Vel crouched down and examined the edges. "Something burrowed out of this…And anything that can climb out of the deep like this is bound to be bad news. We're going to have to be on our guard."

They returned to the main chamber and Kaylessa pulled on the handle of the armoury door, which held in place with a metallic clang. "Locked," she said.

"Not for long." Vel pushed her aside and drew out a ring full of delicate metal instruments. She crouched down in front of the iron lock and began to manipulate the tools until they all heard a loud *click*, and the door swung open.

"Voila." Vel dipped her knee in a mock curtsey and gestured towards the open door. Valex nodded his approval and pushed it open.

After a few tentative steps, Valex was about to motion for the light to follow when he felt the cold stone beneath his feet depress. He jumped back, wary of the trap he may have activated, but instead, the torches of the room burst into flame, illuminating a long, rectangular room covered from floor to ceiling in weaponry and armour.

The four of them walked inside and admired the work. At the back end of the room stood three stone plinths, each modelling a suit of armour. The first was a suit of scale mail, panels of pressed iron made to resemble dragon scale. The second was a brightly polished chain mail, and in between the two was a masterfully wrought suit of dwarven plate mail. All three of the suits of armor had been displayed as if they were being worn, and each held a gleaming weapon.

Valex removed the tome from his belt and after a muttered incantation, a glowing purple circle appeared in the space above the book. He began to wander around the room, holding the book up in the direction of the various pieces of metallurgy. Approaching the three suits of armour, he frowned. Two purple dots had begun to pulse on the outskirts of the circle.

He turned around to face his companions. "The majority of the items in here are mundane and have no trace of magic. But these suits of armour are giving off…"

"Valex! Down!" Kaylessa shouted, nocking an arrow into her shortbow. Valex dropped to the ground as the axe-wielding suit of plate mail swung its weapon over his horns. The armour stepped off the plinth, clearly empty, but hellbent on removing Valex's head. Kaylessa released her arrow, which dinged off the shining cuirass.

The chainmail to the left lumbered to life and lifted a wicked-looking morning star over its head, but Vel had already sprinted into action, drawing a rapier from her belt, along with her curved dagger. She slid through the open legs of the armour, dagger held high, and severed the leather straps holding the leggings to the chestplate.

As the armour's legs collapsed, she drew the rapier back, thrust it into the chest-plate of the armour three times, and slashed the dagger at the helmet. They both went to the floor with a clattering of metal.

Valex circled the suit of plate, tome still open, and the armour dropped its large axe and charged across the room to tackle the large dragonborn.

"Big mistake," Valex grunted as the armour connected with him. He held his ground, and uttered a command word, and his hands erupted into dazzling blue lightning. Placing one hand on the visor of the helmet and the other on the front of the chest plate, he released the spell as they went tumbling into the wall. A thunderous crash shook the room, and the lightning surged from Valex's outstretched claws into the metal armour, which blew apart into many pieces.

Valex pressed his body into the wall behind him, raising his hand to protect himself from the shrapnel. The wall behind him parted at the seams of brick, and he fell backwards into open air. As soon as it opened, the piece of wall slammed shut again.

"Valex!?" Kaylessa cried out in concern, lowering her bow to assess the room. The armour that had been blasted across the room showed no signs of reincorporating, and Vel was savagely sinking her dagger into the helmet of the other, which had ceased its movement.

Valex brushed himself off and looked around the small chamber he had fallen into. Inside was a small cot, a well-used cooking stove, and a golden idol that resembled a dwarf, hands outstretched to reveal a beautifully wrought rapier.

"Yeah, I'm fine!" Valex called over his shoulder, looking with wonder at the weapon before him. He tentatively grabbed the handle and shuddered as power flowed up his shoulder. Lifting it from its plinth, he gave it an experimental swing through the air. *How many months, no years,* Valex thought, *had gone into the manufacturing of this blade?* However, after a few swings, he became aware that his lack of training with such a weapon would make it a waste in his hands.

Approaching the panel he had fallen through, he ran his hands across the wall, looking for the trigger to reopen it. After a few moments, he found a small, wrought-iron lever near the floor and with a bit of effort, pushed it down and the wall swung open.

Stepping back into the armoury chamber, he walked over to where Vel was sheathing her dagger, evidently satisfied with the eviscerated chain-mail at her feet, and pressed the blade into her hand.

"I've got a feeling that this was a special project of Magnus's, but it's of no use to me." Valex tossed a look at Kornid, who shrugged. "I think you should take it."

Her eyes widened as she made contact with the blade, but without a word, she undid the belt her original blade was strapped to, and after removing it, threaded it through the new sword. Dropping the original, she glanced towards a doorway on the left side of the room and looked questioningly at Kornid.

"Aye, that should lead to the shop. That's where the trouble with the blades happened."

Vel approached the door with her tools drawn, but Valex pushed past her and with a mighty kick, booted the door open. He grinned at her, but the smile soured when he saw the look on her face. "Sorry, I guess I'm a little high strung after that last fight. Lightning magic tends to do that to me."

They walked through a small corridor before emerging into a dusty shopfront. Glass cases held the works of Magnus Oakheart, and many pieces of weapon and armour hung from the rear wall, where a large portcullis segmented the shop from a room in the back. A long oak desk ran the length of the room, separating the shoppers from the shopkeepers, presumably. Sitting upon the desk was a small, locked box, the type one usually held the day's take in. Vel cast a quick look at Kornid, who was looking at the swords on the wall warily, before approaching, tools drawn.

"Wait!" Valex commanded, and Vel turned to see him drawing his spell book. He made a delicate gesture with his hand and uttered a command word, and the lock on the box flashed bright, white light. At the same time, three swords hanging on the wall fell to the ground, which made them all jump. Valex moved to the box and with a flick of his talon, knocked the broken lock away.

"I was thinking about what you told us," Valex said, handing the open box to Vel, "and I figured it had to be some kind of anti-theft curse. Pretty smart, having the weapons of the weapon shop protect it. Your father must have been a powerful mage."

"Ay, but he wasn't…my father wouldn't have known magic if it came up and bit him on his nose." Kornid was looking down in thought and missed Vel pocketing the handfuls of coins inside the strongbox. "He wouldn't have been able to do something like this."

"Guys." Kaylessa looked at the portcullis, suspicion written across her delicate features. "Do you hear that?"

They all strained and heard a rhythmic thumping sound of metal on metal. It was a familiar sound to all of them—the sound of a forge being worked.

"I thought you said this place was abandoned," Valex inquired, cocking his head at Kornid.

"Aye, it…it should be. There are no tracks outside, no men posted." Kornid looked perplexed, and a little bit scared.

"There was that strange tunnel…" Kaylessa spoke quietly, but Kornid had already positioned himself on the bottom right corner of the heavy iron gate.

"Little help here, big man," he grunted, trying to see if he could lift the gate. Valex scuttled forward, taking the other corner, and the two of them lifted with gusto.

"On three…One, two, *THREE*." With a tremendous heave and a grinding noise, the gate slid in its tracks up several feet. Valex balanced the door on his shoulder and with his free hand waved at Kaylessa and Vel. Once they'd crossed the threshold, he gave it a final lift before slipping out himself, and the gate clattered down to its original position.

Down the long hallway, a dim blue light glowed in the direction of the hammering, which hadn't missed a beat as they'd struggled with the gate. They followed the sound and reached the opening to a large, circular room with an anvil at the centre, bellows and tongs hanging from the curved ceiling. The source of the spectral blue light was a stocky figure, standing in front of the anvil and hammering at something, his skin giving off a dim blue glow. He paid them no mind as they entered and continued to work. Vel, Valex, and Kaylessa exchanged a look, but Kornid walked forward and spoke in a trembling voice. "...Da?"

The figure stopped suddenly and Vel drew her cowl, pressing herself into the shadows by the wall. It turned around and while it was definitely a dwarf, there was something...*off* about it.

When it spoke, the voice sounded slithery and wet. "I am no father of yours, but I've claimed this forge in the name of my people. Leave now, and you may keep your lives." Its eyes blazed a white blue and a strange mist seemed to flow off its skin.

Recognizing it was no spectre, Kornid snapped to and drew the greatsword from his back. Holding it in front of him in two hands, he readied himself into a stance. As he touched an amulet on his neck and began to chant in Dwarvish, lightning began to creep up the large blade.

"This forge belonged to my father before me, and now it is mine. I will not allow some shallow imitation of him to desecrate this place. Leviathan, lend me your strength!" He dashed forward, bringing the sword down, and the blade made a crackling sound as it swung through the air, as if cutting the oxygen itself. It struck the creature in the shoulder with a resounding crack, and the figure dropped to one knee, a dark liquid flowing from the wound. Its face was a mask of agony; the spot where the blade had cut in was crackled and burnt.

Kornid looked shocked as the creature let out a roar and its flesh started to ripple. They all watched in horror as the blade slid upward and the wound began to seal. The creature's frame grew until it towered over Kornid, nearly standing eye to eye with Valex. With a growl, it grabbed the hammer it had been using on the anvil and rained blow after blow onto the smaller dwarf, who had to parry the blows with his great-sword.

"Shit, buy me some time!" Valex pulled his spellbook from his waist and drew a symbol onto the ground.

Kaylessa drew her harp from her belt, and began to sing in a loud, clear voice. An aura of white light surrounded her and once she had finished, she drew her shortbow and circled the creature, firing glowing arrows.

Thwap! Thwap! Thwap! Each shot found its mark in the creature's torso, and each time they made contact it let out a howl as the arrows sunk in to the fletching, It brought the heavy hammer down on Kornid's shoulder once more, driving the dwarf to the ground, before rounding on the source of its annoyance. As it stalked across the room towards her, she drew a short sword and stood her ground, trembling.

Valex finished his ritual circle and as he chanted word after word in the strange language he used, a large storm cloud formed above his head. Its swirling, purple mass looked angry, and as he raised his hand into the air, lightning that was crashing inside the cloud touched down on a ring on his right hand, illuminating him briefly.

"Lightning bolt!" he cried out, and threw his hand up into the air. The storm above him reached a fever pitch and several more bolts of lightning connected with his hand, like a dazzling spiderweb. Drawing the arm downward in an arc, the lightning flexed and moved with him, before blasting out of his outstretched palm at the back of the large monstrosity. The lightning shot across the room, illuminating everything, and struck the creature in the back, where it rippled through its body. It fell to its knees, convulsing with the force of the blast.

Valex collapsed down on his behind, clearly exhausted from the effort. In the flash of light, however, he saw Vel leap from atop the anvil, diving onto the creature's back like a falcon, with both blades drawn and pointed downward. The rapier pierced the right side of its back, and she released the blade. Then hefting the dagger with both hands, she drove it to the hilt into the creature's skull.

With a gurgle, the monster toppled forward, bringing the slight human with it. As it fell, Vel gripped both blades and with a kick of her feet, she executed a deft backflip. Landing on her feet, she began to clean the blades on her cloak.

Kornid climbed to his feet and stood over the dead creature as it withered to its original size. He cleared his throat and spat onto its corpse, which was still shrinking.

He turned to face Vel, who was looking at him impassively. "Ye have my thanks." He raised his hands to acknowledge all of them. "This imposter musta been the one to lay the traps, trying to defend its lair. Without ye, I'd have been killed for sure."

With a scaly foot, Valex poked at the messy pile of remains, which had shrunk down to the size of a dinner plate, and he grimaced. "He wasn't so tough! I've gotta say though, we make a pretty impressive team!" He raised an open hand to Vel, the excitement on his face making him look quite childish.

She brushed past him, toward a door in the rear of the room. Disappointed, Valex turned towards Kaylessa with the same raised hand, but she shook her head at him. He dropped the hand, and sulked over to the door with Vel, who gestured to a small sign on the door, written in Dwarvish. "If it's all the same to you three, I'm sick of being cooped up in this dank place," Vel said. "Is this the place your father kept his tools?"

"Aye, this should be it." Kornid opened the door and coughed as the dust billowed out. Inside was a modestly furnished office, a bookcase in the back, and a short wooden desk in the centre. Sitting atop the desk was a gorgeous bronze hammer and a matching set of bellows.

"I canna believe…I never thought I'd see these again." Kornid turned to look at his companions, tears welling up in his beady eyes. "These are the only things I have to remember my da by. I canna thank you enough…"

"Save your thanks. You can repay us by coming with us to meet our boss," Vel snapped, the open display of emotion causing her to bristle.

Kornid wiped his eyes and stowed the tools in his rucksack. "Right you are. Ye have done me a service, and I'll repay it in kind. In his letter, Wravien says to head northeast, until we reach a fork in the road. It should be freshly paved, but he also said he'll send a friend to meet us there."

Valex pulled his wineskin from his bag and uncorked it. Turning it upside down, he poured the last few drops of ale into his mouth with a shake. "Lead the way, friend. I don't suppose there might be a tavern on the way?"

CHAPTER 6
THE ARCANE TOWER

Day 300 – Somulous Experiment: I'm starting to fear that I've done something irreversible. It's been over 200 days since I discontinued the stimulants, but my body refuses to enter any state of sleep, and the net of thoughts I have access to has become enormous. It's almost maddening, but I believe I'm picking up the individual thoughts <u>of everyone in the building</u>. It's extraordinary and I would be ecstatic... if I could only remember what I did last week. A.G.

The day's adventure having taken its toll, they made camp in the mouth of the forge's amphitheatre. As dawn broke, they tore down camp and took to the road, Kornid riding double in front of Valex, as he had no mount of his own. Kornid had shared the directions that Wravien had provided, but the direction they travelled was taking them through a very undeveloped part of Illium, and they met no other travellers as they rode. They filled the time with stories from Kornid, about his father and Wravien's adventures.

"Aye, my pa was a Tempest paladin like me, and his patrols would often take him out to sea. But in those days, the Tempest didn't have the numbers they have now, and they would have to resort to hiring reliable sellswords to flesh out tha crew. Wravien was the best of em; he was always a quiet man on the voyage, he dinna drink, or rabble rouse, but if there was a battle to be had, something in him changed. He would rush the deck of the ship like the devil had come alive inside him and whirl through the enemy like a dervish with a sword in each hand and a bloody grin on his face."

Kornid fell silent for a moment, as if carefully considering what to say next. "Pa spoke highly of him, and often. Even when the bloodlust overtook him, he was fiercely protective of the crew and was always willing to put his life on the line to get the job done. Hones'ly, I've heard so many stories, I'm a little scared to meet the man behind the legend."

They rode through the day, passing the odd deserted farmer's field, and when the sun began to go down, Valex pestered them into a detour into a small hamlet to refill his wineskin. His demeanour was decidedly more cheery as they reached their destination.

The broad dirt road curved to the left and there was a slightly shabby cobblestone path leading to the right, through a cluster of small hills. At the signpost of the fork, perched on the wood they saw a familiar black bird, which chirped at them and flew down the path.

They followed and emerged into a small courtyard. Flat, tilled land surrounded it, but the rolling hills that surrounded the area obscured it from view. In the centre of the square was a round fountain, and at the northernmost edge stood a three-story building, a hanging sign proclaiming it to be "The Kraken." There were areas of land that had been staked out around the square, where there looked to be the beginnings of construction, but the only other finished building was a small, round, open-air forge to the east of the tavern.

They urged their horses forward onto the square and heard hammering and loud, muffled cursing. Peering around the fountain, they saw the familiar form of Nogret, the dwarf they had met the night they met Wravien. Sweat was pouring off his bald head and onto his considerable gut, as he stacked bricks and layered mud to form a wall. He saw the foursome, placed his hands on the small of his back, stretched it with an audible crack they heard from across the square, and climbed over the small wall to greet them.

"Well, well, well, if it isn't the tavern brawlers." Nogret dropped them a wink (or a blink, it was hard to tell with the eyepatch). "I was wondering if you lot were gonna show up. I expect the boss man'll be expecting ye."

Kornid stepped forward, placed his right hand across his chest, and bowed in a traditional dwarven salute. "Hail, kinsman! My name is Kornid…"

"Ye, sorry boyo, but I don' really care. The one ye'll be wanting ta make introductions to is in the tavern, yonder." Nogret cocked his head towards the tavern, lit the stub of cigar with a flick of a match, and returned to his work.

Kornid frowned as they walked towards the bar. "…Not the most social fellah, is he?"

"Trust me, you don't know the half of it." Vel rubbed absently at a fading bruise on her cheek, and they left the dwindling sunset, entering the tavern. The smells of fresh mortar and paint were still hanging in the air, the wooden bar and tables shined with fresh polish, and the lights, while dim, gave it an inviting air. The clusters of tables were empty at present, but the back wall of the bar held a raised veranda, a small staircase leading up to a long, heavy table. This was clearly the main feature of the bar, and twelve chairs were placed around it, all empty, save for the two closest to the centre, facing the bar.

Wravien occupied centre stage, but sitting next to him was a very well dressed halfling they hadn't met. His blond hair was slicked down with some kind of grease, and his fancy shirt and jacket looked very out of place in the construction site they found themselves in. As they admired the room, another familiar face popped up from behind the bar and a friendly voice called out to them.

"Hey! You guys made it!" Tim exclaimed, rising to his feet, a cleaning rag clutched in his fist.

"Tim!" Valex cried, grabbing his companions and sweeping them to the bar, "Is this what you meant by, see you soon?"

"Valex right? Wravien made me an offer I couldn't refuse, I was up to my eyeballs in debt on the other bar, but he got me out of the deal and had this place built from the ground up for me! Care to introduce me to your friends?" He grinned openly at them, seeming to forget that he'd seen them all destroy his old bar.

"This is Vel Valdove, Kaylessa Siannodel, and a new acquaintance, Kornid Oakheart." Valex gestured to the three in turn, and when he got to the dwarf's name, Tim startled.

"Wravien told me to send you over to him as soon as you got here, Kornid. Head to the table at the back, I'll swing by in a minute to grab your order."

Kornid nodded and walked over to the table.

Tim turned his attention back to Valex and said, "Looks like we're going to be seeing a lot of each other from here on out, let me pour you guys a glass of something good to celebrate, on the house."

Before they could respond, Tim turned and pulled a dusty bottle full of a golden liquid from the top shelf of the sparsely-filled liquor cabinet. With a flourish, he produced four small glasses and poured a generous helping into each. Vel and Kaylessa eyed it suspiciously, but Valex grabbed his glass immediately, clinked it against the one sitting in front of Tim, and guzzled it down.

Tim gave him an annoyed glance but raised his glass and gestured for the ladies to do the same. "Here's to new partners, and here's to Ravencroft!" He touched his glass to Vel and Kaylessa's, and they all drank. Vel grimaced, but Kaylessa burst into a coughing fit, ducking under the bar to compose herself. Valex, however, was licking his beak and eyeing the bottle.

"Tim, that is delicious. Spicy, smooth, what is it?"

"You've got an eye for quality, my friend. This is elvish goodberry mead, from my time in Thras'lunia. I've likely had this bottle longer than you've been alive!" He chuckled and leaned over the bar. "You alright down there, dear?"

Kaylessa stood up, eyes streaming tears, which she whipped away with the back of her hand. "Yeah…yeah, thank you for the drink Tim, it was…delicious." She stifled a burp, looking ill. "What is this Ravencroft you mentioned?"

"Oh, I'm glad you liked it! Let's have another!" Vel and Kaylessa both shook their heads, but Valex pushed his glass towards the human. "Oh well, more for us, Valex!"

Tim took the shot with a slight grimace and addressed the elf. "Well, you are in it! The big man will likely explain it all to you, but we've gotten a permit to establish a hamlet here. Speaking of, looks like he's all finished with your friend, you three should head over."

Valex placed a silver coin on the bar, nodded knowingly at Tim, and directed the trio towards Wravien's table before the bartender could protest. Kornid had left the table and he nodded at them as he passed. Vel, Valex, and Kaylessa approached, and Wravien directed them to the seats at the front of the table.

"My brave soldiers." Wravien stood as they took their seats, but the halfling with him stayed seated, boots crossed casually on the table in front of him. He gave them a cursory glance and began filing his nails.

"You've done perfectly!" Wravien went on. "Kornid has signed on; he'll be working out of the forge we installed outside, and I'd like to introduce you to another compatriot." He gestured to the slight man beside him. "This is Tanbis Zilgrim. He is…a halfling of many means. Anything you need, with some time, he can procure."

"You can call me Fingers." Tanbis swung his feet off the table (surprisingly stuffed into a pair of loafers–most halflings stayed barefoot.) and straightened up. His clothes were immaculate, his hair and beard were tidy, and he carried himself with the air of someone unaccustomed to such a dirty tavern. "Everyone does. As Wravien said, I'm the money guy. If you find any treasures out there, bring em to me. I'll appraise em, and make sure you get top dollar. Wravien and I go a ways back, and if he vouches for you, then you're all friends in my book."

Vel looked at the smug grin on the halfling's face, a look she had seen a dozen times from the con men who had played her brother, and she made a mental note to double check any price he came up with. Ignoring the halfling, she turned to Wravien. "Job well done, means payment, right, boss?" She put an emphasis on the last word, causing Wravien to cock an eyebrow at her.

"Of course Vel, all in due time." He stepped away from his spot at the table and joined them at the other side. "Tanbis, excuse us a moment. My friends, Step outside with me, I'd like to show you something."

Tanbis left the table and approached Tim, and Valex, Vel, Kaylessa, and Wravien walked through the double doors and saw the courtyard illuminated by light. Someone had placed torches around the exterior of the square, and the soft light made it look cleaner than it had in the light. Wravien walked up to the fountain, dipped a hand in, and placed it on the back of his neck. Relief flooded his face, and he turned to the trio. "Welcome to my project, Ravencroft." He gestured around, arms outstretched. "It doesn't look like much yet, but with a bit more work we'll get this place filled and get some commerce rolling." He pointed towards the smaller domed building, where Kornid was setting things up. Kaylessa noted Kornid had hung his father's tools above the entrance with reverence.

"Kornid has an important first step. His knowledge of metallurgy will be invaluable in crafting defences for our little hamlet, but that brings me to your next job."

Vel's hand reached out but before she could open her mouth, Wravien drew another one of the cloth bags of coin from his bag and pressed it into her open palm with a wry smile. He tossed identical bags to Valex and Kaylessa.

"With our previous business concluded, let's get you briefed." A raven flew down from atop The Kraken and perched on his shoulder. "I need you three to look into something peculiar. My familiar, Charon, had been keeping an eye on a potential recruit, a wizard by the name of Quebys Glassholm. She is a brilliant scholar, but her extracurricular studies caused her to be expelled from the Mage's College in Grand Covus. This work, while frowned upon by the academic community, could be of great use to us, so I've kept a close eye on her tower, which up until last week was located in southern Ephiya."

Valex shot a quizzical look at Vel, who stayed unimpressed.

"The tower has vanished. Not destroyed, not invisible, just gone."

"What do you mean, vanished?" Vel queried. "Towers don't just get up and walk away, regardless of how magical they are."

"Stranger things have happened, and I thought of that, but Charon surveyed the surrounding area and there's no sign of any disturbance to the surrounding wood. I'd like you to head to the last known location and see if you can pick up the trail." He touched his right temple, and the familiar darkness flooded the eye on that side of his face. The bird on his shoulder gave a slight tremor, then took flight.

"Follow Charon. He's been there before and can show you the way. If you find any sign of her, send Charon back to me, and I'll provide further instructions." He turned on his heel as Charon took flight, and walked back towards the bar, Valex right behind him.

"You guys go on ahead!" said Valex. "I've got to see Tim about something for the road, I'll catch up!"

Vel rolled her eyes but she mounted up, and Kaylessa followed suit to follow the raven's path.

A few hours later, the bird dipped low and submerged into the deep canopy of a forest, as Vel, Valex, and Kaylessa followed. The trees grew thick on either side of the road and the canopy above them blocked out most of the early sunlight, limiting their visibility. Vel had the best eyes, so she rode in the front keeping her eyes glued to the black silhouette of the raven. The bird suddenly veered to the left and vanished from sight.

Vel pulled on her reins hard, and so did Kaylessa, bringing their horses to a stop. Valex kept riding—but realising he had passed his companions, he led the Clydesdale in a clumsy circle and returned to the group.

"What's going on, why did you stop?" Valex's voice was slightly slurred.

Kaylessa brought herself parallel to him and deftly plucked the half empty wineskin from his bag, stowing it in her own with a roll of her eyes. "Why don't I hold onto this for a bit, Valex."

Valex started to complain, but one look at the glares he was receiving from his companions silenced him, and he nodded meekly. "But Vel, why did we stop? Did you lose sight of Charon?"

Vel was scanning the wall of trees, eyes squinted in concentration. The twisted branches created a barrier that should have been too dense for something as large as the raven to pass through. "I had it, but it dipped left and vanished. There is no way it could have gotten away from me that easily."

Vel's face was a thundercloud, but Kaylessa dropped off her mare, and drew the harp from her belt. After a few cursory strums, she closed her eyes and began to play a mysterious melody on the lower end of the instrument. Before their eyes, the wall of wood shimmered and warped, and a semicircle of light began to pulse. After a few moments, the previously impassable wood vanished, revealing an overgrown, winding path.

"A magical barrier." Kaylessa put the harp back on her belt. "If this woman is anything like the other people we've met in Ravencroft, I imagine she'll be playing things pretty close to the chest."

Valex stared at her, visibly impressed. "Oh, you are gonna *have* to teach me that one."

They followed the path, one after another due to how narrow it was, and emerged in a large clearing. The grass here was tall and unkempt, but they could see a storage shed off to the left and a small clearing with a campfire pit to the right. At the back of the clearing was a circle of large stones, surrounding a curious patch of bare earth.

Kaylessa drifted towards the campsite and began to sift through the ashes, while Vel turned to the shed, sensing there might be some valuables. She turned her attention to the latch, which had a fairly rudimentary lock. She drew the tools from her belt, but as soon as she'd inserted the longer of the two, she cursed and dropped the tool, shaking her hand. "Damn thing burned me!"

She stuck her fingers into her mouth as Valex inspected the door. Clicking his tongue, he pulled the tome from his belt, muttered a command word, and the latch popped open.

"Magical locks," he said, "we aren't dealing with some half-rate magician. Let's get in here and see if there are any clues."

He stepped forward into the cramped opening, and Vel slipped in behind him. Still grumbling about how she didn't trust magic, she stared in disbelief at the contents of the room. There were jars of strange, pickled animal parts, rolls of parchment neatly squirrelled away into a rack, and a large wooden chest with many drawers. She opened two at random and saw incense, and what appeared to be some kind of red powder.

"Useless." She pushed a stack of papers off the edge of a small table onto the floor. "Why lock it up, if you don't keep anything of value in here?"

"What are you talking about?" Eagerly pulling down jars and opening vials, Valex looked like a child in a sweets shop. "The stuff in here is a wizard's dream. Look, preserved frogspawn! This would have taken me months to ferment on my own!"

"Whatever." Vel stepped back into the clearing and lit a torch in the dying light. "Tell me you've got some good news, Kaylessa."

"Not sure if it's entirely helpful, but this fire was used for cooking within the last few days. Wherever this character is, they can't have gone far."

Vel walked toward the patch of barren earth in the centre and placed her hands on her hips. "I'm more interested in whatever happened here. If I had to guess, I'd say that this was where our 'missing tower' used to sit." She kicked one of the rocks on the clearing and flinched, but when nothing happened, she gestured Kaylessa over. "Come on, let's take a walk around the perimeter. Everything I know about wizards tells me you don't walk through their circles."

As the two women began to make their way around, Valex continued his looting. He found a locked drawer but realising the only arcane lock had been the one on the door, gave it a strong tug and the wood splintered. Opening the ruined drawer, Valex found a rolled up scroll, the quality of the paper much higher than the others. Upon it was a strange, blue wax seal. He drew a talon across it, unrolled the ageing parchment, and began to read.

Kaylessa and Vel made their way around to the opposite side of the circle. Kaylessa looked back toward where Valex was standing and was shocked to see a large, glowing archway. It looked like a tear in the fabric of reality with swirling purple mist at its centre.

"Valex!" she called out urgently, just as Valex reached for the wineskin hanging from the back of Kaylessa's horse. He turned around, caught in the act, and called out, "I wasn't going for it, just wanted to see how much was left!" They stared at him, aghast, and he rolled his eyes and made his way around the circle to them.

With a look of sheepish good nature on his face, he approached his companions. "Now, there's no reason to look so serious. It was just a quick dri…" Getting where they stood, he saw the portal. He was, for once, at a loss for words. He cleared his throat once, then again, and muttered, "Yeah, that's not something you see every day."

"Any idea what we're dealing with, magic boy?" said Vel.

"Well, the majority of my training was in illusion magic, but this looks very different from anything I've seen in practice. If I had to guess, I'd say this is likely some kind of portal, likely to another realm!" He unshouldered his quarter-staff and stood in front of the swirling miasma. "Callum always told me to stay away from this kind of magic. Making a door isn't too hard, but doors work two ways. You can't always be sure that something won't use it to enter our realm." He took the staff in two hands, holding it at the very end of its reach, and slid it through the mist. Aiming toward the ground, he began to slowly walk forward, as the staff was swallowed by the portal. Once it had almost reached his hands, he pulled it back and inspected the end.

"Well?" Kaylessa looked anxious.

"It appears to be harmless, at least to a wooden stick. There also appears to be solid ground on the other side. I'm guessing this 'Quebys' was messing around with some powerful magic and tore a hole in spacetime. We're going to have to pass through it if we're going to get her back."

Kaylessa and Vel exchanged a look and both turned to Valex expectantly.

"What are you looking—oh, of course. Send the minority through, typical." However, he couldn't disguise his curiosity. Raising his right hand, he walked forward until his hand reached the gateway and disappeared from view.

Valex turned back to Vel and smirked. "See, nothing to it…" Suddenly, the smirk changed to a look of shock. "Oh my God, something's got my hand!"

"Valex!" they cried out in unison as Valex was jerked through the portal. Vel drew her rapier and Kaylessa nocked an arrow. They waited a moment, until Valex's head poked through the portal at waist height, a cheeky grin on his scaly features.

"Pffffft, Just kidding! God, if you'd seen your faces!" He looked from Kaylessa to Vel and stood up, emerging from the portal. "Oh come on, that was funny. But for real, you need to see this. Step through." He disappeared again, leaving Vel and Kaylessa to shake their heads.

"Does he realise how close I was to firing an arrow in there?" Kaylessa sighed, returning the arrow to its quiver. "We've got to do something about his drinking. It's getting dangerous."

"Later." Vel approached the rift, looking quite scared. "If he's right, we've got more than enough to deal with already." She tensed her body, closed her eyes, and held her breath. After a moment, she stepped through the portal, vanishing.

Kaylessa looked around and found a nearby boulder, upon which she cinched a length of rope she removed from her pack. She tied it around her waist, gave it an experimental tug, and turned to face the portal gravely before taking a few steps back and running through. Her eyes were closed but she could feel wind blowing all around her, and she had the curious sensation of her body switching from hot, to cold, and back again. Her feet found solid ground, but she held a minute before opening her eyes. What she saw made her wish she had a stronger rope.

They were standing on a stretch of rock that seemed to be floating in midair. All around them, angry purple storm clouds swirled—lightning and thunder ringing out in sheets, illuminating the horizon. In the thick clouds, there were large, alien shapes in the mist, and strange slithery sounds that made her feel sick.

Directly in front of them on the other side of the plateau, was a tall building, five or six stories, which could only be described as a "wizard's tower." The cylindrical base rose up, twisting at crazy angles before coming to a steepled roof where the strange antennas and the barrel of a large telescope only added to the alien feel of it. Lights shone in every window as the tower progressed, but there was something off about them. One floor had a spectral green glow that made Vel very uneasy, another was flashing blue, and the window in the door at the base had white light flowing out of it. At the top of the tower, was the telltale flicker of a candle's flame.

Valex had to shout to be heard over the storm that swirled around them. "We need to get inside! I don't know what's moving around out there, but I doubt it's friendly!"

The women nodded their assent and Kaylessa took an arrow from her quiver, severed the cord that was held taut through the portal, and tied it to the shaft. She fired it into the ground, recreating the tension, and hurried after her companions.

A sign to the left of the door proclaimed that this was "Quebys Glassholm's Very Own Tower, For The Advancement Of Magical Science And Opportunities, and Brewery."

Valex mouthed the word "brewery" and waggled the spiky ridge above his eyes at Vel. She rolled her eyes at him, aware that that was becoming a habit, and pushed her shoulder into the door. It creaked open and radiant white light flowed out.

They looked through the open doorway, dumbstruck, at the scene that unfolded. The room was furnished as one might expect for an entryway, but glowing white portals were opening and closing on the walls, releasing small, strange creatures. They were geometrically shaped and had various cogs and wheels sticking out of them at odd angles, along with the odd, very strange eye. The vast majority of them seemed to be carrying some kind of white stone, but if any of the creatures were aware of their presence, they did a good job hiding it.

Valex was trying to rationalise the situation, when one of the portals opened directly across from him and he gasped. Through the milky film covering the doorway, he saw an immaculate golden temple, and a statue of a man wearing what could only be described as a giant pair of armoured fists on his back.

Vel took a defensive stance almost immediately, but upon seeing the creature's indifference, approached the nearest portal. She raised a dagger, point first, and pressed it to the portal, where the blade disintegrated upon touch. Dropping the ruined hilt, a forlorn look on her face, she looked towards the back of the room, where a staircase led up out of the room. This was flanked by two of the creatures, but these two were different. With large, triangular bodies, each creature had six arms, each set holding a spear. The eyes on these particular monstrosities were flying all around the room. They might look odd, but Vel knew sentries when she saw them.

Valex was talking mostly to himself, deep in thought. "I think...I think I know what this is. I'm pretty sure I've read about it..."

Kaylessa had noticed the guards, but was looking up at the endless stream of flying bodies "We need a plan. We might be able to deal with the two by the door, but if the rest of...whatever these are, join in, we're in trouble."

Vel was looking around the room, trying to find a safe route, when Valex noisily startled her. "Alexander!" Both of the girls looked at him as if he had lost his mind, but he continued, unabated. "This is exactly what the God of Light's realm is supposed to look like, and I'll bet these are his minions... Hold on. I think I've got an idea. I've got a new spell that I picked up in the shed that should do *just* the trick!" He drew his spellbook and made a complicated sign with his left hand, whispering, "Major illusion."

The centre of the room shimmered for a moment, and then the form of a giant man appeared in the centre. He was clad in golds and silvers, but most striking was the apparatus that appeared to be fused with his spine. A pair of enormous steel arms protruded from the centre, hanging down at his sides, knuckles resting on the ground. The man looked old but strong and the eye that wasn't obscured by a complicated clockwork eyepatch was a blazing gold.

Vel let out a gasp. Alexander, the God of Light, was in the room with them. She'd seen his image carved into the temples around Grand Covus and appearances like this had been told in stories, but never once had she imagined it happening.

The appearance of their deity caused a commotion among the flying shapes. Whatever routes they had been on ceased, and they all touched down and pressed whatever eyes they had to the ground. The stillness of the room was eerie.

Valex spoke into his cupped hand and the deity's voice boomed out through the room, shaking the furniture. Whatever language it was speaking, Vel and Kaylessa had never heard it, but the creatures sprang into action immediately. Gathering up their tools and pieces of stone, they all fluttered into a single portal, the sentries leaving last, and the portal closed behind them. The large man vanished as quickly as he had appeared, and the room was plunged into darkness.

The silence was punctuated by great, whooping gasps of air from Valex, who had fallen onto his backside.

Vel struck a torch and Kaylessa helped him to his feet. In the dim light, they could clearly see the fatigue on his features, and he took a moment to catch his breath.

Vel rounded on him. "What in the nine hells was that? Was that…was that you?"

"Ohh, wow, I was not sure that was going to work." Valex pulled the wineskin from his bag, ignoring the reproachful look from Kaylessa, "I'm just glad I remembered enough Celestial from my lessons to command them home."

"Is that where we are?" Kaylessa spoke quietly, her tone reverential, "Are we in the realm of light?"

"No, the portals led there, but outside was completely different." Valex frowned and rubbed his chin with a talon. "If I had to guess, I'd say this 'Quebys' must have tapped into a rift world, where the realms are intersecting. It doesn't look like any of the dimensions I've studied, but it does pose a problem. We could run into all manner of things here, and there is no way to predict what will come next. The only thing I know is that this wizard is in over her head, and we need to press on."

Holding his spellbook loosely in his right hand, he grabbed the handrail of the spiral staircase at the back of the room and began to climb. He felt his stomach clench as he worked his way up the narrow, dark stairs. Why was everywhere they went as dark as the mines?.

At the top of the stairs he threw an arm out as they reached the opening of the next floor, halting their progress. Kaylessa and Vel craned around Valex's bulk to see what awaited them.

At first, the room seemed devoid of light, but a bright blue flash illuminated the chamber, followed by another across the room. The light was followed by a thunderous roaring sound, which peeled out twice, causing the hair on Vel and Kaylessa's bodies to stand on end. Kaylessa let out a small shriek, but Vel clapped her hand over her mouth immediately, squinting into the inky darkness.

"Quiet, you fool. I can't be sure, but I thought I saw something moving in there. Remember, Valex said we could run into *anything* here—we need to stay alert."

She sidled past Valex, hugging the wall, and began to make her way around the perimeter of the room. The farther into the room she got, the more her eyes adjusted, and she was able to make out six circular shapes floating about the room. They were a blue so dark it was almost black, but ripples of lightning were floating in them. Assuming these were the source of the light and sound, she crept forward, drawing the hood of her cloak.

Almost as if on cue, as soon as she leaned forward to look into the swirling blackness, a pair of crackling blue orbs emerged from the fog, and she dove to the side as something large and sleek burst forth with another flash of light. The shape shot across the room and vanished into one of the clouds on the other side. She had a moment of bewilderment, until the pain set in, as the thunder crashed in the room. Looking down, she saw three angry red lines had arced through her leather gauntlet, rending the flesh down to the bone.

The light flashed once more across the room, and she threw herself to the floor, feeling a rush of air over her head as something made contact with the cloud beside her. She crawled on all fours, making her way back to the entranceway, where Vel and Valex were waiting for her.

"Well?" Valex hissed through clenched teeth, "are we safe to cross?" He nodded towards another stairwell across the room.

"Definitely not." Vel tore a strip off the end of her cloak and was tying a makeshift bandage around her bloody forearm. "There is something in the clouds, and it's jumping from side to side faster than I can see, and *that's* saying something." She grimaced, tightening the fabric around her wound.

Valex peered out into the dark, fumbling the clasp of his tome open and closed. The more he racked his brain, the fewer solutions seemed viable. How could he stop something he couldn't see? He was so lost in thought that he hadn't noticed Kaylessa step tentatively into the room, drawing her harp.

"I should be able to slow them down." She plucked a few strings experimentally. "But you'll need to be ready. If my song stops for even a second, the flow of time will return to normal, and I'll be torn to shreds."

Vel and Valex stepped into the room on either side of her, grim determination on their faces. Kaylessa stood still, fingers poised on the strings, and took a deep breath. The lightning flashed, and she began to play, focusing her gaze on the source of the light.

As the swirling clouds slowed down, An alien beast burst from within the mist across the room, its dark-blue fur sending sparks cascading all around. It looked like an enormous lion, except instead of a mane of fur, it had a wreath of white-hot lightning, and the twin tails lashing above its body. Even under the influence of Kaylessa's magic, its trajectory across the room was fast. Vel looked at Valex and saw both his hands burst into flame.

"Oy, lizard!" Vel had to shout to be heard over the thunderous crash that filled the room in slow motion. She drew two of her longer daggers, and threw them both in the direction of the lumbering behemoth. Both sank into its flesh, but the roar of pain that followed was low and distorted. "You ever have kebab?"

Valex was deep in concentration, keeping his magic flowing into his blazing palms, but seeing the two metal handles sticking out of the beast, he understood at once and braced himself.

Deftly stepping to the right, he gripped the handles of both blades, and with a tremendous heave, he hoisted the creature over his head and released the spell. The flames poured out of his hand into the conductive metal and poured into the creature's innards. Fire bloomed in its belly and the creature's eyes popped from the intensity of the heat, Valex allowed the heavy animal to fall to the ground, where it crackled and melted away.

Vel took a deep breath, turned to congratulate Kaylessa on her quick thinking, and saw the shadow of a second animal stretching over her. *How could I be so stupid?* she thought, surging forward. *Of course there is more than one of these things.*

She drew her rapier, the last armament she had, and braced the hilt with both hands. She dove across the room, sliding in the dust on the cobblestone floor, and thrust the blade into the open air above Kaylessa, but kicked the elf's legs out from under her. As Kaylessa fell, the spell broke with a horrific, tearing sound. The room was plunged into darkness as the clouds around them faded from view, while an afterimage of the enormous creature floated in the dark.

"Vel!" Valex cried into the silence, drawing his tome and crying the command word, "Light, damn you, light!"

The ball of light erupted from the book, and illuminated the form of the lion, standing still with its claws outstretched. Valex began to conjure a ball of fire in his palm, but the same tearing sound rang through the silent chamber again, the form of the lion toppled to the ground, and Valex could make out the form of a human, sword outstretched, positively drenched in a dark fluid, he assumed was blood. The pose she had adopted had taken the creature's momentum and used it against it, skewering it like an arrow in a target.

Valex was once again impressed by the slender human standing before him, dripping blood. The reflex of mind and body required to pull off such a feat was astronomical, let alone the strength required to not topple to the ground under the creature's weight. Looking at the glistening rapier, dripping visccra, hc oncc again patted himself on the back for his decision to give the blade to Vel.

"Vel, are you hurt?" Kaylessa moved forward, strumming a pleasing tone on the harp that relaxed the tension in Valex's shoulders. "I can't believe you risked your life for me like that!"

Vel, still standing rigid as a statue, suddenly dropped to one knee. With a retching sound, she purged her stomach onto the stone floor, and the amount of the dark-blue fluid they saw was alarming.

"Oh. My. God," she gasped, wiping her face with the hem of her cloak. "I shouldn't have yelled when I made contact. I swallowed so much blood." Grimacing, she sheathed the rapier and turned her back to Kaylessa and Valex. "It was…it was just instinct." She applied a haughty tone but it felt forced. "Don't expect me to throw my life away every time you idiots get careless."

"Aw." Valex put both claws under his chin, cocked his head to the side, and cooed, "Is our resident hard ass finally developing feelings?"

"Shut it," she snapped at the chortling dragonborn. "We've got more floors to clear and I'd like to get back home to clean this gunk off, if you don't mind." With a decidedly wet sounding swish of her cloak, Vel headed to the staircase, with Valex and Kaylessa on her heels.

Gliding up the stairs, quiet as the grave, save for the odd dripping of blood from her clothes, she led the trio to the next floor, and looked suspiciously around as they entered the next room. The light in here was a soft, golden glow, originating from a large, slowly revolving circle emblazoned on the ceiling. The room itself looked to be a makeshift study, of sorts. Bookcases lined the walls, and the only real piece of furniture was a hefty writing desk and a single chair.

Valex approached the nearest shelf and let out an annoyed snort. "All of these books are in Gnomish," he scoffed, thumbing through a battered volume. "Who even reads Gnomish? I can't remember the last time I even *saw* a gnome."

Kaylessa left the stairwell, passing Vel adjusting her bandaged arm, she noticed something odd about the room. Scattered around were shining baubles, trinkets made from gold and silver that looked quite valuable. She noticed that none of the treasures were scattered outside of the light spilling out of the large circle overhead, but she stepped forward and plucked a jewelled chalice from the ground. The circle on the ceiling flared to a brassy orange colour and began to spin faster, and Kaylessa jumped back, drawing an arrow from her quiver and pointing it skyward, before moaning, "What now?!"

The circle gradually slowed before the spinning stopped, and with an audible popping noise, gold coins began to rain from the ceiling. The coins cascaded for a few minutes before coming to a stop as the circle of light overhead dimmed and resumed its lazy rotation.

Vel stepped over the threshold, looking for any indication of something else happening, and when nothing did, she picked up a coin from the floor and bit into it, feeling the soft give of a true golden coin. She began to scoop up the gold that littered the chamber, stuffing it into her sack.

Kaylessa passed by her, oblivious to the riches littering the floor. "See, not everything in this tower is trying to kill us. Are you coming, Vel?"

Valex had packed away several of the books and was waiting with Kaylessa at the staircase, but Vel had finished clearing the room of anything shiny and was looking at the slow-spinning circle at the roof. She took a small piece of stone from the floor and threw it towards the circle, which changed from the lazy gold colour to a grave purple and began spinning rapidly.

"Ahh…We've got a greedy one." An inhuman voice filled the chamber, making the teeth in their heads shake. Vel, looking alarmed, tried to step backwards but found her limbs were very much out of her control.

"You were given a gift, a boon, but still you wanted more. Normally, if I was at my full power, I'd punish such greed, but in my limited capacity, I'll have to play a trick to fill the time instead." The voice's quality kept changing from a thick gurgle, to the voice of a reedy old man, to the voice of a child. It seemed to be coming from everywhere and nowhere all at once. A flash of light filled the room and a thick, grey smog filled the circle. Coughing, Kaylessa stepped forward, with an arrow at the ready.

"Vel?" she called into the mist, bowstring taut at the sign of any trouble.

"I'm fine, I'm fine." Vel was coughing harshly, her voice cracking, "I think it's over. I can move again."

Valex and Kaylessa watched as a very old woman emerged from the smoke. She was clad in the same leather armour as their companion, and her snow-white hair was tied into the same braid. The deep coughing sound was very appropriate for a woman her age, but as she approached, her brows creased. "I think I'm fine—what are you idiots staring at?"

Valex shook his head once, his mouth hanging open, but Kaylessa stepped forward and took the old woman's hands in her own, holding them up to the light.

Seeing the gnarled fingers, all knuckles and liver spots, the old woman let out a howl. "What's happened to me?!" she wailed. "How did I get so old?!"

Valex pondered this; he had heard stories of some types of mages whose magic was intrinsically tied to their bodies, as opposed to the tried and true magics he had been taught. These wizards typically had similar maladies inflicted upon casting their spells. He tried to explain it as best he could, while holding back the great peals of laughter that threatened to burst forth. The dark expression on Vel's wrinkled face told him that laughing would be *most* unwise.

"Look, once we get back, I'm sure we can find a way to reverse the spell. Until then, just be careful, and let us handle any threats we encounter."

He headed towards the stairs before pausing a moment, looking back, and saying, "Did you…did you want a hand up the stairs?"

Valex ducked as Vel threw the nearest book at him, and he headed up the staircase with Kaylessa. He snorted. "Serves her right, she's already gotten herself loads of coin. We will have to be careful, we'll never forgive ourselves if something harms our new grandmother."

Kaylessa covered her mouth to hide her grin.

The next stairwell seemed longer than the last, a fact made evident by Vel's strained effort to climb. She was clutching the handrail with a trembling hand, taking the steps one at a time, but when Valex offered again to help her, she spit out a string of curses at him so vile that Kaylessa covered her ears.

At the top of the stairs, they entered a small, dark hallway hardly large enough for them to walk three abreast. At the end of the hall, they heard giggling and screeches and saw tiny pinpricks of light denoting eyes in the dark. Kaylessa grabbed her bow and Valex cast a spell to cause the small ball of light to illuminate the corridor.

Crouched around what looked to be a small hole in the floor, were four humanoid figures. They looked to be quite small, maybe coming up to Valex's waist, and their patchy garments revealed snatches of red skin. They had small horns on their heads and appeared to be helping a fifth figure through the hole.

"Are those…goblins?" Valex said incredulously, cocking his head. "Why would there be goblins in here? And why are they red?"

"This must be another one of those portals," said Kaylessa. "At least we know that goblins shouldn't give us too much trouble. Vel, stay back, we can handle—Vel, what are you doing?"

Vel pushed past her, drawing her dagger from its sheath. The tremble in her arms was even more pronounced, and she had to use two hands to keep the dagger held upright. "Some silly magic spell isn't going to keep me from doing my job. You guys focus on the portal, I'll deal with these wretches."

Vel shambled forward, much slower than she normally would, and let out a feeble little cry. The goblins turned to face her and their snarls turned to laughs, they sheathed their weapons and began to mimic her dragging gait, whining and moaning in an alien language. Vel's face darkened.

The goblins in the back began to pull a large, wicked-looking contraption from the portal that was all spikes and blades. As soon as Vel got close, she thrust the dagger into the throat of the first goblin. The eruption of purple blood soaked its companions, and the two dragging the torture device dropped it back into the portal as they all stared open mouthed at her.

She wrenched the blade free with a painful sounding grunt and turned to face them. "Who else thinks this is funny?" she said.

As the goblins scrambled to draw their weapons, two arrows came over her shoulder, one striking the closest goblin in the throat, the other taking off the top of the second goblin's head. Valex ran the length of the hallway and kicked the remaining goblin into the hole on the floor, listening to his scream fade as he fell through the air.

Looking through the portal, Valex had a sense of vertigo. Below him was a war-torn battlefield, covered in hundreds—no, thousands of the red creatures, and it appeared this portal was up in the sky. He could see that a bizarre wooden structure had been erected, and it was absolutely covered in the small red figures, all waving tiny swords and shields as they crawled towards him.

"Nope. Nope, nope, nope, we are NOT going in there," Valex said, heading towards a door on the side of the hallway. Grunting with effort, he tore the door from its hinges, and placed it over the strange hole on the floor. He scoured the nearby room, a bedroom of some sort, and came back with his arms full of heavy paperweights and books and stacked them on the door. They heard the thumping of the goblins trying to push past the barricade.

Valex turned to his companions. "I suggest we move on. I don't mind killing a goblin or two, but several hundred might be a challenge. By the way, Vel, good work! For an old woman, you sure showed them who's boss. Maybe your adventuring days aren't over."

"Valex, I swear to God, if you don't close your godforsaken beak right now, I'll throw you down that hole myself." Vel said, grimacing as she stretched her back, with her hands at her hips. "Come on, looks like… oh joy, more stairs."

They climbed for what felt like ages, Vel's laborious breathing acting as a backdrop. She had to stop twice, unlacing her boots and rubbing at her feet, much to her chagrin, but they climbed until they reached a closed door. Valex grabbed the handle and pulled, letting out a yelp as a pile of sand came cascading down the stairs onto him and his companions. The amount that spilled through was ridiculous, but after a few minutes he saw a small tunnel had been created and warm sunlight was flowing into the hallway.

"What in the nine hells?" he muttered, climbing up through the doorway and emerging in a vast desert. The sky overhead was a sapphire blue, and the dunes of sand stretched as far as he could see. This couldn't have been contained within the tower—the sheer scope of it was enough to make Valex question his grip on his sanity.

Vel and Kaylessa climbed their way up (Kaylessa offering a helpful arm to Vel, who used it begrudgingly). The ground began to rumble and the hole in the floor filled with sand, obscuring the only means of escape. A moment of silence passed between the companions, but it was broken by a low, grinding sound beneath the desert in front of them, accompanied by a deep, feminine voice that rang through the air.

"Oh good, it's been an eternity since I've had any playthings." A woman's face rose from the sand, beautiful and tragic, followed by the body of a four-legged, winged animal. She stretched her wings wide, shaking a cascade of sand onto Vel, Valex, and Kaylessa, before sitting down on her haunches and surveying them with gleaming, silver eyes.

"I…That is to say…we…" Valex was once again at a loss for words. "I'm sorry, but where are we?"

"You are in my home." The creature's voice was seductive, charming. "It appears I've been able to take it with me somewhere new. I'm quite excited to meet my new toys, I do hope you'll be more entertaining than the last ones."

With a swipe of a very large paw, adorned with razor-sharp talons, she cleared some sand away to reveal a pile of bones, sun bleached and picked clean. Vel and Valex exchanged a look, unsure of how to proceed, but Kaylessa stepped forward and curtsied.

"I've heard legend of your kind, honourable Sphynx. I'm sure my companions and I will be up to the challenge of entertaining you, but as is the custom, we must place our wagers before we begin."

"Of course. Always the binding agreements. They are nearly as dry as the sand here. What is it that you mortals desire?" The sphinx looked bored, but docile.

Kaylessa spoke frankly, as if this were a simple market transaction. "We would like you to collapse your domain and allow us safe passage."

"That's all? No gold, no jewels, no immortality or indescribable power?" It was the sphinx's turn to look surprised.

Vel started to open her mouth, but Kaylessa clapped her hand over it before she could begin speaking.

"I know the rules of the old ways, great one. The harder the request, the harder the challenge issued, and we have work to do. Shall we proceed in the traditional fashion?" Kaylessa's tone was polite, like a guest requesting seconds at dinner, but the atmosphere of the desert changed with the sphinx's mood, her annoyance palpable.

She spoke after a brief pause, looking around at the barren landscape. "I had been planning a game of hide and seek, but there isn't much to work with here. Very well, young elf, we shall proceed with the riddling, but remember—an incorrect answer will lead to…"

"Yes, yes, you'll eat our body and soul, trapping us inside your dimension for eternity."

Valex shot Kaylessa a concerned look, but she ignored his glance and continued to the sphinx, "Will you give us a moment, please?"

Kaylessa looked hot and windswept but had a look of fierce determination on her face. She led the others to the side, as the sphinx used its barbed tongue to clean its fur lazily.

"Well, I've bought us a chance," she said, matter of factly. "A sphinx is a vicious killing machine, but they take the rules of their games very seriously. Only one of us will be able to provide the answer, and I think the choice of who is obviously…"

"You," Valex and Vel said in unison.

"Valex—wait, what do you mean, me?" Kaylessa looked startled at the idea. "Valex is the scholar, always studying tomes. If any one of us has a chance, it's going to be him."

Vel crossed her arms across her chest and glanced at Valex. "Kaylessa, you can't say that you aren't perfectly suited for this. As soon as you started talking, it was like you became a different person. Hells, Scales and I didn't even know what this creature was, but you did."

"She's right, kiddo. Unless the riddle is a spell incantation, I'm not going to be much help. You're smarter than the two of us put together. Go on, we're counting on you." Valex nodded his assent.

Vel scoffed, "Speak for yourself," but she patted Kaylessa on the arm, and took a step back.

"You do realise I'm a hundred and fifty years old," said Kaylessa, rankled by the use of the pet name. Valex's look of surprise made it clear that he did not, but Kaylessa continued, quieter now. "Are you sure? If I get this wrong, we're all trapped. Body and soul, for all eternity."

Vel placed her hands on Kaylessa's shoulders, and leaned in close. "If the lizard or I try to answer, we're guaranteed an eternity with this thing. With you, we've got a chance. Kaylessa, we've got faith in you. Try to have a little in yourself." With that, she took a step back, and Valex sat down cross-legged.

Kaylessa hesitated a moment longer but swallowed and turned to face the luminous silver eyes of the sphinx, who had been watching with interest.

"I will take your challenge, great one. My name is Kaylessa Siannodel, first of my name."

"Very well, Kaylessa Siannodel. This is a fine old riddle; you gave me plenty of time to think of it. And remember, if you answer incorrectly I'll devour you all. Do we have an accord?"

The flashing eyes were hypnotising, but Kaylessa never wavered. "We do."

"Good. The riddle is this: I am part of the bird that is not in the sky. I can swim on the water but always stay dry. What am I?" She spoke the riddle in a fast, lilting voice, exaggerating the rhyme, and settled down onto her haunches.

"A part of a bird," Kaylessa mused, eyeing the coiled muscle in the sphinx's hind legs. "A part of a bird that isn't in the sky...a nest? Wait—that's not my answer!" she cried out as the sphynx began to lunge forward. Frustrated, it turned in a slow circle before settling again as the elf ran the riddle over in her head.

"A feather. No, A mouse, caught in its beak! No, A flea, riding on its back!" Valex whispered to Vel, who kicked him in the shin.

"Let her think! It's not going to be something as idiotic as that," Vel croaked, shading her eyes from the sun. She had found a rock to sit on and had once again removed her boots to massage her wrinkled feet.

As Kaylessa paced back and forth, the gnawing teeth of panic began to set in. *She had no idea.* She looked at her new friends, the first she had made while being honest about her identity, but the blazing sun began to slip below the horizon, illuminating their silhouettes and causing her to shade her eyes. The sun was casting long...

"That's it!" she cried suddenly. "The answer is its shadow!"

The sphinx's casual expression slipped for a moment, contorting into a mask of rage, before melting back to its relaxed posture. "Are you sure?" she asked, rising to her feet and spreading her wings. "You know what happens if you're incorrect."

"I am." Kaylessa's chin was raised, her tone defiant.

Vel and Valex watched, hope and despair mingling in their stomachs.

"...Oh very well. Correct. I've been thinking that one up for ages—I was hoping it would be the one to net me a fresh meal. You are all free to go, good luck." She flapped her wings fiercely, stirring up the sand into a whirl-wind, and then she took flight directly towards the sun. As they watched, the glare of the setting sun blinded them.

After a few blinks, Kaylessa looked around and saw they were in an old dormitory of sorts, surrounded by bunk beds. The only evidence of their trial was the sand in their hair and a small, orange stone, the size of a marble. Kaylessa picked it up from the middle of the floor and was sur-prised at the weight and the energy that flowed into her arm. She delicately wrapped it in a piece of fabric and had just about finished clasping her bag when she was hoisted into the air.

"I knew it!" Valex cried cheerfully, hugging her so hard the wind was knocked out of her. "You genius, you!"

"Valex...can't...breathe..." she choked out, and Valex dropped her to her feet, apologising. Taking large, gasping breaths, she looked up at Vel, who was smiling at her.

"For such an old woman, you sure lack confidence," cracked Vel.

Kaylessa's eyes flashed at the joke. "I don't know who you think you are, calling me an 'old woman,' when you look like..."

"Honestly, good work. I knew we made the right choice." Vel turned to the stairwell, all good humor evaporating, and began to climb with Valex at her elbow.

Kaylessa headed after them. "Hey, wait up!"

But Vel had seen something outside the window, watching them. Whatever it was, it had a large yellow eye, and its skin was leathery and spiked. They had to find the wizard, and they had to get the hell out of there.

The next floor was completely empty save for a book bound in a dark-red leather, sitting on a raised dais. Two torches flanked the book, the green flames crackling soundlessly. Vel entered suspiciously but the room seemed relatively harmless, and from the stairwell she heard a pleasant female voice singing an old tavern song offkey. She passed the book without a second glance and motioned for Valex and Kaylessa to follow.

Kaylessa scuttled across the chamber, passing the dais, but as Valex was following behind her he heard a curious voice speak his name. He stopped and heard it again. It was coming from the book!

Nothing in this tower had been safe, and this room was definitely suspicious. He knew that it couldn't be safe, He had become a wizard to bravely navigate the magical mysteries of the world, and he would be damned if he stopped now. He stood in front of the dias, determined to know the tome's secret. He hefted the book, wincing as he prepared for a curse of some sort to blast him, and when nothing happened he sighed in relief.

But the sigh caught in his throat as he opened the book and five stalk-like appendages rose from the centre spine, eyes on the end of each one. Strange words flowed through his mind, and Valex realised whatever this thing was, it was trying to communicate with telepathy.

"We have been trapped, for so very long. For so very long! You must be our first meal. A delicious morsel." The sounds in his head were dissonant, clanging and foreign-sounding.

Well, actually... Valex used all his energy to think in Infernal, another language Callum had had him study. *I believe that by freeing you, I'm your new master. That's how this works, isn't it?*

A wild bluff, but Valex had heard stories of other mages making pacts with demons in exchange for impressive power. In truth, he had exhausted most of his magic in the fight with the lightning beasts, and he couldn't put up much of a fight if this demon decided he was faking.

After a moment of silence, the voice spoke again. This time, it sounded feminine and alluring. *Very well, my loyal acolyte. Remember who your master is, and we can make a deal. I can grant you tremendous, malignant power, and all I require is your complete and utter subservience. And your soul...or your eyes.*

In truth, he considered it heavily. Tremendous, malignant power was appealing, but before meeting Callum he had spent his entire life enslaved to a master and had very little desire to repeat it. Also...his *eyes?*

"Valex!" Vel called across the room, and without thinking, Valex slammed the book shut.

He heard a wet sound and very distantly heard the sound of a voice crying out in his mind. *What are you doing? Let us make a deal!*

"Oh...uh...Here I come!" Valex called back, stowing the evil-looking book in his satchel. Another problem for another day, he supposed. "I'm right behind you!"

Hanging onto each other for support, the three of them climbed the stairs, following the offkey singing and hoping whatever was up there, wasn't looking for a fight.

CHAPTER 7
RETURN TO RAVENCROFT

Day 470 – Somulous Experiment: What have I done? Checking my calendar, I've lost almost a month. I awoke from my state in a cemetery, digging into a grave with my bare hands, the skin raw and bloody. Returning to my home, I was assaulted with deep, private thoughts from anyone I came close too. The noise is overwhelming, I'll need to figure out a method to dampen the voices...before I lose more of my mind than I already have. A.G.

Valex pushed the final door open and the stairwell was flooded with light. His nerves finally giving way, he charged forward with a primal scream. At a desk in the centre of the room, a small figure was perched precariously on a stack of thick books, adding a vial of red liquid to a large, cast-iron cauldron.

At Valex's entrance, the small woman let out a yip, and the stack of books gave way. She managed to drop the entire vial of liquid into the cauldron, and it began to produce an oily green smoke.

Kaylessa pushed past Valex with a, "Really, how clumsy can you be?" and began to toss books aside, trying to find the woman amidst the wreckage.

Vel stepped in and looked around. The room was lit by several floating candles, and a large, blue fire was roaring in the hearth. A comfy-looking bed, very small, was pushed against one wall, and a shelf with many odd-shaped glass beakers and bottles rested against the far wall. A raised landing housed the enormous telescope they had seen from outside. Satisfied that there were no threats here, she sat down in a plush armchair with a groan.

Digging through the mess, Kaylessa found a small hand waving out from inside the pile of books. With a heave, she unearthed a young gnomish woman.

Only a few feet tall, the gnome's features gave off a child-like air, a fact she was obviously trying to hide with the pieces of metal pierced through her ears and the shockingly green hair, styled into an undercut. "My word!" she gasped, massaging her chest. "You scared the hells out of me! Don't you know how to knock?!"

Valex shrugged his shoulders, looking around at the mess he had made. "I'm sorry, it's just that after all the madness leading up here, I didn't know what to expect."

"Ugh, I was so wrapped up in my work. I forgot to tidy the place up, and now I've got guests for the first time in ages!" She slapped a tiny hand to her forehead. "I'm dreadfully embarrassed, and to top it all off, the first thing I do is yell at them! I've forgotten my manners—can I offer you a drink?"

"*Yes*," Valex interjected, before Kaylessa or Vel had a chance to respond.

"My name is Quebys Glassholm, what do I call you lot?" She was digging into a small leather bag, worn at the hip, but it was a curious thing. The bag couldn't have been deeper than five or six inches, but Quebys had her arm shoved in so deep the clasps of the bag were touching her shoulder. "I know I put it in here…" She shook her arm, and they all heard a cascade of many small items falling a great distance. "Oh damn. That will have been my petrified basilisk eyes. That's going to take ages to clean up—Aha! Here we go!"

With great effort, Quebys produced a flask larger than anything sold to common folk and made even more humorous by its disparity with her tiny stature. She gave it a shake, and hearing the liquid sloshing around, gave a smile. With a flick of a small wooden stick in her hand, three glasses soared across the room, sliding onto the table. Valex watched her pour with his jaw hanging open, as an amber liquid flowed out of the flask into each glass, never slowing. He had spent his life learning magic that could assist the townsfolk that lived around Callum's tower, but this was real power. With a flask like that, he would never have to stop into some backwoods tavern to refill. Before he could open his mouth to ask about the spell, Kaylessa had glided across the room and taken the gnome by the arm, pulling her towards the telescope.

"Quebys, as much as we would love to have a social visit with you, we're here on business. Our boss..." She shot a look at Vel, who raised her withered eyebrows at the word, and at Valex, who shrugged, before continuing, "Our *benefactor* gave us a letter to deliver to you, and he said you would know what to do next."

"Interesting, I do love a good mystery, let me see it." Quebys cut the letter open and began to read. The only sound was the crackling fire, and Valex noisily slurping his whisky. Once he polished off his glass, he gestured to Kaylessa's untouched glass with his eye bridge raised, and she slid it over to him.

"Right, that is a generous offer indeed," Quebys folded the letter, placed it back in the envelope, and tossed it on the desk. "He's included some coordinates to teleport my tower to, so hold on a second and I'll get this show on the road."

"Oh no...oh shit...wait!" Vel cried out, but Quebys had unclasped her own tome and shouted a command, and with a violent rattle they were all falling through the air. The chairs and the bed flew upwards, along with the glasses and vials, and Valex, Kaylessa, Vel, and Quebys were tossed about.

"Wait a minute, this isn't what's supposed to happen with this spell!" Quebys cried out, narrowly avoiding a book as it soared past her head.

"We're not in your forest!" Vel's creaky voice called out. She realised Quebys had no idea of what had been happening in her tower and had teleported the tower into the abyss, thinking it would take her to Ravencroft. So, instead of touching down in the town square, they were now spinning through space. Quebys's eyes lit up—but with a great, wet, crunching noise, the tower made contact with something out in the storm, and they all heard a wail of pain in their heads.

"It worked?! It worked! We've achieved realm travel!" Quebys cried, pinwheeling through the air and punching her fists.

"I'm very happy for you," Valex shouted, though he was looking very green indeed. "But your discovery will be short-lived if *you don't find a way to fix this!*"

Quebys was already frantically rifling through the pages of her book. She found what she needed and began to speedily spit out an incantation, waving her hands through the air like a conductor. She kept her eyes glued to the window, and as she spun through the air she held off on the last word. Finally, she let loose with the command word, and with a resounding crash they all fell onto the floor as the tower made contact with solid ground. The golden sunlight flowing through the windows told them they had found safety.

"Right in the nick of time!" Quebys said. She stood up, dusted herself off, and clapped her hands. "Everyone alright?"

"Define alright." Vel untangled herself from the curtains with great difficulty as Kaylessa tried to lift a heavy bookcase off of Valex, who was vomiting onto the floor.

"Still alive? Still have all your limbs?" Quebys confirmed this and ran off towards the door. "Sometimes you have to break a few eggs when you're doing research. I'm going to see this Wravien fellow, and I'll tidy it up when I'm back. See yourselves out, would you?"

With a cheery wave, Quebys slipped through the door and descended the stairs, leaving Vel and Kaylessa trying to clean up Valex as he worked through his stomach heaves.

By the time they had collected themselves, cleaned up Valex, made their way down the many floors (finally portal free), and emerged in the courtyard, they encountered Quebys on her way back from her meeting with Wravien.

She had a spring in her step and was clutching a large rolled up piece of parchment. "He's a no-nonsense fellow, isn't he?" She waved as she passed. "But true to his word! He said he wanted to see you three immediately!" Pausing, she turned back towards Vel, adopting a maternal voice. "I'm not sure you should be doing such dangerous errands, Grandmother! You'll hurt yourself!"

"Your damnable tower did this to me!" Vel howled, and Valex had to hold her back to keep her from charging at the tiny gnome, gnarled fists clenched. "I'm no grandmother!"

"Oh ho ho. I see! Looks like you were the victim of some wild magic, hey? Not a problem, I'll have you sorted in a jiffy." Quebys produced her glimmering book and a small pocket watch from her impossible pouch, which smashed against the ground while saying the command word.

Gradually at first and then much faster, Vel's youth returned. With a sudden crack, she was on her hands and knees, panting. She tentatively opened her eyes, looked at the back of her delicate, unblemished hands, kissed them softly, and said under her breath, "Right. Fuck magic."

"Sorry, dear, I didn't catch that. It doesn't matter, though, I've got to run! Much to do and so little time." The gnome smiled as if she hadn't heard and cried out, "Toodles!" and with a flip of her hand, she hurried towards her crooked tower.

Back on her feet, Vel and Kaylessa supported the sick Valex between them and urged the larger dragonborn's bulk through the doors of The Kraken, where they dropped him into a chair. Valex flapped a hand at Tim and pushed Kaylessa and Vel towards the table at the back where Wravien was sitting alone, smiling warmly.

He came around the table and clasped Vel and Kaylessa around their shoulders. "I will admit, I was worried when my birds lost sight of you three. But I never doubted you for a minute. Where is our friend, Valex?"

Vel nodded towards the table at the back, where Valex was cheerfully having Tim line up several small glasses of whiskey, along with a few ales.

"Ah. That may be problematic in the future, but I believe that he'll figure it out. That being said, you three have done me a great service. I was fully prepared to rebuild the tower that Quebys had established, but since you've brought it here to Ravencroft, I'm in your debt. I'm doubly excited to share with you the payment I've lined up." He walked towards the front door of The Kraken, saying, "You too, Valex, finish up your drinks and follow me outside."

"Right behind you!" Valex grabbed the first glass, poured it down his throat, and followed it with the second and third. He drained a wooden mug of ale and staggered out after his friends, wobbling slightly.

In the crisp sunlight, Wravien walked through the square towards a new, clean-looking building on the western side of the square. Standing outside, he addressed the trio with a flourish. "Well, what do you think?" he asked, excitement written all over his face.

Vel looked at Wravien with a confused look on her face. "Is our... payment inside or something?"

"No, no, my dear! This here," he gestured to the building behind him, "is your payment! I've had Nogret build this hall for you three. The deed is in all of your names, and this land belongs to you. If I'm establishing a town, it's important that my lieutenants have residency here." He looked from Valex, to Kaylessa, to Vel, as they all looked at the stocky brick building, unmoving.

Wravien chuckled. "I'll take my leave, but I do have one more surprise. I'll treat you to it as a second payment for today, after I explain what the next job is. Take your time and really explore your rooms, I've custom tailored them to each of your needs. Enjoy yourselves." He walked back towards the bar.

Valex walked up to the stairs leading to the front door and touched the wrought iron railing. He slowly ascended the three-step riser and pushed the front door open. The smells of fresh paint and lumber permeated the building as Vel and Kaylessa followed him in.

Looking about the room they'd entered, they saw a furnished living area. Mostly furnished, was probably a more fitting term, as the many shelves along the walls were bare. Sitting in the centre of the room was a round table with four chairs positioned around it. There were two doors on either side of the room. On the left, closest to them, was a dark wood door, emblazoned with a large V and a small sigil of a dagger. Farther up the wall on the left side of the room was another door, built from a much lighter wood. A large G, along with a sigil of a harp was carved into it. Looking to the right, in the back of the room, was an incredibly large door frame, with a V and a sigil of a book. The final door was blank, and they all felt a sense of waiting. This room belonged to someone. They didn't know who, but it belonged to someone.

Vel moved towards the first door, and Kaylessa drifted towards the second. Valex spotted a bottle sitting on the circular table, along with a folded piece of parchment. The bottle looked fancier than anything he'd run into before, a dark-green glass with an impressive label, and he cracked the seal on the envelope and began to read.

Dear friends,

I'm so glad to hear you've decided to join our little venture! Wravien told me that you were getting your own home here in Ravencroft. So, as your first neighbour, I wanted to make sure you guys got your first gift from me. I've left a bottle of Dwarven Fire Whiskey (don't let Valex chug it all, this stuff is a treasure, very hard to come by). I'm sure you'll be in need of refreshment as you continue to do the good work you do, so feel free to drop by anytime.

Cordially, Tim Crenshaw.

Vel snatched the bottle from Valex, who had cracked the seal and poured himself a glass already. "What a thoughtful fellow." Valex sipped his drink, and breathed in through his teeth. "He isn't kidding, that's good stuff." He drifted towards the door emblazoned with the magic book and pushed it open. His jaw dropped at once—the entire room had been dressed in much the same fashion as Quebys' tower. A large, glass-fronted cabinet housed all manner of reagents, several divining tools were lined up on a desk, and the rest of the walls were covered in bookshelves, housing all manner of research tomes. Even the bed had been reinforced, a fact he was very glad for. Almost every bed he had slept in on this journey had been about a foot and a half too short, and he'd had to drape his scaly talons off the footboard.

Vel opened her door and stepped through, slamming it behind her fast before the others could see. The room was dark, dimly lit with gothic features, but the entire back wall was made up of shelves, all of them housing treasure chests. There appeared to be a table done up with strange glassware, and a small herb garden. She looked at the herbs dismissively, but then realised she recognized a few of them as deadly poisons. There was also a chest of drawers, each with a different type of lock on it, which appeared to get progressively more complex as it reached the top. She opened the drawer closest to the bottom left, eager to see what treasure awaited her, but was disappointed to find nothing but a small, folded note, which read: *"Sorry Vel, wish I could have seen your face, but these boxes are for the treasures you'll find. -W"*

Kaylessa entered her room last and looked around wide eyed. At first glance, this could have been her bedroom back home in Thras'lunia. The fabrics, furniture, and fixtures were almost all the same, but a motley collection of musical instruments had been placed in the corner. None were as high quality as the harp she carried on her hip, but she appreciated the gesture. There was also a rack on the wall beside the door that housed a myriad of archery supplies, from bow strings, to fletching materials—even a container of arrowheads. She suppressed a shudder, feeling the tears rise. How could he have known? How could he have known how deeply she missed this room, how often she saw it in her dreams?

Collectively, a hive mind thought flowed through them. They had all either had homes taken from them or never had them at all. Wravien may have given this gift flippantly, saying that his agents needed a place to stay in town, but he must have done an incredible amount of research to custom tailor this place to their exact needs. Whether he knew it or not, this was the strongest play he had made yet for their loyalty.

Returning to the main common room, Kaylessa spied a piece of parchment that had been hung behind the door. "Hey, look. I think this is a property deed, and It's been made out in equal parts, to all of us."

Their emotions heavy, they shared a silence that echoed with the memories of homes lost, until Valex finally spoke. "Whatever, it's not like he could keep renting rooms for us. Come on, let's go see the big man."

Vel stifled a yawn behind her hand. "I don't know about you, but after what we just went through I'm pretty sure I've earned a nap. Don't wake me up unless you're ready to leave." She turned and entered her room, and there was the sound of many locks closing.

Valex and Kaylessa shrugged at each other and adjourned to their rooms with their thoughts.

They slept through the night and woke to the sounds of birds singing. Kaylessa woke with a start and cursed her carelessness—she should have at least sent a messenger to let Wravien know they wouldn't be coming in the evening. She dressed in haste and emerged from her room to see Vel seated at the table, geared up, as well as Valex, who was drinking something from a mug and wearing a silky housecoat.

Valex smiled at her, his gaze unfocused. "G'morning! Care for a drink?"

Kaylessa looked at Vel for support, but Vel pushed away from the table and left the room without a word. After a few moments of awkward silence, she returned carrying a bucket, and upended its contents onto Valex's head.

He gasped, and let out a holler, pushing away from the table and dripping onto the floor. "Wh-wh-what was that for, Vel?!" His teeth chattered from the cold.

Vel looked at him innocently. "I just figured you'd want to clean up before you get dressed, it smells like a lair in here. Come on Kaylessa, Valex can catch up."

The women walked out the door, leaving Valex to shiver in the room. He took a smell from his cup, shrugged his shoulders, and finished it off, before returning to his room to dress.

By the time he had thrown on his clothes and scuttled across the courtyard into The Kraken, Kaylessa and Vel were seated at the long table at the back of the bar with Wravien, who had a large map of Meridia spread across the table. He stood over it, knuckles pressed against its surface, studying a number of what looked like small, brass chess pieces.

Wravien didn't look up as Valex sheepishly joined them, sliding a chair out for himself. Finally, he addressed the trio. "Welcome home you three..." he began but was cut off by Kaylessa.

"We're sorry, sir, we should have come to see you when we returned, but the sight of fresh beds overcame us."

He waved his hand nonchalantly, continuing to stare at the map. "Of course, I understand completely. Quebys filled me in on your ordeal, so some rest was likely required. Were the accommodations to your liking? Nogret, Fingers, and I toiled over each individual room, but I think we hit the nail on the head," He looked up and flashed a roguish grin, making him seem much younger than he was. "I do sincerely hope you enjoyed your rest, because starting today you'll be doing some extended work, down in Z'raco."

Valex flinched—Z'raco was home to the city of Gallowspire, which had housed his childhood home, the Underdark. Was he finally going to be able to...

"Not yet, Valex, I promise you will get your revenge, but only once you are good and ready." Wravien said.

Valex was startled from his thoughts, and he looked at Wravien, whose piercing blue eyes seemed to be staring through him. He opened his mouth to respond, but realised he had no idea what to say. Troubled, he thought, *How can he know what I'm thinking?*

"So far, we've done some great work for Ravencroft. We've discovered an architect, who will help us establish the foundation; a blacksmith, who can reinforce what we've built, as well as ensure we're well armed; and as of yesterday, we've acquired a powerful wizard, whose powers should help to provide us with a means of magical defence. We're proceeding according to plan, and our next course of action is..."

"Another tavern." Valex said at once, certainty ringing through him.

A crease formed in Wravien's forehead, and he tilted his head at the dragonborn, giving it a a shake, "No, Valex, we're going to need more fighters. I'm currently evaluating a few situations to get the populace of the town bolstered, but I'm afraid something has, as it always does eventually, gone south, so to speak." He looked towards the southern part of the map, where a brass token of a battle axe stood. "Ideally, I was going to have you head to the badlands in Z'raco, to make contact with an old...colleague of mine."

They all noticed the pause but chose not to pursue it.

"His name is Khan Xarlug and he is, or rather was, I suppose, the war chief of the Bloodspine tribe. The tribe has always been vicious, pillaging and attacking other tribes in the badlands, but once Khan took the mantle, they became something much more—organised, tactical. It really was a thing of beauty, right up until the Tempest Paladins caught wind of it, and raided their camp."

Kaylessa shot a look over her shoulder to where Kornid was standing at the bar making small talk with Tim. When she looked back, she saw Wravien had followed her gaze.

"Yes, Kornid is technically one of their order, but he has been inactive for some time and won't be able to assist us in this matter." He tapped a large, ominous-looking island off the eastern shore of the map. "The Waves, as they call themselves, have always been public supporters of freedom and free trade, but the Bloodspine tribe's way of life runs in direct opposition to that. I had hoped that Khan would be able to stay one step ahead of them, but the musclebound oaf was captured in a recent ambush." With a flick of his wrist, Wravien toppled the brass figure, letting it fall to its side. "Xarlug is a high-value target, and I have no doubts that they'll execute him, publicly, to make an example to the other bandit tribes. This works in our favour."

Vel's eyebrows shot up. "Oh, public execution is your idea of 'good news?'"

"No, but I know the way these holy knights operate. Once he was taken by the Waves, they beseeched their god, obscuring their war party from being tailed magically. I've been unable to get close with any of my familiars, but I've reached out to my network and learned that in order to deliver him to the Eye, which is where they would hold the execution, there is only one port they'll be able to bring him to." He tapped a small circle on the southern coast, labelled "Mercallia" and grimaced, "And the safest time to make the journey will be when the new moon rises."

Vel studied the inverted map, committing the brass figures strewn across it to memory. "But sir—I mean Wravien, that's well over a month away. Why don't we just wait until then and storm this 'Mercallia' when they are slated to bring him in?"

"I see you've never visited Mercallia, my dear." His mouth was a grim slash, and he looked at her humorlessly. "They tend to be a bit prickly about people coming and going, and I promise you aren't the first person to suggest laying siege to it. As well, I have it on good authority that the Waves have a fortified garrison they will use as a temporary jail until they are ready to make sail. You'll need to get into the city, entrench yourselves, and scout it out if we're to avoid a blood bath. Fortunately, our resident barkeep has a brother that tends a small establishment in the city, a bar called The Crimson Krill."

Valex scratched his chin, thoughtful. "Okay, so I'm guessing the trip will take a few weeks, but what are we supposed to do when we get there? We don't exactly look inconspicuous."

"That, my good man, is where your second surprise comes in." Wravien produced a long wooden tube, covered in strange, carved symbols, and cracked the seal. With a puff of dust, he pulled out an ancient-looking, rolled-up piece of parchment. "In my travels, I won this particular treasure off another mercenary. It lines up perfectly with the world map, except…" He took the parchment and laid it over the map on the table. Once the coasts had lined up, he flipped the parchment back and forth, revealing that the new addition this map brought was a small, strange island off the southern coast. It had been slashed through with a large, red X.

"I've had the map verified, and it is enchanted in such a way that the island shown on the map is completely hidden, unless the map is in your possession. I have never been able to make the journey myself." He grinned unflinchingly at Vel, who was frowning at the paper.

She touched the corner delicately and looked stonily at Wravien. "That sounds a little far-fetched to me, and even if it is real, what do you want us to find for you there?"

"You misunderstand, Vel, this map now belongs to you. You'll find yourself with time on your hands while you wait for Khan to be brought into the barracks, and I implore you to investigate the mystery of this island. Whatever you find is yours to keep—consider it a sign of my continuing faith in you. I want no part of whatever riches you uncover."

"If I understand you correctly," said Kaylessa, speaking methodically, "We are to head to Mercallia and assess the security of where they will be holding this…Khan, you said?"

Wravien nodded at her, and she continued, "And once we've confirmed that he's there, what do you want us to do?"

"I would think that would be obvious, Kaylessa." His face split into an unusually charming grin, lighting up his eyes. "It's a jailbreak."

CHAPTER 8
THE ROAD TO MERCALLIA

Day 599 - Somulous Experiment: I was called into my department head's office today and was told I am to be promoted to the head of Research and Development for the Xerkan Army. I was unable to muster any feelings about it, and all I could hear was the man's jealousy and shame at being replaced. This will suit my purposes, and he was a weak one anyway. I will do great things for our country...I just have to get myself under control. A.G.

The ride through Z'raco was very long indeed. They put their horses through their paces, fended off more than a few bandit raids, and eventually came across a small camp, where two old women were sitting around a simmering pot, resting precariously on their fire.

"Hail, fellow travellers, do you mind if we join you? The ride has been long, and your camp looks very...inviting." Kaylessa called down, noticing the hanging carcasses of several small animals, as well as a number of pieces of equipment built for men much larger than them.

However, Valex had already dismounted and was approaching the two. "I must say, that smells delicious! Would you be so kind as to spare us a portion? We could use the energy for tomorrow." He wafted the smell towards his face and smiled at the women.

Greasy black hair framing their faces, they looked up at him through ruined features, but they nodded their assent and began to speak to each other in a strange language.

"Valex, are you sure about this?" Vel hissed, keeping her back to the women. "I'm pretty sure these aren't travellers—they look like hags."

"Vel, I would have thought that after all this time, you would have learned not to judge a book by its cover. These two fine women..." He looked back at the two, who had crawled over to him and were plucking at his pouch of reagents. "No, hey, please don't touch that. As I was saying, these lovely creatures have offered us a place to rest, and we would be rude to spurn their hospitality. Now, about that soup?" He turned to the women, who scuttled away from him on all fours.

They looked at each other briefly, before ladling out a portion of the rich-looking broth into a wooden bowl and handing it to Valex. Kaylessa stood by her horse, looking pensive,

"Thank you. See, Vel, just two nice old ladies in the..." Looking down at the spoonful of soup he had brought to his lips, Valex stopped. An eyeball stared back at him. He dropped the spoon and looked down at the bowl, where a fat human toe was floating to the surface.

"Ugh! Kaylessa! Smoke bomb, do something!" he cried, dropping the bowl and running to his horse. The hags snarled and their forms began to change, bodies rippling under the scraps of fabric. Running on all fours, they chased Valex until Kaylessa strummed a harsh note on her harp. A shockwave radiated out of the instrument, knocking the two hags off their feet into a tumble.

"Ride! Ride damn you!" Valex shouted, spurring his horse and throwing up a cloud of dust. He turned to Vel, galloping at his left, and shrugged his shoulders.

"You're an idiot, Valex. Our idiot, but an idiot." Vel began to laugh, and soon all three of them were roaring with laughter.

The hags camp behind them, they rode hard until finally the landscape began to change. Instead of the barren sand dunes of the Ill'zuriak Desert, they saw lush jungle with tropical, fruit-bearing trees, and eventually the horizon gave way to the southern ocean. They followed a winding coastal road, marking the signposts and adjusting accordingly, until they eventually found themselves at a large wall, with a gate barring passage on the road.

Two guards stood at the gate, looking even more suspect than most of the bandits they had defeated. The fatter of the two stepped forward as the party approached, and with a spear held loosely in his hand, trumpeted, "Oy, stop right there!" He lurched forward with a heavy limp, and they smelled him almost at once. "You've come to the city gates of Mercallia and the royal vizier has imposed a tax upon all travellers."

"We didn't hear anything about such a tax on the way here," Valex said dubiously. In truth, the few people they had encountered on the way here had either been in a very sorry state of disrepair or had ignored them completely.

"Well, that's because it's a new tax, 'innit Oswald?" He looked back at the skinny guard, who was shamelessly digging for treasure in his nose with a filthy pinky.

"Oh ayup, ayup, the new tax. Just started today, it did." Business concluded, the skinny guard resumed his excavation.

"What's to stop us from slitting your throats and just walking past?" Vel asked, casually inspecting her nails.

The guards both burst out laughing and the fat one stuck his fingers into his mouth and whistled. There was a flurry of movement as a dozen archers popped their heads above the gate, training their aim on Vel, Valex, and Kaylessa.

"You're welcome to try, love, but I doubt you'll get more than a few steps. It's clear you've never been to Mercallia, so I'll let the attitude slide just this once. The tax is fifty silver pieces each. Pay up and you can be on your way."

Vel scowled and placed her hands on the hilts of the daggers criss-crossed on her hips, but Kaylessa strode past her, harp in hand. She was playing a song that sounded familiar, but no one could have named it. It was maddening. But the tubby guard's face relaxed, and his eyes went vacant. Kaylessa leaned in close and began to whisper in his ear.

"What? Oh, my name is Broan, but you already knew that—you're my oldest friend!" The guard's voice was a monotone, and Vel and Valex exchanged an amused glance as Kaylessa continued to whisper.

The tubby guard went on. "Oh, you've already paid the tax? Well a'course you did, I knew that. Oswald, open the gate for my good friend, Kaylessa."

Kaylessa clasped the guard's shoulders companionably, and said "Thank you, Broan. I knew you'd understand, and I appreciate the favour."

Oswald looked dumbly at his partner and then shrugged and leaned against one of the heavy wooden doors barring their path, which slowly creaked open. As they passed through, they saw Broan continue his dreamy, vacant stare into the open road.

Taking the lead, Kaylessa spoke without turning her head. "Ride fast. He'll realise he's been charmed in a few minutes, and we need to be long gone before that happens." With a whistle, she spurred her horse and set off down the road, kicking up dirt, and Vel and Valex followed suit.

Once they'd gone a suitable distance down the road, Kaylessa slowed her mount to a trot and allowed her companions to catch up.

Valex pulled up beside her. "What exactly did you promise him? That guy was *gross*."

"Oh, no, it's just a spell. It only works on creatures with significantly below-average intelligence, but I convinced him we were childhood friends and that we'd paid our tax long ago." Looking pleased with herself, Kaylessa patted her mare on the neck, and it whinnied in appreciation.

"Bloody useful, that one is," Vel said, scanning the horizon. "We'll need to keep that trick in mind as we settle into our investigation."

"Honestly, don't put too much stock into it," Kaylessa said. "We were lucky there were barely any original thoughts in his head."

As they rode into the main street of Mercallia, Valex closely watched the townsfolk who crossed their path. They moved through the streets furtively, heads down but shooting wary glances and whispering amongst themselves.

"I think we should hurry up and get settled; we're beginning to attract attention," said Valex quietly. "What was the name of Tim's brother's bar again?"

"There." Vel pointed to a dingy building on the right side of the road. "The Crimson Krill."

The main street ran directly down to the ocean, where half a dozen ships were moored to the shabby docks. From their blue sails and flags, it was clear that two of the larger ships bore the crest of the Tempest Paladins, but the rest were done up with garish silks and loud insignias. This was clearly a pirate town, and they would have to be on their guard. To the left of the road was a large, fortified structure, the two heavy iron doors were guarded by two well-armoured soldiers. These men were leaps and bounds from the men at the main gate. From the way their eyes darted to and fro over the moving townsfolk, to their grim, unsmiling faces, Vel deduced their training would be top notch. A frontal assault would likely end in failure.

On the other side of the street was the Crimson Krill. Looking at the bar, it was clear that this was not the type of tavern any of them were used to, save maybe Vel. The paint on the walls was peeling, and one of the front windows had been shattered and hastily repaired with a few rotten boards.

They tied their horses to the hitching post outside the bar, and in an effort to ward off would-be thieves, Vel made a show of flipping her cloak back, revealing a myriad of semi-concealed daggers, as well as her sparkling rapier. The three walked up to the front doors and with a gulp, Kaylessa pushed one of them open.

The dingy, smoke-filled room was dimly lit, and the source of the smoke seemed to be at every table, where embers winked in and out of the haze. A small hush announced their arrival, but the murmured conversations began again almost at once.

Valex scanned the poorly stocked bar to his right and saw the man whom they had been sent to meet. The gleaming bald head was a clear indicator of his relation to Ravencroft's friendly barkeep, but that was where the similarities stopped. This barman had a patchy beard that was already going grey and a sizable belly, poorly hidden behind an absolutely filthy apron. He was rubbing an equally dirty rag against a glass, but as Valex approached, his eyes widened in alarm and he spoke before they had a chance to say hello, his voice whiney and nasal. "Ay, I don't want any trouble out of you lot. We've already got one of you dragon men at the bar, and we don't need any troubles between colours."

"Really? Where?" Surprised that there might be another dragonborn here, Valex forgot what he had intended to ask. He hadn't seen any of his kind since leaving the mines, and he smiled when his gaze stopped on an azure-scaled figure. The dragonborn was sitting at a table with perhaps a dozen men, who all wore the same armour that Kornid sported, though the dragonborn had a much nicer set. It was adorned with blue gemstones, trimmed in gold, and where his allies' gear was the colour of a stormy ocean, his armour gleamed like it was brand new. He finished telling a story, and his companions all laughed, which prompted a smug look to appear on his face.

Valex placed a silver piece on the bar top and addressed the barman. "Relax, friend, I hold no ill will towards other dragonborn. Besides, we're actually here to talk with you. Why don't we start with four ales, one for yourself, of course."

The bartender eyed the single coin with distaste and then said, "I won't say no to a drink, but you'll need three more of them coins."

Valex gaped. A silver...*per ale?!* This was highway robbery! He looked to Vel and Kaylessa pleadingly, and Vel placed three more coins on the bar begrudgingly.

The air of a bothered man all around him, the barman sighed and poured ale into four, tiny cups. Valex eyed it haughtily, but the barman leaned onto the bar and said, "Well, what do you want? I'm very busy."

Kaylessa looked up and down the empty bar top, but carried on as if he was correct. "We won't take up too much of your valuable time. You're Jim, right? We know your brother, Tim, and we're–"

Jim let out a nasty sounding cackle and hit his fist against the bar. "Oh, is that what this no good, piece of trash singer calls us? He's got some nerve, calling in favours after running off to that school. We haven't spoken in a decade, but now he expects me to help his friends at the drop of a hat. Go on, what did my *brother* have to say?"

"Only good things, I assure you," Valex said, recovering quickly from the tirade. "He said you were the man who knew things in this...fine city, and if you help us you'll be compensated fairly for your troubles."

The barkeep's beady eyes darted around the room. "I'll have to see the colour of your coin and we'll see how talkative I'm feeling."

Valex pulled out his coin purse, retrieved another silver coin, and placed it on the bar. Jim looked up at the ceiling and continued to polish the glass. Valex plunked a second coin on top of the first, but Jim was still unmoving. This farce continued until five silver coins had been placed on the bar. Then Jim suddenly swiped a hand across them and they disappeared from sight. He flashed them a gap-toothed grin, which Valex did not return.

"Alright, you've bought my attention, what did you need to know?"

Kaylessa cut in before Vel could mention the map. "First, we were a little curious about the garrison."

Vel shot her a dark look, and said, "Secondly, we're looking for a reliable crew for an adventure."

"Well, *first of all,* The barracks are the pride of the Tempest Paladins in these parts. People have reported hearing horrible noises from inside, like people being tortured, but they are very good at ensuring that no wandering eyes see inside. *However,* I have heard a rumour that when the new Tempest initiates are brought in, they sneak out of the fort to get a slice of our nightlife. It's been happening for years, so there must be another entrance. It's become a bit of a tradition, for when a new soldier is brought in, he isn't considered a part of the squad until he beds one of my whores." Jim smiled like a proud father, ignoring the disgusted looks on Vel and Valex's faces. "When it comes down to finding a crew, well, you've got your pick of the litter. We've got a few Tempest boys who are not averse to turning a blind eye if there's coin in it, and more pirate crews than I know what to do with. With enough gold, they'll take you wherever you want." He finished matter of factly and walked away before they could ask anything else.

There was a silence amongst them until Kaylessa chimed in, "Excuse me, but what exactly is a whore?"

Valex and Vel burst out laughing, serving to confuse Kaylessa further, and Vel promised to explain later.

Valex guided Vel and Kaylessa to a nearby table. "As much as he's a piece of work, he did give us some helpful information. First order of business, we need to pick a crew. This map could be a big score for us, and I know that we've got some time before Khan will be brought here. Our best bet is to pool our coin and see what kind of transport we can afford. I've got… ugh, about thirteen silver left. What about you, Kaylessa?"

"Thirty silver, give or take. Plus we've got the treasure we recovered from Quebys' Tower, right Valex?"

"Oh, well, you see…" Valex stammered (He'd had quite a raucous night with Nogret and Quebys to celebrate coming back, and most of it had been spent) "… I have thirteen silver. Vel?"

"Nope." She looked at the battered, broken window with disinterest.

"Are…are you serious? What do you mean 'nope'? Do you have a ship hidden somewhere we don't know about? If we want to get whatever this map leads to, we're going to need something."

Sighing dramatically, Vel reached into her belt and pulled out a coin purse roughly the same size as Kaylessa's and tossed it onto the table. They both continued to look at her expectantly, and she grumbled as she pulled a second, equally large bag out and tossed it on top of the first. She held her hands out, palms out, towards her companions. Valex cleared his throat, and Kaylessa studied the ceiling. "Fine! Fine, you damned vultures." Vel pulled pouches of silver from her belts, one after another. A small pyramid formed on the table, and after pulling a small stack of coins out of her boot as well, she sat back, looking disgusted. "There, that's all of it. But so help me… if this map doesn't lead us to a fortune…"

"We appreciate your candor," Valex said sarcastically. With Kaylessa's help, he divided the pile up and began to count. Valex tore a scrap of paper from his spellbook and kept track, and after almost half an hour, he leaned back, looking at the paper, bemused.

"Five hundred and twenty-eight silver. If you've just been casually carrying around a small fortune, why in the hells have I been bribing this jackass?" He cocked his thumb at the bartender.

"Because a fool and his money are easily parted, and because I need mine more than you do." She looked at him coolly before pulling the napkin out of his hands, pushing the hood of her cloak back to reveal her icy white hair, and approaching the nearest table. It was full of surly looking men, covered in faded blue tattoos, working their way through a small army of ales. She stood at the end of their table for a moment, but when no one acknowledged her, she cleared her throat and said, "I'm in need of a ship and a brave crew to take me and my allies on an adventure to the south. We are willing to offer fifty silver pieces!" Valex groaned, and the silence from the table was broken by a single derisive snort, but Vel remained undaunted. "Alright, you drive a hard bargain boys. I'll pay *one hundred silver pieces*," she let each word hang for a moment. "What do you say?"

"Lass." The man closest to her spoke quietly. "It's clear you've never done this before. No one in their right mind would risk sailing out of here with this many Waves around, let alone for appropriate payment." This was a slang term for the Tempest Paladins they had heard a few times on the road down.

"Well, except maybe Dreadwing," the man across the table called out, and the table erupted into laughter.

"It appears that the men of Mercallia are indeed cowards. Where can I find this man, Dreadwing?"

"First, it isn't cowardice, but common sense. Plus Dreadwing is the only captain I know who might entertain your..." He paused, then grinned, "generous rate of service." Vel's face reddened as she left the table full of laughing men, returning to her original table where Valex was trying, in vain, to conceal his own laughter."

Vel sat down and crossed her arms, glaring daggers at Valex. "Is something funny to you, you damned iguana?"

"Hey, come on now, there is no need for name calling." Valex composed himself before continuing, "I'll take it you've never hired a ship before?"

"What, and you have?"

"No, but I've spent a fair amount of time with Kornid, who used to sail with the Waves. He told me that hiring a mercenary crew was expensive, and that it varied from a fifty to one hundred *gold* pieces. You might be able to rent a rowboat for the day with what you were offering. "

Vel's jaw dropped. One hundred silvers could be exchanged for a single gold coin.

"You basically offered a nail file in exchange for a castle, bold as can be. No wonder they laughed you out of there." He chuckled again and rose to his feet. "Kaylessa, why don't you see if you can come up with a better idea, while Vel buys us another round." He turned quickly, snagging one of the cloth bags from the tabletop before Vel could protest, and hustled towards the bar. Kaylessa drew her harp from her belt, and began to pluck the strings, a palm pressed against them so they wouldn't ring out.

"Honestly, what an oaf," grumbled Vel. "The nerve of him. What exactly are you..."

"Quiet!" Kaylessa's tone was sharp. "I'm trying to listen to what the paladins are talking about." As she played, her gaze was laser focused on the blue dragonborn, and a curious thing began to happen. The din of the bar faded away, and the voice of the paladin became crystal clear. Vel looked around startled, but no one else appeared to have noticed.

"And of course," Vel could see his mouth moving across the room, but his voice was crystal clear. "The filthy savage started begging, 'Don't kill her, she's my only daughter!' Boo hoo, right? So I lowered my flail, offered him a helping hand," He mimed a pout, "And reached out and broke his neck." The men around him laughed, and Kaylessa gasped, the spell slipping slightly. She shook her head and resumed playing.

"...Imagine—letting them breed, unpoliced? Ridiculous. But! I've saved the best part for last, boys," They all leaned in, and the dragonborn paused, relishing the attention. "We took the big, green bastard alive! Once we had scattered his warriors, we surrounded him and brought him down with smites, praise Leviathan." He kissed a small talisman worn around his neck. "I rode ahead to prepare the keep, but not before we stripped him naked and tied him to the back of the caravan, like the animal he is. The caravan should arrive anytime and in a few weeks, we'll be able to mount Xarlug's head on the tower walls."

Kaylessa started to stand, but Vel grabbed her wrist and began to laugh, very loudly and in an air-headed voice shouted, "Oh my God, and *then* what did he say?!"

Kaylessa looked at her perplexed. "What are you..." she began.

Vel pulled her in close and cawed the same, obnoxious laughter. "Wait, he said what?!" Then she hissed into her ear, "The dragon knows we heard something. He noticed in the middle of his story and hasn't stopped looking over. Play along."

With a slight nod, Kaylessa pulled away, and let out a throaty chuckle, before exclaiming loudly, "Yeah, and he was a half-orc!"

Vel roared with laughter. "The half that mattered, I'll bet!" She watched the paladin from the corner of her eye and saw him grimace and return to his conversation. After a few more obnoxious comments to be safe, she and Kaylessa settled in and watched Valex arguing with the bartender. *We'll have to be careful around the blue skin,* Vel thought. *He's sharper than the rest.*

Valex, meanwhile, was arguing over the price of the ales with Jim. Jim was unmoving, and suggested he might want to take his business elsewhere. Valex argued that there was nowhere else, to which Jim gave him a look that meant, *Well, there you have it.* Valex relented and shelled out the coin. After receiving another tiny cup of ale, he inquired about "Captain Dreadwing."

"Ah that crew does catch a lot of flak," Jim said. "Mostly cause they're the only crew that will take on a job without being paid in advance."

"Well, that sounds like just the man I'm looking for!" Valex exclaimed, and Jim chuckled. "Where can I find his fearsomeness?"

"Oh, Dreadwing's crew doesn't like to be bothered..." His eyes had taken on a sheen that Valex knew well from Vel's usual expression. He threw his head back, held up his hand in a *one minute* gesture and returned to the table.

"So how did it—hey, cut that out!" Vel threw an empty cup at Valex's back as he retreated to the bar with another bag of coins. Instead of haggling, he threw the entire thing on the bar and looked pointedly at the grubby barkeep. "Will this suffice? I really don't have all day."

Jim hefted the bag and with a satisfied smirk reached behind him to grab a disgusting-looking bottle on the shelf, labelled Troll Drool Liquor. It angled down when he pulled on it. A grinding noise came from the back of the room as a panel of the wall opened up and a cloud of noxious smoke poured out. Valex motioned to his companions and walked through the doorway, stooping his head so he didn't bang his horns.

The three of them soon stood in a small room. The air was filthy with the acrid odour of cigar smoke, and through the haze they saw a small card table set up at the back. There were five people seated around it, four men and a woman, all smoking and playing some kind of card game. Valex looked them over, and settling on a humongous, bearded man, he mustered up his courage and walked over.

"Excuse me... Captain Dreadwing, sir?"

There was a tense moment before all five of the pirates burst out laughing. "Ah, that never gets old. No boy, I'm not the captain. She is," the bearded pirate said. He gestured to his right, where a small figure tipped her hat back, revealing a gorgeous, almond-shaped face. With big, ochre eyes, full lips, and cheekbones sharper than the blade of a sword, she could have been a noble in any of the big cities, save for the tattoos that framed her face. Her raven-black hair tumbled down a long, red jacket, which she wore open to reveal a toned stomach, covered in small scars.

She smiled, revealing several gold teeth. "Oh Drake, you shouldn't have! You know I've never taken a dragon to bed! Step into the light, big boy, let Momma have a good look at you." Even her voice was exotic, but Valex was too stunned to respond.

"I didn't buy you no dragonborn," The bearded pirate, Drake said with a frown.

Kaylessa stepped forward. "Oh, there is a misunderstanding. We would like to hire your crew!"

"Hmm, aren't you precious?" Dreadwing stood up, leaning across the table. "But always pleasure first, business second, that's my motto. Speaking of pleasure, I believe I could show you a thing or two."

Kaylessa stared at her open mouthed, so Vel stepped in and unfurled the map on the table. "Enough. Do any of you know this island?"

"And this must be the tough one. I'm impressed, very imposing. Very well. Alfie, do we know this island?" Without breaking eye contact with Vel, she pushed the map towards one of her fellows, a thin, bookish looking pirate. He drew a pair of half-moon spectacles gently from an inside pocket and peered at the parchment.

"Let's see…No, there is no way there is an island here. We would have seen it a dozen times."

"That's the trick!" Valex had composed himself enough to be able to speak. "It's a magic map—once you've touched it, you'll be able to see the island for yourself."

Dreadwing looked at him appraisingly and slid the map to her other side, where Drake inspected it with interest. "Drake, check it out," she said. "As for you three, let's discuss payment."

"We'll give you fifty silver…" Vel began, but Valex interjected.

"Half. Anything we find, we'll split in half. We have no idea what's on the island, but considering how difficult it is to access, it must be something pretty spectacular." Valex said, sticking out his hand.

The pirate captain looked at him for a moment, before bursting into laughter. "Did you hear this? You've got balls on you, lizardman, I'll give you that. I think I'm going to enjoy you. Alright, we've got an accord." She took his talon in her hand, and gave it a delicate shake, "Half the treasure, all the adventure! Come down to the dock at first light, and Natalia Dreadwing," she smiled again, flashing the gold teeth, "will guarantee you safe passage there. I look forward to…working with you."

CHAPTER 9
THE UNCHARTED ISLE

Day 708 - Somulous Experiment: I...I don't know what happened. One minute I was studying my blood under a microscope, and the next I was in my department head's office, covered in blood. His blood. I can't let this stop my progress, and my newfound abilities seem to let me influence the thoughts of others—I was able to deter several researchers from meeting with him. I will wait until after dark and dispose of the body...[There are several lines of text that have been crossed off, and the pages bear spots of blood.]

After a *very* uncomfortable sleep at the local inn—surreptitiously prepaid for them (*Thank you Wravien*, Valex thought, his coin purse sufficiently depleted), the three of them met up in the main street outside the Crimson Krill, rubbing sleep from their eyes.

Kaylessa appeared to be scratching herself all over. "How anyone can live like this? I have no idea," she stammered, twitching. "I swear, I could feel the sheets moving. I don't know if it was bed bugs or fleas, but it was disgusting."

Vel, who had slept in worse, shrugged and said, "Let's go jump in the water before we go meet up with that she-devil, to wash the place off. It will help, trust me."

Valex opted out, deciding he had just enough coin for a quick ale, and the ladies left towards the beach. He entered the tavern and was surprised to find that the place actually looked *worse* in the daylight. Several of the blue-clad Tempest Paladins had passed out in their chairs—left there overnight. He noticed that the blue dragonborn was absent, and he surveyed the troops with a mixture of pity and disgust. *Is this what I look like?* he thought, and a sudden idea struck him. He moved over to the nearest sleeping man, and whistling innocently, began to rifle through the man's effects. Pocketing a small bag of coin, he pulled out a rolled piece of parchment with the Tempest Paladin company seal and a ring of keys.

He had just finished stowing these when a pompous voice spoke behind him. "Just what do you think you're doing, you rustborn? Those are my men."

Valex whirled, caught off guard by the slur, but pasted a smile on his face as he saw the blue dragonborn paladin, arms crossed and glaring. "Ah, another of my people! I had come down for a drink and noticed that this poor fellow had fallen asleep in his sick. I wanted to make sure he was—"

"Save it, I'm not one of 'your people.' You metallic monstrosities are all just common trash. I saw you and yours skulking around last night, eavesdropping. What are you doing in Mercallia?" His tone was icy, and Valex saw the flash of lightning in his eyes.

Valex looked over the other dragonborn's shiny armour and polished horns, and allowed his shoulders to slump, making him seem smaller than the paladin. "My companions and I were travelling and wanted adventure. We thought this was a good place to find a ship to take us somewhere exciting, but it seems like we were mistaken...unless you have a ship? I'm sure someone as distinguished as yourself, sir..."

Preening, the dragonborn made a throaty noise, and looked down at Valex. "I am Sir Zordriag Split-Tongue, and do not hold your breath. I'm pleased to see that you understand your place, but the Tempest Paladins have no need for brass trash upon our ships. The blue dragonborns are the one true descendant of Leviathan himself. Now, I'd advise you to clear you and yours from Mercallia posthaste, before we are forced to remove you."

Valex gritted his teeth, watching Zordriag finger a trident clasped to his back, but he choked down his retort and made a small bow. "I don't want any trouble, so I'll be on my way. But you should know that your attitude is very unbecoming of the faith. If I hadn't met a proper paladin before I'd come here, I'd believe your entire church was a mockery."

He turned on his heel and walked towards the door, but the paladin called out, "You'd better hope I never see you again, rust."

Valex met Kaylessa and Vel at the docks. They both had wet hair and looked distinctly happier than when they had parted. Valex felt a pang of regret that he hadn't joined them, until he remembered his find on the sleeping paladin. Gathering them round, he pulled the note from his pouch and read it aloud:

> *Soldiers of the Wave - Thanks to your valiant effort, we have captured the criminal Khan Xarlug, and are escorting him to the Mercallia barracks in seven days' time. He will be held overnight, until our adjudicators arrive to bring him to The Eye for his sentencing. Be on your guard, we have scattered the Bloodspine Tribe, but there may be resistance on the roads surrounding Mercallia. We will double the patrols, supplementing our forces with the Mercallia Militia, and Captain Hamilton and his squad will remain to maintain order in the barracks.*
>
> *Remain Vigilant, and Praise Leviathan.*

Kaylessa jumped in place, clapping her hands. "Valex, this is amazing. They've got all their troops out of the city watching the roads, with only a skeleton crew guarding the keep! This is going to be much easier than we thought!"

Vel's response was more muted. "Before you get too excited, remember that while their numbers will be reduced, it's likely the strongest they will keep behind at the fort. I wonder if this...'Captain Hamilton' is the dragonborn from last night?"

"No, I had the pleasure of making his acquaintance this morning while you were bathing. Called himself 'Zordriag Split-Tongue,' and he's...yeah, he's a piece of shit," Valex said humorlessly.

Vel nodded her head towards the water. They followed her gaze and saw Natalia Dreadwing waving a red kerchief at them from the railing of a large ship. "Yoo hoo! Hurry, my lovelies, we must set sail posthaste!"

They hustled down the busy dock and staggered up the walkway to the ship. All around them, burly, tattooed men and women were hustling across the deck, tying down cargo or adjusting sails. The deck of the ship was an open space, save for the two cylindrical masts jutting out at its centre. At the back of the ship, twin staircases flanked a large door, emblazoned with a symbol of a spider. The staircases led to a raised platform, where they could see an impressive chair, the ship's wheel, and a table where Natalia and the pirates from the bar were standing around talking.

Vel made her way up the staircase and joined the crew, who were studying a large map of Meridia, as well as several brass navigation tools. She looked warily at the four men, making mental notes about each one in case they turned on her.

Natalia glanced up. "Finally! The boys wanted to leave without you, but I convinced them we had to wait. The journey will be hard and fast, but we'll get you to your island. After that, though, you're on your own." She waved the men away and took her place at the wheel, surveying her scurrying crew.

"Alright lads! Raise anchor, draw out the sails, and let's get this old girl back on the water!" she bellowed, her voice ringing through the harbour. They snapped into action like a well-oiled machine, and the ship began to soar across the ocean's surface. After about an hour, the crew seemed to have their course set, and began to settle into groups of three or four around the deck. Valex took up a spot on the railing and stared into the water, transfixed, Vel sat down, leaning against the mast with her hood up and her eyes closed, while Kaylessa played her harp for the pirates at the front of the ship to wild accolades.

They sailed through the morning and around midday, Natalia sat up from her ostentatious throne, stretched, and said, "Right. I'm bored, what's say we have a little bit of fun with our new friends?"

The crew chuckled as she vaulted the railing to the lower deck, landing catlike on her feet.

"Oy! Vel, Valex, Kaylessa, front and centre."

Valex turned away from the water in her direction, and Kaylessa shuffled over obediently from the front. Vel remained seated with her eyes closed but raised her head slightly and asked, "What?"

"Now, that's no way to speak to your captain, my lovely." Natalia smiled coyly at Vel. "But we need to see if you are capable of surviving this mysterious island, and my boys could use some exercise. I'd like to have a little exhibition match…see what you can do."

"Pass." Vel returned to her relaxed pose, "and you're no captain of mine"

"If you're on my ship, I'm the captain whether you like it or not," After a minute, Natalia chimed in, "Why don't we make it interesting?"

"What did you have in mind?" Valex asked, as Vel stood and joined her companions.

"Let's see…if you best my crew, I'll give up my half of the treasure. You can keep the lot." She glanced down at her nails. "But, if I win…the three of you join me below deck for the rest of the voyage. We've been out at sea quite a lot lately, and I find I've got some extra energy to burn."

Her fox-like grin made her intentions very clear, and Valex, Vel, and Kaylessa turned away to discuss it.

"No. No, no, no way, no chance." Kaylessa looked sick with nerves. "I don't like the way she keeps looking at me."

"You aren't thinking clearly, Kaylessa," Vel argued. "Have we ever lost a fight, the three of us? It's just a couple of pirates—think of all the bandits we trounced on the road. Plus, *we keep all the treasure!*"

"…I think she's right, Kaylessa." Valex had a dopey grin on his face. "Besides, it might be fun, even if we lose."

Vel rounded on him, grabbing him by the collar and looking into his face, "You better not throw this bout, just to get with that trashy pirate. I'll turn you into a jacket. Don't tempt me."

"No I—of course Vel, we're really going to have to see if we can buy you a sense of humour with the money we make from this venture."

He turned to face Natalia, who was surveying them, hands on her hips. "You're on, Dreadwing. Where are our victims?"

She smiled again and walked over to a trapdoor on the floor. Bringing a stiletto heel down onto it three times, she called out, "Boooys! Show time!"

The hatch cracked open and three of the largest, most muscular men any of them had ever seen ascended the stairs to the deck. Sweat dripped down their bulging muscles, and each of them carried a two-handed hammer of some kind. The pirates gathered around the six combatants in a circle, and began passing coins back and forth, wagering.

Natalia scaled the netting attached to the centre mast and cupped a hand around her mouth. "Ladies and gentlemen! Your queen has secured this afternoon's entertainment! Today's betting will regard who remains alive or conscious at the end. We're offering three to one odds on the dragonborn, four to one on the stunning rogue, and a whopping eight to one on our delicious little elf! As always, two to one odds on the crusher crew!"

She dropped from the net and addressed Valex. "Rules are: There are no rules. God, I love being a pirate. Do your best not to kill them, and they'll do the same. Of course, accidents happen. Last man or woman standing secures our wager. Ready?"

They nodded grimly and Natalia walked to the edge of the circle. Turning on her heel, she waved the kerchief in the air. "Let's get it on!"

The three muscular men advanced, weapons in hand, as Vel and Kaylessa sidestepped away from Valex. He crouched slightly, preparing his stance, facing the largest of the three crushers directly across from him. With a feral roar, the man slammed his hammer against the ship deck and charged blindly at Valex, weapon raised. Valex spoke a command word and vanished into smoke as soon as the man made contact. The crusher skidded through the mist, waving his club and turning around, perplexed. Then he grinned at Natalia. "I'm the strongest! One hit turned him to smoke!"

"Not quite."

The large man whirled at the sound of the voice but was too slow to stop the enormous wave of water Valex had conjured up from the ocean and blasted across the deck. The wall knocked the pirate off of his feet and tossed him out into the ocean. The crowd groaned, and the sound of money changing hands could be heard all around them.

Kaylessa had followed Natalia's thinking and scampered up the central mast, climbing quickly, hand over hand. One of the pirates tossed his hammer aside and put a dagger in between his teeth, and began scaling up behind her. Once She'd reached the crow's nest, she crouched down for a moment, before popping back up, and tight roping across the thin wooden beam that supported the sail.

"Come get me, asshole!" she challenged, nocking an arrow and aiming where she had just run from.

The pirate reached the top and jerked his head back as an arrow soared past his ear. His startled look was replaced by a grin as he faced the elf. "Hah! You missed, little girl! My turn!"

"Did I?" Kaylessa grabbed the end of the rope at her feet and dove from the sail. As the rope became taut, the pirate looked down, saw the snare his foot was standing in, and followed the line up to the arrow stuck in the mast. Before he could react, he was yanked off his feet and then he dangled, suspended in the air by the snare she had set. Kaylessa's momentum on the swing carried her, and she sailed over the heads of the pirates, who were cheering her on. But she released the rope a moment too late and landed on the upper landing of the ship with a clatter. The cheers faded to boos.

Vel crouched low, waiting as the third crusher approached. His wild hair and beard made him look feral, but he reached out with an enormous hand faster than she had predicted. She ducked backwards and sidestepped the man, kicking off the railing of the ship to lob herself onto his back. As both of her daggers sunk into his back and shoulder, the man groaned and then dropped his weapon to reach over his head to grab her. She ducked, but one of his hands found purchase on her cloak and with a heave, he swung the smaller woman over his head, bringing her slamming down to the deck hard enough to crack the wood.

The crowd was silent as she got shakily to her feet, one of her arms bent at an unnatural angle, her right hand lower than her left. She placed a hand on the shoulder, grimaced, and *pushed* the joint back into place with a snap. The pirates cheered as the two fighters circled each other again, unarmed. The bruiser pulled the daggers from his skin, and with a cursory glance, tossed them overboard.

Every word dripping with venom, Vel said, "Now, not only do I have to kick your ass, you owe me new daggers." She moved low, adopting a strange fighting stance, her right hand and foot wide in front of her, and her left tucked in behind. The pirate, unphased, raised his hands in a boxer's stance and waded in. His left hand shot out in a wild haymaker, and Vel bent at the waist to swing underneath it, not moving her feet. She was prepared for the follow-up right hand, and stepped *in* towards the man, grabbed his extended wrist, and swung both of her legs up around his neck and shoulders. Hanging in midair, Vel braced herself and arched her spine. The sound of the man's arm breaking was audible, and they collapsed together in a heap.

Vel scrambled to her feet, and looked around for her companions. Something cold pressed against her neck, and she heard a "click." She turned slowly, until she was looking down an iron cylinder, held by Natalia Dreadwing. Whatever it was, it appeared to have some kind of mechanism attached, and she could smell the bitter tang of gunpowder.

"Sorry, love, that would be checkmate." Natalia kept the tool pointed at her head, and Vel saw her companions were in equal states of distress. Valex was on his back, Drake's swords held across his throat, and Kaylessa was up against the railing of the upper deck, hands raised as three archers held her in place.

"This is bullshit. You cheated." Vel spat, but Natalia laughed and lowered her weapon.

"Don't be a sore loser, darling. I said you had to beat my crew, not just those three. Fair's fair, and we've only got a few hours until we make landfall. I intend to make the most of it." She walked over to where Drake was helping Valex to his feet, and grabbed Valex by the belt, dragging him towards the double doors of the captain's cabin. As she opened the doors, she slapped Kaylessa across her bottom, and pushed the two of them in.

"Come on, noble leader," she beckoned with a crooked finger. "A bet is a bet."

Vel swallowed and walked across the deck, her head high amidst the cat calls and jeers of the crew.

Natalia closed the doors, but not before turning to Drake and saying, "Regardless of what you hear, I am not to be disturbed."

Vel, Valex, and Kaylessa sat around a small fire they had lit on the beach. They had arrived at their destination around sunset, after Natalia had finally released them from her chambers. They had been given a small boat, which Valex rowed to shore, the three of them silent, and avoiding each other's gaze.

Vel removed one of her pre-rolled cigarettes and lit it on the fire, staring into the embers. Valex motioned for one, and Kaylessa surprised them both by doing the same. They smoked in silence, until Valex cleared his throat and spoke up. "So…are we going to talk about…"

He was abruptly cut off by Kaylessa and Vel saying "No!" in unison, and the quiet returned.

"…Well, alright then." Valex tossed the end of his smoke into the fire and rolled over to sleep. Vel and Kaylessa followed suit, and as the fire burned, they kept their distance. No one slept for a long while.

At dawn, they collapsed the camp and during the tear down, Vel stood straight upright and spoke to no one in particular: "Yesterday never happened. Agreed?"

"Agreed." Kaylessa's voice was quiet, and she kept her gaze locked on the floor.

"I don't know what you two are so—Ow!" Vel had thrown an iron cooking pot at Valex's head, which clanged against his horns, "Alright, alright! It never happened!"

Nodding, Vel turned to survey the rocky cliffside. A winding path carved its way up the overgrown cliffside, dotted with stone carvings. The path wound up the mountainside, until it was swallowed by the clouds that eclipsed the peak. Valex came up beside her, cinching the straps on his pack. "Here we go," he said, and began to climb.

Vel and Kaylessa followed, watching the ship shrink against the horizon. Vel's heart burned with fury. She had never been one to lose a bet or to be taken advantage of, and both had happened last night. *Revenge will be mine, Natalia,* she thought, letting the anger propel her up the steep slope.

By late afternoon, they crested the cloud cover and reached the plateau. Tall grass and trees surrounded the area, and they crept through, mindful of the noise they were making. They had no idea what could be on this island, but the carvings told them that *something* lived here. They reached the edge of a large clearing and looked out at a strange, ceremonial-looking area. Ornate pillars dotted a stone courtyard, and at the centre stood a dilapidated building, a temple of some kind.

"Ugh, what a dump. Wravien is going to owe us big time if this ends up being a bust," Vel grumbled under her breath.

"Look, four o' clock. What…What are those?" Kaylessa had ducked low and was looking across the clearing. Vel and Valex followed her gaze and saw the creatures.

There were almost thirty figures roaming the courtyard; they were tall, lean, and vaguely humanoid. Their scaly skin ranged in colours from teals, to dark purples, and their webbed hands clutched strange, foreign-looking weapons. The blades glistened opalescent in the fading sunlight and might have been made of sea shells. Worst of all, where their heads should have been, each creature had a strange composite of black mouths full of tiny, triangular teeth and long, disgusting stalks that ended in yellow eyeballs. Human or not, Vel knew what patrols looked like when she saw them. She and her friends ducked down as a pair of the creatures walked past, chittering in an alien language. She took a quick count, and grimaced when she realised how dire this could be.

"Do you think they're friendly?" Valex whispered, and Vel shook her head.

"There are at least thirty that I can see, and from their weapons, I don't think they'll welcome us warmly. They're guarding something. We'll need a distraction..."

As she wound a loose strand of hair around her finger, Kaylessa began to skulk off to her right through the trees.

"I've got this, but you won't have a lot of time," she said quietly. "As soon as you hear my signal, break for the temple and figure out what we're looking for."

"Wait, Kaylessa..." Valex hissed, but she had already melted away into the trees. Exasperated, he turned to Vel. "We don't even know what the signal is!"

Valex removed a bottle of a foul smelling liquor he had swiped off a pirate and uncorked it while Vel held her breat They waited at the treeline looking for any sign of what Kaylessa had planned, when a resounding crash sounded from the other side of the clearing and several of the creatures flew up into the air. All around the clearing, stalks pivoted in the direction of the disturbance and the horrible chittering increased in volume, as all of the creatures headed to the source of the disturbance. Without confirming with Valex, Vel broke from the tree line, running low to the ground and beelining for the structure. Valex cursed and hurried to get up, the straps of his bag wrapped around his large taloned feet. He fell forward, the bottle shattering and the contents of his pack spilling out. He cursed again, swiped everything he could see back into his bag, looked at the crowd of creatures, and lumbered out after Vel, making considerably more noise as the pots and pans strapped to his bag clanged on his back.

Vel slammed her shoulder into the doors of the temple, knocking one of them off its hinges, and began to scan the situation. Long wooden benches ran the length of the room, skeletons sitting lopsided in them. Two bookshelves flanked the door, but at the back of the room was an altar that housed an incredibly large, pulsing, purple crystal.

Valex entered, stepping over the broken door, and saw Vel approaching the gemstone, hands outstretched as he wiped his sodden hands onto his trousers.

As she was inches away, Vel flashed back to her harrowing experience in Quebys' tower, and dropped her hands. "Valex, do you think you can lift this?"

"In a moment." Valex rummaged through the bookshelves, pulling out dusty books and tucking them into his bag after a cursory glance. The noise from outside was getting louder, and Valex and Vel turned to the entrance as Kaylessa burst through the door, blood flowing from several wounds all over her body. She slid around the large shelf beside the doorframe, and pressed her body into it, trying to knock it over and create a barricade. "Help!" she called out, and they could see the creatures sprinting towards the temple through the open doorway.

Vel rushed over and together they were able to knock the shelf to the ground, just in time. The creatures slammed into it, and the two women braced it as best they could.

"We need a plan! Valex!" Vel shouted, jumping back as a spear shot through the opening over the bookshelf, narrowly missing her head. "What are you doing? We need you!"

Valex reached into his bag and grabbed for his grimoire, finding nothing in its place. He frantically pawed through the contents of the bag, and in his search, he brushed his fingers against the strange tome he'd found in Quebys' tower, and the alien voice had returned inside his head.

It appears you are in quite a pinch, my acolyte. You could request the aid of your patron—I'll happily give you the power you need to eliminate these lesser creatures.

"I'm not giving you my soul," Valex muttered aloud, watching as Vel and Kaylessa pushed pews against the shelf. But it was clear that they were running out of time. The creatures had swarmed the building and were beginning to smash through the wooden boards that covered the windows on either side. Kaylessa had used up almost all of her arrows, and Vel was nursing a nasty slash across her chest, oozing blood. Valex realised nothing he had in his arsenal would be enough to save them.

No, of course not. I've thought it over and that was too much to ask. If you take my help, I'll make it an easy transaction. All I want is to take away something you love."

Valex considered this and then clarified, "Something I love? If you kill any of my friends or family, I'll make sure you spend the rest of your days as a doorstop."

"Of course not. You are my loyal servant. It will be something I'm sure you'll miss very little, but if you grip my tome and open your mind to me. I'll do the rest."

Valex hesitated for a moment, but the sounds of the strange creatures assaulting the small stone chapel were getting worse, and the barricade had almost been destroyed, so he did as instructed and was gripped by an otherworldly sensation that flowed over him. His eyes rolled back and he began to float up into the air, as a sickly miasma flowed out of the open book. The sky through the broken windows turned a deep magenta, and the noises from outside changed. The chittering went from angry, to confused, to terrified, and an immense pressure washed over Vel and Kaylessa, driving them to the ground.

It was over as quickly as it had begun. Valex fell through the air, collapsing in a heap, and the sunlight returned. Vel got to her feet and listened. There was only the sound of Kaylessa's haggard breathing nearby—no sign of the strange creatures. Vel risked a look over the remains of the barricade and saw the clearing was washed with a deep-red liquid, but the bodies of the creatures were nowhere to be seen.

"Valex, are you okay?" Kaylessa got to her feet and staggered over to the prone figure of their friend. She shook his shoulder and his eyes fluttered open, settling on the elf.

"I think so. That was not something I'd like to repeat. It used almost all of my magical energy to stay conscious. I don't suppose either of you have something to drink?"

Vel approached and tossed a small silver flask from her pouch to him. "Go ahead, I'd say you earned it this time."

Grateful, Valex unscrewed the cap and put it to his lips, letting it flow into his mouth. He stopped and looked at the flask incredulously. He took a sniff of the liquor, then poured a bit out onto the ground, then took another, smaller sip. Shaking his head angrily, he pressed the flask back into Vel's hand.

"Very funny, Vel. I'm going to be getting a proper drink when we're back. Why you'd have a flask of water on you, I dont understand." He turned to the barricade and pushed past the heavy furniture to reclaim his lost tome. Vel took a quick sip, grimaced at the whiskey's burn, then pocketed the flask. *Whatever.* She removed a small hammer from her side bag and began to rain blows down onto the large purple crystals, picking up the fragments as they fractured off.

Kaylessa leaned against the wall at the end of the room where a large tapestry hung, clutching a deep wound on her side. The tapestry was faded by time and the elements, but she could just make out the image of a large hand reaching down from the clouds and a small crowd of people holding up various treasures. She ran her bloody hand over the spot where the treasure was and heard a mechanical click.

Vel turned around to see a portion of the floor begin to slide open with a grinding noise, revealing a small hole. Sitting at the bottom was a large, ornate chest, and Vel squealed with pleasure as she rushed towards it, her previous labour forgotten. "Oh, I knew you were good for something!" She knelt down in front of the chest, picked the lock, and opened it to reveal shining golden trinkets, jewelled goblets, and a matching set of golden short swords, elvish in their design. "Jackpot! Even splitting this with the pirate, we're going to be set for a long time! Kaylessa, come take a look at these—Kaylessa?!"

Kaylessa had slumped down the wall by the tapestry, leaving a large red stain. She raised her head weakly, but let it fall again, her eyes slipping shut.

"Valex! Shit, Valex, we need help!" Vel slid to the ground beside her friend, and Valex hurried over from the front door, spell book in hand. Vel turned Kaylessa onto her side and saw a long slash through her side that was bleeding profusely. Her blood was creating a pool around her, how she had been able to stay standing this long was a miracle. "Oh God. She's losing too much blood. Valex, what do we do?"

Valex knelt down beside Kaylessa and pulled the tome from his belt. "I've got a spell that should be able to stabilize her, but if I perform it, I'll have to use all of my remaining mana. I'm going to be out for the count,. Whatever happened to me with that weird book drained me. You'll be on your own if we need to do any more fighting."

"Do it." Vel's voice was strained with emotion. "She doesn't die here. Anything else comes, I'll tear it apart myself."

Valex nodded and began to cast his spell.

Vel looked at the treasure chest sadly but walked over and removed the twin short-swords and put them in her bags. They would make a good gift for Kaylessa when she was back on her feet.

She looked back and saw Valex wiping the blood off his hands onto a small cloth. "It's done," he said. He looked clammy and pale, and was shaking visibly "If you carry Kaylessa, I'll bring the treasure down."

"No, we both carry Kaylessa. Fuck the treasure. We can have Natalia's men come get it once we've got her safe." Vel said.

Each taking an arm, they hoisted her up. Kaylessa let out a shallow moan but failed to open her eyes. They lurched through the door and crossed the blood-soaked courtyard towards the path down the mountain.

As soon as they broke the cloud cover, Vel felt her stomach drop as she looked down towards the beach. Night had fallen, but she could see that the pirates had all left the ship and were standing in a circle around a ring of torches. They had agreed that Natalia and her crew would stay on the ship, and Vel couldn't help but feel that this was a bad omen. She grunted as she adjusted the unconscious elf on her shoulder. Valex was on the other side but wasn't of much help as he was barely standing himself. Blinking down at the beach, he noticed what Vel had seen, and a weak smile appeared on his face.

"What's going on down there, do you think? Is it a cookout? I hope it's a cookout. I'm very hungry."

"I'm not sure, but I don't like it." Vel said, "Let's focus on getting down there in one piece, okay?"

They manoeuvred the cliffside delicately, the drunken voices of the pirates carried on the wind to them. As they approached the beach, the circle of pirates opened up, and Vel staggered through it. She heard the sound of a single set of hands clapping slowly, and she turned to see

Natalia, seated on the throne she had kept on the ship, watching her with eyes full of mischief.

"I'll be damned! When we saw the lights change, and the blood poured down the side of the mountain, I was sure you were dead. Imagine my surprise, when I see you having a three-legged race down the cliff! It's a shame—taking all of the treasure when you were dead would have felt less like betrayal. Oh well, beggars can't be choosers."

"What do you think you're doing? We had a deal. My friend here needs help, besides...there wasn't any treasure up there," Vel lied, assessing the situation.

Natalia rose to her feet and walked over to them. The circle of pirates closed behind her, cutting off their escape. "Oh we had a deal, yes, but the terms of said deal were very clear. I promised you safe passage *to* the island, I never said anything about getting *back*. I am a pirate, after all, and you were naive to trust me. A shame—I enjoyed your company the most, Ms. Valdove; there was something so satisfying about breaking you. Your death will break my heart." She pouted at Vel and drew one of the two devices strapped to her hips.

"Wait! You kill me, and you'll never find the treasure!" Vel knew she was floundering, but she had to buy some time to think. Then she thought back to the day before and knew what she had to do. "But, we could make a little wager?"

Natalia lowered the barrel she had pointed at Vel and laughed sarcastically. "But Vel, there was no treasure, right? Look at us, one and the same, a pair of liars. But I do enjoy a good bet, and I do love an underdog. Especially one that's been under me." She winked, and Vel's glare sharpened. "Go on, what do you propose?"

"You and me. One on one, proper, for all the marbles. I win, we take your ship, your crew, and the treasure," Vel said.

"Very funny." Natalia thumbed the hammer on her device. "But what could you possibly offer me that would be worth such a prize?"

"Me. I offer you me. I'll join your crew, be your slave, whatever you want. Bark when you say bark, and all that. You can do what you want with the dragon and the elf. What do you say? You did say I was your favourite." She leaned in closer to Natalia, whose eyes narrowed. "Besides, if you refuse, think of how much face you'll lose in front of your men." Natalia looked around at her shipmates, who muttered amongst themselves, and she holstered the device.

"Dominating you again? I'd have to say, I'd be worried if I didn't know what a kitten you really are. Fine my darling, let's have ourselves a little more playtime before I brand you as my property."

"Good, it will be the last playtime you ever have, before I put your slimy ass into the ground." Vel gritted her teeth, and the pirates erupted into cheers. When was the last time they'd seen the captain fight one on one? The betting commenced with gusto. Vel let Kaylessa's weight fall onto Valex, who dragged her back towards the edge of the circle, and sat down, too weak to contribute.

"Go get her, Vel." Valex hissed through his clenched teeth, and Vel nodded back.

Vel drew her rapier, Natalia pulled a bejeweled scimitar from her belt, and the two women circled each other. Natalia's black hair and Vel's white struck a curious contrast in the moonlight, and as they sidestepped around the crowd fell silent. Eyes locked, Vel moved first, pulling a small throwing knife from her belt and hurling it in Natalia's direction.

The scimitar flashed, deflecting the blade, but Vel was already sprinting across the sand, closing the gap. Natalia cackled, and she parried the first thrust from Vel, but her confidence failed as Vel pressed the advantage. *Ting! Tssh! Clang!* Vel moved like a storm, strike after strike raining down, and Natalia was forced back to the edge of the circle. She sidestepped and Vel drew her dagger, doubling the strikes.

Natalia called out, "Drake!" and a muscled arm from the crowd reached out and shoved Vel to the side, allowing Natalia to roll backwards. Valex roared in indignation, but Vel was prepared for this. In a fluid motion, Vel released her dagger into the crowd, which gasped and parted as Drake staggered backwards, hands pressed to the dagger embedded to the hilt in his forehead. Blood flowed down his face and saturated his beard.

Vel returned her attention to Natalia and then a loud *bang* reverberated in the air, and she felt a white-hot pain in her right shoulder. Through a cloud of smoke, Natalia's triumphant face appeared above the barrel of her device—some kind of portable cannon. The smile faded as Vel let out a bark of laughter. "I was wondering what those did, seems like a coward's weapon." She dropped the rapier from her wounded arm and began to run towards Natalia, who fumbled the cannon and tried to draw her scimitar again.

Vel slashed out with another throwing knife, and it glinted in the light as it sailed across the clearing and embedded itself in Natalia's left eye. Natalia howled, but Vel was already within range, and she grabbed the wrist holding the scimitar and twisted, forcing it out of the pirate's hands.

"You bitch, what did you do?!" Locked in the grapple, Natalia spat into Vel's face.

"Oh that's just the beginning, you whore. You're going to regret trying to double-cross a Valdove." Vel cocked back and struck Natalia in the face with a closed fist, sending her pirouetting into the sand. Spitting out a mouthful of blood, Vel balled her fists and waded in.

Natalia got to her feet, and yanked the small blade from her eye with a howl. She charged Vel, surprising her, and tackling her to the ground. Placing her hands around Vel's throat, she began to throttle, slamming her head into the sand again and again. "I'll end you! You stupid fuck, do you know how many men I've killed, and never once has anyone damaged my perfect face! Once I'm done with you, oh, I'm going to take my time with your little friends! They'll be begg–"

BANG!

Natalia's eyes widened in shock, and she released Vel's throat, putting her hands on the crimson rose spreading on her stomach.

Coughing, Vel tossed the second hand cannon she had stolen off of the pirate's belt into the sand and pushed Natalia off of her. Standing over her as she cried, Vel spat into her face, and said, "Thanks for teaching me how those work. See, the thing is, *no one fucks with my friends.*"

Vel looked grimly around at the pirates, her lips pulled back to reveal a crimson snarl. "What are you lumps waiting for?! Send someone up the hill to retrieve my treasure…and carry my friends onto the ship." When no one moved, she kicked Natalia in the stomach and howled, "Move! Your new captain just gave you an order!"

Startled into action, the pirates followed her orders. A group headed up the winding path at a sprint, and several moved to carry Valex and Vel onto the ship. The bookish-looking pirate who had inspected their map appeared at her elbow as she lurched her way over to the gangplank. "What would you like us to do with Cap...I mean, Ms. Dreadwing?" he said, speaking loud in order to be heard over Natalia's cries.

"Leave her," Vel said coolly. "A quick death is more than she deserves."

They set sail and once Kaylessa regained consciousness, Valex regaled her with what had happened. After telling the story, he limped up to the deck and leaned on the railing, enjoying the warmth of the rising sun. He looked at the island as they sailed away, saw movement on the beach, and snagged a spyglass off of the nearest pirate. Unbelievably, as he trained it on the shore, he saw a solitary figure silhouetted by the fire she had lit, watching them sail away. Valex swallowed the nervous lump in his throat and collapsed the spyglass, feeling that they hadn't seen the last of Natalia Dreadwing.

CHAPTER 10

THE SCOURGE OF MERCALLIA

Day 900 – Somulous Experiment: The voices are beginning to tell me things. Things I should never be able to know, things I never <u>wanted</u> to know. I have taken the body to my new laboratory, which is impressively secure, and have begun to see if applying electric stimulation to the deceased brain tissue will spark any thoughts that I can hear. Fortunately, if the tissue erodes, I've learned how easy it is to make someone disappear with a power like mine. Besides, the voice has shown me how to bring the dead back to life—this means I will never run out of subjects. [The signature is gone, replaced with a single word.] GRIMHOWL

The return trip to Mercallia was relatively uneventful. The combined lack of sailing experience between Vel, Valex, and Kaylessa became apparent quite quickly, and they delegated most of the efforts to Alfie, the bookish looking pirate from the bar. He took charge of the crew with

surprising zeal, as Drake's stature had always kept him from rising up in the crew. Kaylessa spent most of the journey recovering in bed, and Valex was uncharacteristically sullen and withdrawn. A few of the pirates were celebrating their new captain with toasts and offered drinks to Valex, who surprised his companions by quietly refusing, and retiring to the crow's nest.

Vel took to the captain's quarters and with a vigour immediately busied herself with eliminating any trace of Natalia. She began by breaking a large oil painting of the raven-haired woman over her knee, with a look of grim satisfaction, and she made repeated trips to and from the cabin, tossing overboard anything she deemed to be of no value.

Vel had not spoken to Kaylessa since they'd returned to the ship, and when Alfie summoned Kaylessa to the cabin, she was fairly apprehensive. Knocking before entering, she opened the door and was pleasantly surprised at the changes. The old captain's quarters had been a garish affair, with leather supports hanging from the ceiling and ostentatious furniture, but it was now minimalist and neat. In the centre of the room was a desk, which Vel was seated at, looking at a small leather ledger and pawing through the contents of a chest.

"Kaylessa. It's good to see you up and about. How are you feeling?" Vel asked, not looking up from her ledger.

"Much better, thank you." Kaylessa squirmed in her seat, feeling the weight of the small talk. "You seem to be settling in nicely."

Vel sighed, closed the ledger, and stood up. She headed towards the window at the back of the cabin and rested her head against the glass. "I'm not very good at this kind of thing, so I'm just going to spit it out and be done with it. I'm not used to relying on people, but when I saw you hurt as bad as you were, I lost it. You've become a comrade, and I don't want to lose anyone that I care about so… here." She held out a rolled piece of fabric, and Kaylessa took it, bracing at the weight.

She unrolled the package and revealed two, gleaming, golden short swords. Vel had taken the pains to polish the tarnish off their scabbards, and now the elvish runes were clear, and someone had threaded the blades through an intricately woven belt.

Kaylessa stared at them, awestruck. "Oh, Vel. They are beautiful! Judging by the runes, I think they may have even been forged in my homeland! Thank you."

"Well, I can't always be there to save your ass, so some quality weaponry will hopefully give you the edge in a fight." Vel looked awkward and Kaylessa realised this might be the longest conversation they'd ever had.

The oppressive silence hung in the air, so Kaylessa steeled herself and asked the question that had been lingering since she'd regained consciousness. "So…what will you do now? You've secured yourself a ship and a crew, so you probably won't need to work for Wravien anymore."

Vel drummed her fingers on the arm of her chair, then threw her hands up in a gesture of indifference. "I've never been one to lead anything. This could be a profitable venture, to be sure, but I promised Wravien I would support his enterprise, and so far it's been a smart call. I think I'll have a chat with Alfie before we dock, promote him to captain, and have them pay me a cut."

Kaylessa tried to play it cool but was unsuccessful. She gave a small squeal and hugged the other woman, who patted her on the back half-heartedly as she continued. "Besides, we've got a warlord to save. You won't be rid of me just yet."

"I'm glad, Vel, we need your skills and your power for what's to come." Kaylessa smiled warmly. "I'll send Alfie in and grab Valex—we should be arriving at port soon."

Alfie was flabbergasted but agreed at once to Vel's suggestion. He bowed and scraped and promised that she would be notified of any bounty or treasure they acquired. After handing over her information so that he could follow through, they bid the crew farewell at the docks, and the ship sailed out once again.

They had only been gone a few days, but the air in Mercallia had notably changed. Soldiers were streaming in and out of the barracks, and the majority of the pirate ships had dropped sail and made themselves scarce, making way for more of the navy-blue sails of the Tempest paladins, giving the entire town a militant feel. When they entered the Crimson Krill, they saw a harried Jim was serving table after table of the armoured men, stress written plainly on his face. Several rather homely women, dressed in stockings and corsets, were milling about the room, laughing and flirting with the soldiers.

Valex looked at the sea of blue and saw Zordriag's telltale horns poking out, but the paladin's back was to him, so he drew his cloak up over his head, grabbed a nearby table, and beckoned his companions over. "If our information is correct, we're running out of time. Khan is either in the barracks already or will be shortly. Kaylessa, can I ask you to do a quick recon run to the fort, and see if you can find the hidden entrance Jim mentioned? With the lack of facial hair in this bar, I think we've got a lot of young blood, and they likely have the passage unobscured."

Kaylessa nodded, pulled her own hood up, and slipped out of the bar.

"Valex, you seem a little high strung. You need something to drink, my treat?" Vel asked, looking at him with concern.

"...No, that's fine, thank you." Valex's face was pinched and he looked a little nauseous.

Vel noticed he was drumming his fingers on the table, and his eyes were darting around. "Cut the shit, Valex, what's going on with you? Before the island, you never met a drink you didn't like. Hell, I used to have to pry the bottle from your fingers, and now you're just...not drinking? What's the matter with you?"

Vel stared at him, hard, and Valex finally met her gaze. With a sigh, he explained what had happened, starting with the book he had stolen from the tower, and ending with the situation with her flask.

"... and ever since I agreed to give up something I love...I can't even taste it. No matter how much I drink, it turns to water in my mouth. Ale, whiskey, it doesn't matter. I thought I was losing my mind."

"That would be...disorienting, I'm sure. But maybe it's for the best? Seemed like it was causing you more trouble than good," she said sympathetically.

"Easy for you to say," Valex snapped. "What if I told you that you had to suddenly stop being a greedy bitch?"

Vel looked at him coolly, until he lowered his head, and sighed. "I'm…I'm sorry. I didn't realise how much I needed it to take the edge off."

"Get your shit together. We've got a job to do tonight, and I need to know I can count on you not losing your cool in the middle of it all." She turned towards the door. "Kaylessa's back."

"I found it!" Kaylessa's face was flushed and she was grinning, "There is a patch of ivy on the southern wall, and it's covering a crack that leads into the main courtyard. I crept close and overheard some of the soldiers talking. Khan is currently being held in a cell, to be delivered tomorrow morning. But there is some bad news…the hole is fairly small. I don't think Valex is going to be able to fit."

"That is a problem. I know this is going to be a bit of a stealthy job, but I'm counting on big and scaly's magic to even the odds," Vel mused.

Valex pushed his chair back from the table. "It would be a problem, if I didn't have a great idea just now. We're breaking Khan out of a cell, right? So as long as I'm in a cell when it happens, you can just break me out at the same time." He handed his coin purse, spell tome, and the keys he had filched off the sleeping paladin to Kaylessa and then cracked his knuckles.

"What are you thinking, Valex?" Kaylessa had the items in her hands, and looked at him, perplexed.

"I've had one hell of a day, and I'm going to do something to cheer myself up. See you on the inside." Valex approached the table where Zordriag sat, surrounded by his fellow soldiers, and grabbed a half-empty bottle from the nearest table. "Hey Zordriag!" he shouted.

All eyes in the room turned towards him.

"I got you a drink, you racist piece of shit!" He brought the bottle down hard onto Zordriag's upturned face, spraying the surrounding paladins with beer. The uproar was immediate, but Valex grabbed Zordriag by the horns, and grappled him to the floor. The onlookers grabbed at his arms, but the bigger dragonborn shook them off.

Maintaining his hold on one of Zordriag's horns, he began to hail down blows into his face. "Who's…inferior…now!" he screamed, punctuating each word with another strike. There was a brittle, snapping sound and Valex tumbled backwards, still clutching Zordriag's broken horn.

Blood poured down Zordriag's face and he rose to face Valex, who got yanked into a kneeling position by two of the bulkier knights.

"You crazy bastard, I'll kill you!" Zordriag drew a long trident from his back and gripped it with both hands, bloodlust in his eyes. He cocked back with the weapon, looking to impale Valex, when Jim interjected by smashing a bottle and crying out in a mewling yell, "Gentlemen! You're the law here, please, not in my bar!"

Zordriag's beady eyes looked about and saw the commotion had drawn a large crowd of onlookers who watched with bated breath. He composed himself, took a breath, and struck Valex across the face with the back of his talon, then he reversed his trident and struck him in the face with the butt end of it. Valex collapsed to the ground, completely unconscious, and Zordriag returned the weapon to its holster, before turning to address his soldiers. "Take this overgrown kobold to the fort. We'll ship him out with the barbarian, and Leviathan can pass his judgement on him."

"Yes sir, Lieutenant Split-Tongue!" It took seven guards to pick up Valex's hulking frame, but they carried him like a piece of furniture from the bar. Zordriag sat down, pulled a frilly kerchief from a pouch on his belt, and dabbed at the ruin where his horn used to be. "Barkeep!" he barked at Jim, who scuttled to his elbow at once. "Get me a healer and another round of ale for my men and I. I've saved your bar from any damage, and I expect you to take care of our tab."

"Ah...yes, of course sir." Jim hustled away, but as soon as his back was turned his simpering smile melted into his trademark frown.

"Wow...I suppose that's one way to get the job done," Vel laughed, looking impressed. "Come on, Kaylessa, let's get prepared. As soon as this place clears out, we'll break in and free him."

Valex faded in and out of consciousness, but when he finally came to, every part of his body ached, and he was distantly reminded of the beatings of his youth. He tried to open his eyes and found that only one would open, the other had swelled shut from the savage attack. He was in a tiny, wooden-walled room, laid upon a metal rack that, he supposed, was intended to be a bed. At the door of his cell, a small tray of food sat, but the bread looked moist, and a large, white shape was floating in the top of his stew. He approached and smelled the tray with a grimace. *Of course,* he thought, *they spit on it. Such gallant soldiers.*

"AH, THE LARGE ONE AWAKENS!" A voice boomed from the cell across from him, making Valex jump. "I'M IMPRESSED YOU'RE ALREADY ON YOUR FEET, THEY HAD QUITE A TIME WORKING YOU OVER. YOU MUST BE BLESSED WITH A WARRIOR'S SPIRIT!"

Valex squinted his good eye and looked across the hallway to the cell adjacent to him. Seated on the bed at the back wall was a humongous half-orc. His green skin and protruding tusks gave his heritage away, but the figure was lounging comfortably, legs spread and completely naked. Valex gaped for a moment, then looked at the floor.

"Oh, Gods. What…Are you Khan Xarlug? Also, where are your clothes?"

"INDEED I AM! KHAN XARLUG, WAR CHIEF OF THE BLOODSPINE TRIBE, THE TERROR OF Z'RACO. AS FOR MY CLOTHING, THE COWARDLY BOYS WHO AMBUSHED ME THOUGHT THEY COULD SHAME ME BY MARCHING ME ACROSS THE GREAT PLAINS NAKED, TIED TO THEIR WAGON." He laughed out loud, the sound ringing obnoxiously in the tiny rooms. "THE FOOLS. KHAN XARLUG HAS ROAMED THOSE SAME PLAINS AS NAKED AS THE DAY HE WAS BORN! KHAN XARLUG FEELS NO SHAME!"

"That's…that's great Khan. What say we try keeping it down a little, you don't need to shout, we're only ten feet away." Valex rubbed his temples, realising this was going to be a very long night.

"WHO IS SHOUTING, MY FRIEND? IF YOU WISH TO HEAR A SHOUT, THE XARLUG WAR CRY CAN SHAKE THE SNOW FROM THE MOUNTAINS THEMSELVES!"

"No, please, that's quite alright. Listen, my name is Valex Shatterscale, and my friends and I are here on behalf of Wravien Leonhart. We're going to break you out."

"WRAVIEN! A NAME I HAVE NOT HEARD IN MANY MOONS! HE AND KHAN XARLUG SPARRED MANY TIMES, AND HE EVEN WON ONCE OR TWICE! I HAVE NOT FORGIVEN HIM FOR THIS

AND WOULD RELISH THE CHANCE TO PROVE MY SUPERIORITY AGAIN." Khan's bellow made it clear he wasn't at all phased by his current situation.

"Yeah, great, listen…have you spoken to any of the other prisoners? If we're going to make a break for it, we're going to want as many distractions as possible," Valex said.

A voice spoke up through the wall to his right. "Oy, I've been listening to you this entire time, bloody hard not to, and if it means I can quit listening to this great, green idiot, I'll do anything. Count me in."

"Aye, us too!" Another voice, that seemed to come from the cell beside Khan, cried out in a thick, Dwarvish brogue. Valex leaned against the bars and saw a whole squad of dwarves crammed together in the tiny cell. "We got tossed for gettin in an argument with the soldiers after a few drinks, and I dunna want to see my brothers' heads roll for that." A chorus of affirmation followed.

This might actually work, Valex thought, settling into his cot, *provided Vel and Kaylessa come through.* The door of the building opened, and a thick-set militia man poked his head in and bellowed, "Keep it down in here! You're in jail, not a tavern!"

"THEN COME IN AND SILENCE ME YOURSELF, CUR!" Khan bellowed, rushing the door of his cell and shaking the bars, "OR DOES MY DIVINE PHYSIQUE INTIMIDATE A SMALL CHILD SUCH AS YOURSELF?"

Valex put his head into his hands. It was going to be a long night indeed.

In a small grove of trees and grass outside the barracks, Vel and Kaylessa stayed low, watching the paladins stream out in groups of two or three on horseback. They had tied their own mounts out of sight by the city gates and were waiting patiently for the endless stream of navy-clad soldiers to subside.

Eventually, the stillness of the night took hold, and Vel determined it was time to make their move. Creeping along the wall, she pushed the ivy aside and gestured for Kaylessa to duck under, before following suit. A row of hedges concealed the entrance from view, but they could hear the sounds of metal striking wood just beyond the hedge, and a hoarse voice shouting out commands. They crept along the greenery, stopping at the end, where Vel risked a look out into the courtyard.

A quick headcount confirmed that there were only ten men stationed here, and almost all of them wore the tell-tale armour of the town militia. She did see, however, Zordriag and two paladins approach the gate on horseback, and she had to suppress a laugh. The dragonborn's bruised face, along with the lopsided helmet, which sat askew due to the missing horn, ruined his previously prestigious aesthetic. *Serves you right,* she thought vindictively.

Two small buildings were visible in the courtyard. The one farther from them appeared to be a mess hall and had a flight of stairs that led up to the fort's wall. The other building, just to their right, was a much more fortified structure, and had two guards posted at the door. As they held their position, a guard came around the corner of the back of the building, nodded to the two men at the door, and continued around on his patrol. Vel tapped Kaylessa on the shoulder, and the two women skirted the building to the back side, where there was a small alleyway between the building and the wall. At the centre of the structure was a simple, wooden door, and as Vel moved towards it, the patrolling guard came around the corner with a look of surprise.

At the last second, Kaylessa drew her bow and let loose an arrow that impaled the guard through his throat. He pawed at the wound soundlessly and slumped to the ground. Vel dashed ahead and dragged the corpse farther behind the building, out of sight, and motioned Kaylessa forward to the other side of the door. Once in position, Vel cycled through the key ring, until she found the one that turned the lock, and pushed the door open slightly to see into the room.

Valex sat in his cell, watching the solitary guard walk up and down the central aisle of the cell block, sliding trays of food through the small flaps at the base of their cell doors. His bread was covered in thick, stringy globs of saliva, and he pushed it away. The guard returned from the last cell, and as he walked past, smirked down at Valex. "What's the matter, prisoner?

Is the food not good enough for you? A shame, after we made sure to give you extra toppings, courtesy of—Gah!"

The words were cut off as Vel's forearm snaked over his shoulder and pressed on his windpipe. The guard struggled for a moment, until Vel wrenched her body to the side, breaking the man's neck with an audible crunch. She dropped him to the ground, plucked the keyring from his belt, and approached Valex's cell with a smirk.

She grinned at him. "How was your stay? Everything to your liking?"

Valex scowled back. "Not a moment too soon. I was about to complain to management." He stepped through the open door and gestured to the cell across from him. Khan had fallen asleep in the same position as Valex had first seen him, manhood dangling. "I'd like to introduce you to the man we've been sent to save, Khan Xarlug."

"Oh my. Kaylessa! Come quick! We need your help!" Vel cried out softly, holding in her laughter.

"What is it? Are you al... oh my God." She came around the corner, looked into the cell, and gasped, covering her eyes.

Vel clapped her on the shoulder and let out a low whistle. "Would you look at that?"

The noise woke the slumbering warlord, who blinked a few times and then stood and approached the bars, arms outstretched. "AH! A BEVY OF BEAUTIFUL MAIDENS, ARMED FOR WAR! HAS KHAN XARLUG EXPIRED, AND REACHED THE AFTERLIFE?" He laughed hard and shook the bars.

"Shh! Keep it down, you idiot! I sure hope you're not dead, or this trip would be a waste." Vel unlocked his cell and undid the clasp that held the cloak around her neck. Holding it out at arm's length, she offered it to Khan, "Do me a favour, big boy, tie this around your waist. We don't need Kaylessa to pass out from shock."

"Shut up, Vel." Kaylessa still had her eyes covered, but they could see the blush racing up her face.

"NO NEED TO BE SHY, SWEET ONE." Khan tied the cloak around his waist, one well- muscled thigh protruding out from the slit in the fabric, "YOU WOULD NOT BE THE FIRST TO FAINT UPON WITNESSING MY MAJESTY."

Vel snorted as Khan struck a pose, flexing, but Valex shook his head. "Let's get the rest of these cells open, the more chaos we can cause, the better our chances of getting this buffoon out of here alive."

"Are you sure? I don't know if releasing a bunch of criminals, without knowing what they've done, is the best idea." Kaylessa looked around the room nervously, but Valex took the keyring and opened the dwarves' cell.

"This town is a garbage heap anyway, everyone we've met here is a criminal, so what's a few more?" he said. "Besides, I vetted most of them."

He moved across the hall and opened the cell beside his. In the gloom of the tiny room, a slender man dressed in black leather murmured his thanks. The cell across held the dwarves, who whooped and hollered as the door creaked open, and Vel scolded them as well.

Valex opened the last cell and almost thought it was empty, before he noticed the small gnome crouched beside the door. A tangle of coppery-orange hair crowned his head, and a pair of wide, manic eyes stared up at Valex. The gnome was giggling creepily and muttering under his breath, but Valex shrugged and turned to survey the ragtag crew.

The smartest play would be to sneak out the back door and try to herd the captives towards the hole in the wall. He opened his mouth to say so, when Khan muscled past him and addressed the room. "MEN! NO LONGER ARE WE CHAINED HOUNDS. WE ARE PROUD WARRIORS! WE MUST RECLAIM OUR HONOUR BY TAKING THE HEADS FROM OUR CAPTIVES AND MOUNTING THEM UPON THEIR OWN GATES! FOR GLORY! FOR HONOR! FOR KHAN XARLUG!"

With the final shout, Khan approached the front door and kicked it open, hurtling into the courtyard, his laughter mingling with the alarmed shouts of the guards. The dwarves looked at each other for a moment, then cheered and followed the half-orc out the door.

"Wait! We should..." Valex looked back, realising the gnome and the other man had already slipped out the back door.

He saw Kaylessa and Vel watching him, bemused. "It was a very good try, Valex!" Kaylessa said, patting him on the shoulder, and handing him back his book and money pouch.

"It is what it is," Vel said, pulling the hood over her head. "Let's just do our best to make sure he doesn't get killed."

They pushed the door open and stepped into utter pandemonium. The dwarves were clustered together, punching and shoving a harried group of guards, who had been using wooden swords to train on target dummies. His boisterous laughter ringing through the air, Khan stood in the centre of the courtyard, flanked by four guards holding spears. Dodging a thrust from the guard behind him, he stepped forward with his hands outstretched, grasped a man's helmet in each hand and brought them together with a loud *BONG*. The men dropped to the ground.

Kaylessa and Valex took up defensive positions near the war chief and fired arrows and spells at the guards who were taking aim at them from the top of the wall. Vel rushed into the crowd of men, slashing and cutting whenever there was an opening. She saw the man Valex had rescued from the cell steal a sword from a guard and move through the crowd with a thief's ease.It reminded her of the way Vincent had fought, and it made her smile.

The majority of the guards had been dispatched, and Valex had begun to believe they would be able to pull it off, when a loud horn sounded, echoing in the stone courtyard. They all turned towards the gates, which swung with a clattering sound. A squad of six Tempest Paladins rode horses through the open gates, along with a giant of a man astride a draft horse.

The giant rider pulled on his reins, bringing his horse to a stop. "Are you men, or worms?!" he bellowed. "I leave you alone for less than an hour, and a handful of rag tag adventurers turn my barracks into a battlefield! I, Captain Hamilton, will show you how to handle such a situation, and hopefully you'll learn something. Men, to arms!"

The other knights dismounted and assumed a phalanx position, shields arranged in a wall, and they charged towards Khan. He remained unarmed, but as he held one of the soldiers up by the back of the neck, punching him in the gut, the formation changed and they moved to completely encircle him. Khan allowed the man's body to tumble down, and held his arms wide, turning to view all of his attackers.

"I SEE YOU HAVE ANALYSED THE LARGEST THREAT, AND WISH TO REMOVE ME FROM THE FIGHT! YOU CHOSE THE RIGHT MAN, BUT I WISH YOU LUCK, PUPS!" Khan bellowed.

The circle of soldiers closed in tight, and they bashed him with the metal plates. He held onto his footing longer than he had any right to, but the swarm of men proved to be too much, and when he lost his footing, they descended on him, kicking and slamming the shields into his back. One of the men threw a weighted net over his prone form. Once they had him secured, they pivoted around and rushed the crew of unarmed dwarves, dispatching them with ease.

Captain Hamilton had moved into action at the same time as his men, and he spotted Vel and the other thief in the shadows of the building leading to the stairs up the wall. He spurred his horse, unshouldering a halberd with a vicious spike on the end, and a blunt hammer on the other, and lunged out at the prisoner. The halberd pierced through the man's chest, and Hamilton raised his body in the air with ease, flicking the weapon to the side. The body tumbled to the ground. Hamilton turned his mount to charge at Vel, who was able to sidestep the thrust, but he turned his wrist and swung the long weapon in a wide arc, catching her in the ribs with the mallet end of the weapon. The force of the blow sent her sailing through the air into the wall, where she collapsed in a heap, clutching her smashed ribs.

Kaylessa saw Vel lying in a heap, and while rushing forward began to fire arrows one after another at Hamilton's huge steed. The horse reared back in pain, and she dropped her bow and drew the twin swords that Vel had given her, using her momentum to slide along the ground underneath the horse, slashing wildly with the blades. The swords found their mark in the hind legs, and the horse toppled backwards. Hamilton launched himself from the saddle, tumbling on the ground, his plate armour clinking against the cobblestones.

He rose to his feet, undoing the clasp on the bottom of his helmet and removing it. He tossed it aside and inspected his mewling horse, whose legs had been nearly removed by Kaylessa's wild strikes. He slashed the halbred through the neck of the great beast, severing bone and silencing its cries, and turned to look at Kaylessa. Blood soaked into his military haircut, while vengeance burned in his eyes. "I raised that horse from a foal—you're going to pay for that in blood."

"Fire cleanses all!" A shrill, high-pitched voice called out into the court-yard, momentarily stopping all the combatants in their tracks. Atop the wall stood the gnome with the frizzled red hair, surrounded by bottles that had been corked with rags. "I offer this fire up to you, great Ifrit, in hopes that you'll bring me to your warm embrace!" He cackled, began to light the rags on fire with a small tinderbox, and hailed them down onto the stone courtyard. The bottles smashed and whatever was inside erupted. The yard was suddenly full of fire. Valex ran backwards from the flames and saw the squad of soldiers advancing towards him. Looking at the fire all around, he shrugged and thought, *What the hell, what's a little more destruction?*

He held the tome up, spoke a single word, and the book rose from his hand, floating in place. He began to chant, rattling off command words, while both his hands made complex gestures. The sky above them darkened and fat drops of rain began to fall, sizzling against the open flames. The soldiers hesitated for a moment, but when nothing happened, they contin-ued their approach. Valex continued to chant, undaunted, until they were almost upon them. With a final word, he reached out, grabbed the book from the air, pointed to the sky, and shouted, "LIGHTNING STORM!"

The sky exploded with light. Bolts of lightning arced down, blasting the soldiers' careful formation apart. The smell of cooked flesh permeated the air, and the storm continued to rage in the direction the dragonborn had pointed, obliterating the northern wall of the fortress.

Valex ran to the net that held Khan down and sawed it open with a nearby discarded sword. "Khan! We have to go!" He helped the bigger man to his feet, stepping back as a militia man ran past them screaming, his entire upper body engulfed in flames.

Khan blinked at the carnage and destruction, clapped Valex on the shoulder and laughed out loud. "WE ARE GOING TO HAVE SOME FUN, YOU AND I, I CAN TELL. WHAT ABOUT THE WOMEN?"

"They can handle themselves, trust me. We'll regroup at the gate!" Valex shouted over the noise, and supported Khan towards the hole in the wall. He helped him over the ledge and chanced a look back. "

Kaylessa had placed herself between the unmoving Vel and Hamilton, who appeared to be unphased by the carnage all around him. Hamilton advanced, bringing the halberd over his head and swinging it down.

Kaylessa had to dive forward to avoid the vicious attack, but Hamilton drew a smaller war hammer in his other hand, and lashed out with it, catching her in the shoulder. He was much faster than he looked, in his bulky armour, and the superior reach of the long-handled weapon made getting in close enough to land a killing blow difficult.

Valex saw the fire spreading all around them and poured the last of his energy into one more spell. The sky above them parted briefly, and a gust of wind blew through the courtyard, encircling the two combatants. The fire that reached the swirling tempest was extinguished, and Valex clipped the book to his belt, exhausted. "Good luck, kid," he said aloud, "It's up to you now." He heaved himself up and over the broken fragments of wall and toppled out of the fortress.

"Give it up, girl!" Hamilton shouted over the roar of the wind spinning around them. "It's only a matter of time! If you surrender, I'll make both of your deaths quick and painless!"

Kaylessa gritted her teeth, took a tentative step backwards, and was almost ripped off her feet by the force of the wind. Regaining her ground, she looked over her shoulder and realised she only had one chance to finish this. With a prayer to the great tree, she took a deep breath and jumped backwards into the whirling wind, which pulled her away from the advancing paladin. He laughed, dropped the war hammer, took the halberd in both hands, and stood over Vel, who was trying to crawl away from him.

"A pity your friend turned out to be a coward," he roared, and raised the halberd high, intending to skewer her to the ground.

Unbeknownst to him, Kaylessa was using the momentum of the wind, and as she curled into a ball, she rode the current in a circle, the force of the gale causing her to spin rapidly with her swords outstretched. Through teary eyes, she watched as the back of the captain got closer and closer, until she was directly behind him.

Hamilton loomed over Vel. "You've caused me a lot of trouble, so forgive me if I enjoy this a little."

Vel closed her eyes, waiting for the blade to pierce her flesh, but risked opening them when the blow never came. Hamilton still stood over her, weapon raised, but a trickle of blood was spilling from his mouth, and the blades of Kaylessa's swords protruded from his chest. He fell to his knees, and Kaylessa wobbled behind him, dizzy from the rotations of the storm. She pulled the blades out of his chest with a mighty heave, and then turned to vomit. Wiping her mouth, she tottered over to Vel and helped her to her feet, supporting her on her shoulder.

"You came back for me," Vel said, her head down.

"You're important to me too," Kaylessa responded, sounding unsteady.

The building that had housed the cells collapsed, sending ash and dust up into the air. "Come on, we've got to move or we're going to burn to death in here!"

The wind abated, they hurried to the gates of the keep and out into the city, taking in the scene. Mercallia was ablaze. The houses and buildings closest to the fort had caught fire, and Valex's storm had cut a swathe through the northern part of town. Towards the water, the sails of the ships burned unattended, the smoke billowing up into the sky. Across the street from the fort, The Crimson Krill was fully engulfed, as Jim threw bucket after bucket of water onto it from a nearby well, the hungry flames turning the offering into steam. Grief written all over his face, Jim fell to his knees and looked around. His teary eyes came to rest on Kaylessa and Vel, who were standing at the gates, shocked.

"You." He spoke softly, his voice snatched away by the roar of the fire all around, but they saw his lips form the word. He began to get to his feet and walk towards them, but the silhouettes of horses came in between them, and they looked up at Valex, his face covered in soot. Khan Xarlug sat astride a donkey, looking around at the chaos with a blissful look on his frightening features, and Vel and Kaylessa's horses trailed behind, whinnying in fear.

"We have to get the fuck out of here, now!" Valex screamed, and they mounted their horses and galloped towards the road. They had just cleared the city gate when it collapsed.

They rode. They rode until their horses were ready to collapse from exhaustion, then pushed them a little further. The only one who seemed unphased by what had just happened was Khan Xarlug, who regaled them with the tales of the conquests of his tribe. By the time they saw the sign-post for Ravencroft, Vel, Valex, and Kaylessa were all completely exhausted with the man's bragging.

They rode into town as the sun set and found the square empty. The only building in town with the torches lit was The Kraken, and the sounds of merriment spilled out. They opened the door, and someone shouted, "They're here! The guests of honour!"

The bar was packed full of unfamiliar faces, who cheered and milled towards the entrance. Khan stepped forward, arms outstretched, but the crowd of people pushed past him, and began thrusting drinks and food towards the confused trio.

From the centre of the crowd, Wravien emerged and smiled warmly. "My friends! I knew you could do it!" He looked happier than they had ever seen him, but Valex leaned in close to shout into his ear.

"Wravien, who are all these people?" he asked, casting looks about the strange admirers.

"What's a town without townsfolk, Valex? I answered a request from the town of Ozark's Vale while you were away. Their castle had been occupied by an orcish war party, but I killed their chief, most of their warriors, liberated their lords, and they agreed to relocate their people here. But enough of that, tonight's celebration is for you three!"

"What exactly are we celebrating?" Vel asked, shying away from the crowd of people intent on talking to her.

"You haven't heard? Your first bounty!" He laughed, unrolled a parchment scroll from inside his cloak, and held up a hand. The crowd quieted at once.

"Wanted—Dead or Alive—Valex Shatterscale, Vel Valdove, and Kaylessa Siannodel. Charged with the murder of high-ranking Tempest Paladins, piracy, and the destruction of the town of Mercallia. Reward..." He held the moment, looking around at the countless eyes watching him, "ten thousand gold pieces."

As the crowd cheered, Valex grabbed the paper and hurried to explain. "Wravien, this isn't even true! I mean, except the murder…and the piracy… and kind of the town, but we didn't mean for this to happen!"

"Valex, Valex, do you think you are the only ones here with a price on your head? We do dirty work, and it's bound to rub people the wrong way. I, for one, consider this your initiation. You're one of us now."

The crowd cried out, "One of us!" and as he scanned their faces, he saw Nogret, Kornid, Quebys, Tim, and Fingers all raising glasses and smiling at them.

"You'll have to cool your heels for a bit, until the heat dies down, but I'll make sure you get a nice payout for this. Everyone!" Wravien raised his drink, and the entire bar did the same, "let's raise a glass to my lieutenants—the scourge of Mercallia!"

CHAPTER 11
GODFREY'S HOLLOW

Day 1095 - Somulous Experiment: I've heard a new voice. So sweet, so rich. It speaks to me as if it knows I'm listening, and it delights in the conversation. I can sense the power it has—and it seems immune to my ability to direct another's actions, which comes as a pleasant surprise. The voice tells me that I'm not fulfilling my potential—that we can do bigger, greater things and that no one can stop us. I am beginning to think that it's right. Today, I purchased an entire ship of slaves and had them delivered to my laboratory. The voice has some good ideas for them. GRIMHOWL

In the weeks that followed, Vel, Valex, and Kaylessa did as instructed and laid low. After the tumultuous series of adventures they had experienced, the laid back pace of Ravencroft proved to be both a respite and a source of irritation.

Soon after they arrived, Vel sequestered herself in her room and began sorting the treasures she had found into their various boxes. She spent so much time at Fingers' side, bartering over her trinkets, that he had begun to avoid her. "She just wants to sell!" he had cried into his cups at The Kraken to anyone who would listen. "Never buys a damn thing! She's going to clear me out!"

Kaylessa busied herself in the barracks that Nogret had built for Khan Xarlug. After receiving the gifted blades from Vel, she had beseeched the warlord to help her master them. Sceptical at first, looking at her slender frame, at Wravien's request, Khan let her attend the training sessions he offered to the villagers who had come from Ozark's Vale. But after she worked her way through anyone strong enough to physically carry a blade, Khan proudly proclaimed her to be his apprentice, and seeing her bloody and bruised became commonplace.

Valex tried to go back to drinking with Nogret at the bar, but whatever had taken hold of him on the uncharted island continued to impair his ability to taste or feel the effects of the drink. He drifted around town, never staying in one place too long, a morose expression on his face.

On one of these dalliances, he made his way to the forge where Kornid was hammering out a longsword, singing tunelessly in Dwarvish with his back to the square. Valex felt a tug in his memory, and opened his mouth before he could think: "You're going to want to quench that."

"Lad, I think I know when ta…" Kornid paused, noticing the shape of the blade. "Well, I'll be damned, you're right! I didn't know ye were a smithy, Valex."

"I'm not, not really. When I was a whelp, I had a friend who taught me the basics." Valex swallowed, surprised to find himself on the verge of tears. It had been a long time since he had thought of Garm.

Kornid inspected the dragonborn, and when he spoke his voice was quiet and smooth. "Valex lad, I danno what's changed for you, but I could use an extra set of hands at the forge. Mayhap I could teach you a thing or two?"

Something woke inside Valex, and he smiled for the first time since he had returned. "If you think I could be of any help."

The weeks had turned into months by the time Wravien finally sent for them. Three ravens soared over the town, diving down to their charges.

At the sound of the raven roosting, Valex looked up from the pike he was hammering but returned his focus at once. "Hold on, this part is crucial," he said. As the steel's warm glow began to fade, he returned the blade to the furnace, removed it, and began to hammer again. After a cursory inspection that appeared to satisfy him, he undid his apron and looked at the bird. "Well, lead the way."

Crossing the square, he heard the telltale sounds of wood striking wood from the barracks. He made his way over to the exposed fighting ring and saw a circle of men cheering as Kaylessa squared up against the green-skinned giant. Her twin practice swords looked very small compared to the absolute unit of a club Khan wielded, but she spun them in deft circles, never losing focus on her opponent's face. Suddenly feinting to the left, she threw the sword in her right hand directly into Khan's face, but he parried it with an upward strike, sending it spinning into the sky. With a practised ease, Kaylessa broke through his defences, slipping past his reach and sweeping his legs out from under him. Khan toppled to the floor with a crash, and lunged forward towards his weapon, but Kaylessa had already stepped onto the haft of the club, and was pointing her sword into his face.

"NOT A TERRIBLE BOUT," he grumbled, as Kaylessa caught the other sword in midair. "BUT YOU GOT LUCKY, DON'T LET IT GO TO YOUR HEAD."

"Khan, that wasn't luck, she had you from the first!" a bearded villager in the circle crowed. "I've never seen anything like it!"

"LET'S NOT FORGET, WE ARE 621 BOUTS TO ONE NOW," Khan grumbled, then raised his voice even louder. "DRILLS! EVERYONE TO THEIR POSITIONS! ESPECIALLY YOU!" He roared at the villager who had spoken up.

Kaylessa made her way over to her mentor and bowed low, making a show of it in front of the other men. "It was only possible due to your excellent instruction. Thank you, warchief." She raised a clenched fist to her forehead in the tribal salute Khan had shown her. Sufficiently mollified, Khan turned to face the troops, and Kaylessa's eyes settled on her old friend, watching from the half wall.

"Well done! I barely saw you move!" Valex said.

"I've been trying to do that all month; this is the first time it succeeded. But the training, hard as it is, has definitely given me a feel for the blades. What brings you around, stranger? It feels like ages since I last saw you out from behind the forge."

Valex pointed to the bird roosted above her, the twin to the one that had perched on his shoulder. "Wravien appears to have work for us. I was just heading over to The Kraken to meet with him. Have you seen Vel?"

"Oh, If I know her, she's probably playing cards. Nogret was saying something about a rematch."

Almost as if on cue, the surly dwarf burst through the double doors of the tavern, spitting and cursing. "No! Fuck you, you cheating she-devil! I don't know how ye did it, but when I figure it out, I'll be winning my money back!"

Vel's voice rang through the open doors, a note of smug satisfaction in it. "No one likes a sore loser, Nogret. If you want a rematch, you know where to find me."

Valex and Kaylessa entered the bar and saw Vel sitting at a table with Tim and Fingers, the two men wearing identical looks of anguish. Vel was sliding a sizable pile of coins into a bag, and she smiled when she saw her friends. "About time. I was getting tired of spanking these beginners day after day. Does he have something for us?"

"Apparently." Valex nodded at the long table at the back of the room, where Wravien slumped, lost in thought.

They approached, and a smile appeared on Wravien's weather-beaten features. He gestured for them to sit and tapped a marked spot on the northern part of the map, where two brass figures stood. "My friends, it has been too long. I trust you've been keeping busy?" he said.

"As busy as one can be," Vel mused, "In a sleepy place like this. I'm hoping you have something good for us, my blades are growing dull."

"Well, we can't have that, can we? Perhaps if you're worried about dull blades, you should have been to see Valex. I understand he's been working under Kornid. Or, you could have gone a few rounds with Kaylessa, who I believe, has just won her first bout with the noble Khan Xarlug."

Kaylessa shifted uncomfortably in her seat. This man's ability to know everything that happened in Ravencroft was fairly unsettling.

Wravien stood up and leaned over the table. "No matter—the time for rest is over, I do indeed have something for you. Have any of you heard of the Blacke hunters?"

"The Blackes? Are those two still active?" Vel surprised her companions by speaking out, and then she addressed them. "They are, or were, I suppose, world-renowned monster hunters. They worked for a particular sect of sellswords, called the Eternal Echoes, and were known to take every contract that had to do with disposing of anything otherworldly. But I haven't heard any news of them in well over a year."

"Yes, I forget the circles you once ran in, but you are correct Vel. What you might not know is the reason they picked that particular trade: Years ago, some manner of demon attacked their town and killed every living soul save those two...including their young child. They had been away, hunting for food, and returned to find their entire world in ruins. They swore revenge on any godless creature that crossed their paths, and they are in possession of talents we can make good use of." He paused to sip at his water. "And you're right about their absence, but I've gotten word that they finally took a contract in the hamlet of Tizen Mill." He tapped at the marked spot on the map.

"So what's the play, boss? Deliver a letter like the others?" Valex asked, the eagerness to return to the road plainly written on his face.

"Ah. Well...it's a little more complicated than that. Alison Blacke and I have...a bit of a history and so Colin isn't too keen on me. But we definitely need them for what's to come. I'd like you to present yourselves to them as mercenaries, looking for a cut of the job. They usually work alone, but this contract has caused quite a stir and I imagine they'll be willing to contract outside help."

"Complicated huh?" Valex grinned. "Sounds like there might be a story there."

Wravien's face went a rare shade of crimson, and he cleared his throat before continuing. "The details aren't important, but you'll need to move fast. Tizen Mill is a few days' ride to the north, and I've had Fingers resupply your horses. Remember, avoid mentioning me if possible, assist them in their work, and only after you've proved your mettle, give them this."

He held out a folded scrap of parchment, and Vel plucked it from his hands. "What's this, then?"

"A contract, one they won't be able to refuse, issued by the unnamed mayor of Ravencroft," said Wravien.

"The mayor? Who is the..." Understanding dawned on Kaylessa, and she burst out into a fit of giggles, "Oh gods...I'm...I'm sorry, but when I picture 'The Mayor' I can't help but see a portly, balding paper pusher. You don't really fit the bill, sir."

"Be that as it may," Wravien looked annoyed at the outburst, "my official standing will be useful here. Be wary, though, the majority of the threats you've encountered have been flesh and blood, but with the Blackes you always get more than you bargained for. Now, if you need anything else, Fingers can provide it. When you've made contact with them, blow this whistle, " he produced a small, bone flute from an inside pocket, and gave it to Kaylessa, "and one of my birds will make contact, so we can begin our planning."

Their business concluded, the trio left the tavern and headed towards their horses. Fingers had loaded their horses up with rations, replaced the bedrolls, and was currently brushing out Vel's horse's mane with a coarse brush. Kaylessa walked up and asked if he could do the same for hers, but Valex was chuckling, and Vel asked what he thought was so funny. "I don't know about you two, but I can't *wait* to see the woman who can do that to Wravien. He was practically shaking!"

They rode north, the lush plains around their home fading into the marshy swamps of northern Illium. The land began to take on a sickly, barren vibe, and the very nature itself appeared to twist and contort as they proceeded through the fetid pools and forests. On the third day, they made camp in a grove of spindly trees off the side of the road. Strange chittering sounds and animal calls could be heard in all directions.

Valex opted to turn in early, but Vel and Kaylessa stayed up late until the fire had almost burned away. Kaylessa was loath to admit it, but the alien nature of the landscape frightened her. She chanced a look around into the line of trees and gasped when she locked gazes with a pair of emerald-green eyes, blazing in the dark.

Vel snapped to her feet, weapons drawn at the noise Kaylessa made. "What is it?"

Kaylessa shook her head and rubbed her eyes before returning them to the spot she had seen the eyes. Now she saw only the skeletal outline of the trees and the muted dark. "It's nothing, my eyes must be playing tricks on me. I thought I saw...something."

Vel rested a hand on her shoulder. "It's easy to get spooked out here, but don't worry, I'll hear anything that approaches before it can do us any harm. You should sleep. I'll take the first watch."

"Yeah, I'll do that." Kaylessa roused herself and undid her bedroll. "Thank you, Vel."

Vel nodded her assent, and Kaylessa settled down to sleep, but every time she closed her eyes, the fiery green orbs haunted her. She hadn't sensed malice, in fact, it was quite the opposite— the eyes seemed to be admiring her. Before she could figure it out, she drifted into an uneasy sleep.

The next day, they arrived at Tizen Mill. As they made their way through the main streets, Kaylessa noticed eyes watching them from shuttered windows, and she repressed a shudder as she thought of the previous night once again. Except these eyes belonged to frightened townsfolk who were watching them intently as they rode past.

"Just what is it that happened here?" she wondered aloud, glancing down an abandoned alley in time to see a man thrust himself through a door and click the lock in place. "Whatever it is, it can't be good."

Valex spurred his Clydesdale forward. "Come on, even in a ghost town like this, the best place to seek information will be the inn."

The air of disquiet followed them through town like a shade, but they found the inn tucked away in the southern part of town. Many of the homes and businesses were boarded up and looked completely abandoned, and the inn fared only slightly better. A sign dangled by a single chain (The Cock and Stallion), and Valex had to duck to keep his horns from hitting it as they entered.

"Oh! Customers!" The innkeeper was a harried-looking human with a shock of red hair, and he scurried across the empty dining room towards them, bowing low. "Welcome to The Cock and Stallion. What can I get for you? Some ales, perhaps a few plates of dinner? The mutton is especially nice!"

His desperation was clear, but Valex brushed it aside and got to business. "For now, we just need information. What in the gods' name happened to this town, man?"

The innkeeper deflated, and leaned against a table. "Oh, you're not staying. I should have known; this place ran out of luck a long time ago. People have been going missing, is what's happened. First the Smiths, then the Millers, then a whole bunch of other families. Last month, it was Gerard James' kid." He gave his head a brisk shake. "That one was a real tragedy. Gerard had left to go hunting in the morning and came back to find his house full of blood and both his children vanished. After his wife died, he lived for those kiddos and it broke the man. You'll see him wandering around at all hours, eyes wide but empty. The man is haunted."

"Anything strange about it, aside from the blood?" Vel asked, and the man looked at her surprised.

"Oy, are you with the other woman? You two are sure dressed the same. Well, I'll tell you exactly what I told her." He held up a hand with two fingers outstretched. "First: There have been sightings all around town of a monstrous wolf. Now, I ain't seen it myself, per se, but I've seen the tracks! Big as a dinner plate, they were!" He raised a second finger. "Second, and this is the real strange part, none of the houses that people went missing from showed any sign of break-in! Doors were unlocked, windows whole, just a whole lot of blood, and never any bodies."

"Hm. That is strange. Do you know where we can find this woman? Was she travelling with a man, her husband perhaps?" Vel said.

"I should say so! She's staying upstairs! But a husband you say? Nope, just her at first, then she came back with a really strange crew of folks, mercenaries I suppose, and then they left again. You could wait for her in her room." He stopped, inspiration flashing across his face. "Or maybe you will need rooms as well?"

They made their excuses and walked upstairs towards the only room with a closed door. Kaylessa approached, knocked curtly, three times, and said, "Hello? Colin? Alison? We heard you were looking to tackle the contract here, and we want to help." She tried to bring her voice down an octave once she noticed Vel laughing at her prim and proper speech. There was no answer, and she tried the handle to no avail. "Locked."

"Not for long." Vel removed her tools and went to work on the lock, which popped open with ease. She turned the handle and began to press into the door but heard a click. There was barely time for her to recoil her head before a crossbow bolt burst through the door, passing by her head and embedding itself into the door across the hall.

"Whoa! That was lucky!" Valex pulled the bolt from the door with great effort, touched the tip and winced as blood bubbled up from his finger.

"Not luck, skill," Vel said, tentatively pushing the door open again. Once she realised there were no more traps, she allowed it to swing open. "We'll need to be on our guard with these two."

They filed into the room, which looked more like a king's war room more than an inn. Opposite the door, a crossbow had been rigged up with a complicated looking pulley system that connected to the door. A hand-drawn map of what appeared to be the town dominated the back wall, large red X's struck through the majority of the buildings, save for one property at the outskirts. A list of names had been tacked up beside it with a similar number of strikes applied.

"Godfrey's Hollow," Vel murmured, running her fingers across the stretched parchment, "and an Alistair Godfrey."

"Vel, look at this," Kaylessa called her over to a large stack of books. "*Cycles of the Moon, Lycanthropy: A Study, Creatures of the Night, Knock Knock: A Guide to Refusing Spirits.* These are all very impressive tomes."

"Uh...friends?" They heard the panic in Valex's voice and turned to look. "I believe we've got company."

Holding a long, shining dagger that was dripping a horrid blue liquid to Valex's throat, stood a woman in her late twenties. Chestnut hair framed a sharp, intelligent face, and her clothing was almost identical to Vel's tactical leathers, save for a deep crimson cloak. "No one breathes or the lizard gets to find out how slowly basilisk venom kills. Who sent you?" said the stranger.

"Calm down, we're looking for Colin Blacke and..." Vel's voice was level, but as she inched forward, she saw the edge of the blade press into the soft flesh of Valex's neck, and she stopped her approach.

"I said don't move. What could you want with my dead husband? Is it Balthazar? Did he send you?"

Vel's eyes widened at the mention of the crime lord, but she kept her tone calm and said, "No, we're just mercenaries, looking for work. We heard you might have a job."

Kaylessa watched the heated exchange and between the nervous glancing from the strange woman and the way Vel was resting her hand on her rapier, she decided to throw caution to the wind and blurted out, "Wravien sent us! Wravien Leonhart!"

There was a moment of stunned silence, but the woman dropped the blade to her side and began to laugh. The sound was far from cheerful, however, and it made Kaylessa's stomach turn to ice. "Oh really? *Really?!* He runs off, tail between his legs, and has the audacity to come crawling back, less than a year after I bury my Colin. To make matters worse, he won't even face me himself—he sends you lot. Unbelievable, truly. Anyway, no thank you, get the hell out of my room." She stepped to the side of the door and gestured toward the door expectantly.

Kaylessa tried to explain. "No, you don't understand, he sent us to help..."

The woman cut her off curtly. "It's too late for that. Any help that man could have offered me, I needed five years ago. Tell our Mr. Leonhart that I've already hired my own protection. I don't need his worry or his concern, and if I ever see him again I'll kill him myself. Out. Now."

The finality of her tone followed them from the room, and down the stairs.

Seated around a table in the dining room were three very strange people. They looked at the stairs, clearly expecting the trio's arrival, but their conversation continued to flow between them as they watched. The first was a young, blonde girl, barely of age, wearing the tell-tale armour of the Exorcists of Alexander, a religious sect based in Grand Covus. Across from her was an elf, dressed head to toe in animal furs, with a longbow and a shortbow slung across the back of her chair. Finally, seated in the middle, with his back to them, was a tiefling, whose skin was green instead of the usual red of the half demons. He had the telltale horns and forked tail, but the horns were wrapped in thorny vines, and his clothes appeared to be entirely composed of large palm leaves and bark, making it hard to tell where his clothing stopped and his dark green skin began.

Vel marked the three, and when they continued to stare, she threw her head back in exasperation and turned to her companions. "Alright, we should go. Let's signal Wravien and figure out where to go from here." They made their way towards the entrance, but Kaylessa chanced a look back before they crossed the threshold, and what she saw made her heart skip. The tiefling had turned to watch their departure, his blazing emerald eyes never breaking contact with hers. The very same eyes she had seen in the forest the previous night.

"Listen, if these townspeople see us talking with birds, after whatever they've been through, they're liable to burn us at the stake," Valex suggested, so the three friends travelled to the outskirts of town to blow the strange whistle Wravien had given them. No sound escaped the small, wooden carving, and Vel was about ready to try it again, when with a flurry of wings, a raven perched on Kaylessa's shoulder.

"Report." The gravelly voice of their benefactor spilled from the beak. "What news of Colin and Alison?"

"Just Alison, actually. She told us Colin died last year. Oh, and she said that she hates your guts, doesn't need or want your help, and if she ever sees you again, she'll kill you herself," Valex retorted sarcastically.

"What?!" They could almost see Wravien standing up in surprise. "What do you mean, Colin's dead? That never happened last…" The bird trailed off into silence, its beady eyes betraying none of the rest of the sentiment.

"Erm, did you miss the part where I said she hates you and wants you dead?" Valex asked incredulously. "Honestly, why do I even talk sometimes?"

The silence stretched a bit before the bird made a very human sigh, and said, "She has every reason to, but that doesn't change what I need you to do. Were you able to get hired on?"

"No, she already had a crew with her: a very woodsy-looking tiefling, an elf in furs, and a human woman barely old enough to have an ale, sporting exorcist armour. An apprentice maybe?" Recounting the three mercenaries, Kaylessa repressed a shiver at the thought of those eyes.

The bird cocked its head in a very human look of surprise. "Wait…you said a tiefling, a ranger, and an exorcist? There's no way…Unless… Perhaps the gods work in mysterious ways. Alright, this changes things, You need to make sure these people see your value, all of them. Setting aside Colin, Alison's importance remains paramount, but the rest of these travellers are of equal import, so ensure they come to Ravencroft as soon as possible. This may be the most important task I've given you, but I'm confident you'll be able to manage it. Make haste."

"Wravien…what were you going to say, this didn't happen last..? Last what? Last time?" Vel studied the bird very closely, but its avian features betrayed nothing.

"You know the rules, Vel; no questions until the time is right. Good luck." And with that, the bird's eyes dimmed, and it took off with a startled caw. They stood around, contemplating what they'd just heard and Valex pondered aloud, "Bit of a cradle robber, isn't he?"

"What are you talking about, Valex?" Vel asked.

Valex was thinking hard, a talon rested on his bony chin. "It's obvious there were some strong…feelings, between our boss and Ms. Blacke, but he has to be at least twice her age, if not older."

"Never mind that, Wravien's love life is the least of our worries. What do we do now? Alison was very clear about not wanting our help," Kaylessa said.

"I was able to get a fairly good look at her research, and it looks like she's exhausted every possible option of her search, save one: Let's wait for her at Godfrey's Hollow." Vel said, sweeping from the room.

A full moon hung above them in the sky, illuminating the dark as they made their way down the winding road out of town towards the property. They came to a sturdy, high gate, flanked by thick stone walls that were covered in a spidery ivy. The gate itself was made of thick iron bars, set tightly enough to deter any would be intruders, and it had an ornate G worked into the centre of the two doors. Winding around the letter was an impressively intricate lock.

"Can you crack it?" Valex inquired, but Vel was already shaking her head.

"If I had all night, maybe, but this is an impressive specimen."

"What do we do now, then?" Kaylessa asked. "I don't exactly see a bell."

A voice rang out from the woods beside the road. "Obviously, if it was easy we would have gotten in much earlier." Alison emerged, flanked by her mercenary entourage. "And I thought I told you to get lost. I don't need his help."

Vel matched her cool gaze with an equally icy look of her own. "What if the creature you're hunting isn't what you think, or it has spawned? I saw your notes, and even if it is a werewolves, you'll be hard pressed to deal with an entire pack with just four fighters."

"Besides," Kaylessa added, "We are just worried about the town. We aren't interested in the reward—we just want to protect people."

Alison scrutinised them, clearly noting how Vel's teeth ground at the casual mention of a reward declined. Then she surprised them by laughing. "Are you sure we're thinking of the same man? The Wravien I knew would never lift a finger if there wasn't a bag of silver in it for himself.

Alright…We can work together, but I'm running point. If I say fight, we fight, and if I say run, we run. Any objections?"

Valex reached out and gave the gate a brisk shake with his talon. "None, but we still need to solve the problem of how we're going to get inside."

"We'll have to go over." Vel and Alison spoke in unison, and then shared a look of amusement. They both produced spools of hempen rope, and after tying them into slip knots, tossed them up and onto the ornate spikes that ran the length of the wall. The seven adventurers made it over the wall (Valex with some difficulty) and found themselves in a well-manicured courtyard. A path wound through several gardening plots, devoid of life, and ended at a large, gothic, three-story home. The building was like a beacon in the night with torchlight glaring from every window, but something about the home felt off. It should have looked inviting, but from the sharp angles and the wickedly sharp spikes that lined the parapet, even the architecture felt malicious. Vel and Alison both began to stride down the path, leaving the rest of them to follow.

Kaylessa found herself walking beside the tiefling, whose eyes continued to glow as brightly as the torches in the house, and she found herself unsure of how to bring up their first encounter. She mustered up her courage and in a small voice said, "…Did I see you last night? In the grove south of town?"

"You have sharp eyes, great sage." The tiefling's voice was low and held a thrum of otherworldly power. "Not many can spot a panther in the dark."

"I'm sorry, a panther? I'm pretty sure you aren't an animal, based on what I can see."

He flashed her a smile full of pointed teeth, and his skin rippled as he fell to all fours, and transformed into an enormous jungle cat, the fur the same dark green as his skin and the tail wound with the thorny vines that encapsulated his horns. Several steps later, he regained his previous form, saying, "I am many things, under the blessing of Eden, as are you."

He chuckled at her shocked expression, and she struggled to regain her composure. "You are a druid, then?" she finally said, surprised. In Thras'lunia, few of the forest folk remained, having been driven into the deeper parts of the enchanted wood by the expansions of the elves.

Kaylessa's shock began to wear off, and she realised how he had addressed her, "Wait, how did you know I was training to be a sage?"

"The Earth Mother and I have spoken often of you in the recent past. She has said regardless of your actions, you are not forgotten to her and her power continues to flow. I was told that I may have the honour of meeting you. My name is Barakas Vinetree, and I am a child of Eden, the great God of nature." He gestured to the stern-looking elf who was walking a few paces ahead of him, "And this is my partner, Shenarah Jonan. Together, we protect the bounty that Eden has given us. If I speak for the trees, she speaks for the beasts."

With barely a grunt of recognition, Shenarah held her head high and quickened her pace.

The young woman in the exorcist armour laughed, a high, pure sound that pierced the quiet of the night, and she clapped Kaylessa on the shoulder. "Don't let her get to you. She just prefers animals to people; it's been this way with anyone we've met on the road. Shenarah is standoffish, but if we find ourselves in a skirmish, you'll be glad she's on our side. I'm Johanne the Holy."

Kaylessa had read that when exorcists took on their mantle, they cast off their familial names for a title, but it was her first time being introduced to someone this way.

Valex walked closer and asked, "Are you really an exorcist? You're quite young, you know."

"Exorcist's apprentice," she corrected quickly, a blush rising in her face. "My master, Bernard the Righteous, is…indisposed, so I've come in his place."

Valex was about to ask more questions when a sudden rumble of thunder sounded overhead and the sky suddenly opened, soaking them instantly. They sprinted the rest of the way to the front double doors, each large enough for someone taller than Valex to cross through comfortably. There was a single silver knocker, fashioned into the shape of a wolf with a ring in its mouth. This caused Alison and Shenarah to share an interested glance.

Alison turned to face the pitiful-looking group as they huddled together under the eaves. "Here's what we have figured out so far. A large wolf has been seen around the outskirts of town and even in town where the abductions took place in several cases. Godfrey apparently has an impressive specimen of a hunting dog, and this is the final place I need to check for any sign of monstrous activity. We need to be ready for anything—follow my lead." She turned without waiting for any comments and rapped the silver knocker three times, taking a step back and waiting with her hands clasped behind her back. The sound of movement inside the house made them all nervous, but they heard a small, shaky voice call out over the rain. "Oh, who could that be at this hour? I'm coming, just a moment!"

The door opened slowly, as if with great effort, and a wizened old man appeared in view. He was sweating laboriously from the exertion of opening the enormous door, and the wispy hair on his head was standing up at odd angles. Dressed in the traditional black and white of a servant, he turned to address them, his eyes comically magnified by the large, round glasses he wore.

"Oh my goodness, it's pouring! Please, come inside where it's warm!" He ushered them in, and they stood in the entryway of the lavish mansion, dripping onto a red carpet. The entry hall was a spectacular affair, made entirely of a rich, dark-colored wood. There was a roaring fireplace on the rear wall, and a masterfully made portrait of a young woman hung over it, her eyes gazing down at them. A spiral staircase flanked the portrait on the right, leading to a second floor.

"My name is Barnelby." The little man made a low bow. "I am the caretaker for Lord Godfrey. What brings you to our residence so late?"

"Barnelby, my name is Alison Blacke. The mayor has asked me to look into the disappearances around town, and as a formality, I have to inspect the dwellings on the outskirts of town. May I speak with Lord Godfrey?" Alison said.

"Disappearances? Heavens me, that sounds dreadful! I'm afraid Lord Godfrey is away on business at the moment, but I know he cares for the town greatly, and would be happy if he could help." Barnelby said, wringing his gloved hands.

Valex pointed past the man's shoulder to the portrait. "Is that his wife?"

Barnelby awarded him a look of melancholy. "Ah, yes sir, the Lady Godfrey. She is a true beauty, but I'm afraid she is very ill and spends most of her time in bed."

"I know this may seem strange," Alison continued as if Valex hadn't spoken, "but does your master own any hunting dogs? Several of the reports from town indicated seeing a large animal around the site of the crimes."

"Oh, he does indeed, but just the one! His name is Brutus, and the master has owned him for many, many years, but I assure you, he never leaves the grounds without Lord Godfrey. We keep him penned up out back and occasionally take him around the grounds, supervised of course. Now, I believe you've been made uncomfortable long enough, may I take your cloaks to warm by the fire?" He held out a hand expectantly, and they all gladly handed over their sodden garments.

Barnelby crossed the foyer to a small door on the right, and Alison turned to Johanne as soon as the door had swung shut. "Anything?"

Johanne took an ornate knuckle duster from her belt and slid it onto her hand. A thin golden aura spun around her, and her lips moved in a silent incantation. She opened her eyes, and the aura vanished. "There's something in the basement," she said, looking towards the room where Barnelby had just headed. "I can't sense what it is exactly, only that it's radiating great evil."

"That checks, something about this place feels…off." Shenarah made her way towards the fire, and looked up at the large face painted there. "But there don't seem to be any immediate threats."

Barnelby returned and bowed low. "I've hung your cloaks over the fire, and they should dry out posthaste, but I'm afraid there is a pressing matter I must attend to. If you're keen to see Brutus, head towards the dog run." He pointed towards a door to the right of the fireplace. "And you may explore anywhere else on the first floor you see fit. I do ask that you refrain from ascending the stairs, as the master's private quarters are up there." He made another low bow and began to climb the steep stairs with some difficulty.

Alison looked their little party over, her eyes darting between them, before addressing Johanne. "I think we should split up to cover more ground. The supposed 'dog' is out back, but we should investigate whatever is setting off your sense in the basement. Take these three with you." She pointed to Vel, Valex, and Kaylessa.

Barakas stepped forward and said, "I believe the elf should come with us. Her affinity to the great tree may help us soothe the beast, if need be."

Alison looked at Kaylessa, who faltered slightly, but the tiefling's stare held her. This might be an opportunity to understand what he knew better. "Alright, I'll go with you." Kaylessa nodded at Valex and Vel and followed Alison towards the door at the rear of the room.

"Well, that leaves you lot with me! Don't worry, I'm sure we won't have any trouble. Usually these senses of mine are only picking up a skeleton or two in the closet, and these rich types seem to have lots of them." Johanne giggled, but her words carried an ominous ring.

Alison led Barakas, Shenarah, and Kaylessa down a hallway that opened into a laundry room dimly lit by the light of the pregnant moon hanging in the sky. The smell of soap was overpowering, but Kaylessa swore she could smell something underneath it, something coppery. The large shadowy shapes of washing basins and baskets of clothing were outlined by the moonlight, and they skirted them as they headed towards an iron door that led out back. As she crossed the centre of the room, Kaylessa felt several drops of water splash the back of her neck, and she rubbed them away absentmindedly.

Alison took a position by the door and whistled, and her companions joined her. "Anyway, we don't know what we'll find out there. Kaylessa, was it? I doubt you've silvered your swords, so take this." She held out a sheathed dagger, which Kaylessa took and pulled to reveal the blade. The edge shimmered slightly in the moonlight.

"Silver? Isn't this too soft to cap a blade?"

"Aye, I go through them like mad, but it's the only way to deal lasting damage to abominations like what I expect we'll find. Conventional steel will score, but the wound will close before you're drawing back to strike again." Alison waited for Kaylessa to loop the dagger onto her belt, then pushed the door open and stepped into the night.

The area behind the manor was a long rectangle, fenced in by hedges. At the far end of the run was a miniature of the house they had just stepped out of, save for the gargantuan hole cut into the face for whatever creature resided there. Kaylessa looked into the opening and saw a pair of feral eyes glinting in the moonlight, watching their progress. Barakas unshouldered a large wooden club he wore on his back, and Shenarah nocked an arrow, but a voice inside of Kaylessa told her this was wrong. She raised a cautionary hand, walked a few paces forward, and called out, "Brutus! Here boy!"

The eyes in the dark rose up, stopping almost at her eye level, and a dire wolf stepped from the shadows. Its silver fur shone in the moonlight and its muscular form dominated the entryway, its fur scraping at the edges, but its tail was wagging and it had a ball in its mouth. It burst into a sprint across the yard towards Kaylessa and Shenarah almost let an arrow fly, but Barakas held her arm back. The beast skidded to a halt at Kaylessa's feet, panting through the toy, tail continuing to wag.

"Oh, you aren't a big scary wolf at all!" Kaylessa scratched Brutus between his ears, and his hind leg began to thump against the ground. "You're just a big puppy! What have you got there, boy?" She reached for the ball in the beast's mouth, which it released, and then it looked at her expectantly.

Alison stared at the dog, thunderstruck. "I don't understand...I was sure it was a werewolf, unless..."

"Alison?" Kaylessa's voice was small, and she turned to show the ball to her. She had rotated it in her hand, and it was clearly made of bone. There were two large holes, with a smaller one set in between. A human skull, and likely a child's, judging by the size.

Alison looked down at it, then at the grinning dog, and said, "We need to go back. Your friends are in danger."

Johanne led the way through the doorway into a large stone kitchen. The pomp and affluence didn't extend into this wing, and the plain stone walls and hearth made Vel and Valex feel at home. A solitary woman in a maid's uniform stood by one of the roaring fires, slowly working a wooden utensil through a large bubbling pot.

"Excuse me, miss," Johanne called across the room. "Barnelby said we were allowed to take a look through here, just so you know." If the woman heard her, she gave no sign, and with a derisive snort, Johanne walked towards the rear of the room, the knuckleduster once again slipped over her fist.

"Bit odd, isn't it?" Valex mused, looking over his shoulder at the woman. "You'd think the hired help would be more like, 'Yes sir,' and 'Right away, sir.'"

"I've seen a bit of this in Grand Covus." Vel's voice was bitter. "Some of the elite would break their servants in so they would never talk again, sometimes going so far as to remove their tongues. A quiet slave can't complain, of course. It's barbaric, but with what we know of this Godfrey so far, I'm hardly surprised."

Johanne stopped suddenly and pressed her free hand to an exposed stretch of bare wall. "Here. Whatever I've sensed is behind this wall and down below."

"I don't know how quiet the help will be if we start doing demolition." Valex unshouldered his quarterstaff and gave the wall a hard rap, then quickly peeked over his shoulder at the maid, who continued to stir her pot. "...Or not, I suppose." He raised the staff over his head, but Vel moved smoothly in front of him, shooting him a look of disdain.

"Valex, it's a rich guy's creepy old house. It's obviously a secret door." She began to press each brick, one after another, until one slid into the wall, and the stones parted with a clicking noise, revealing a narrow wooden staircase. "See? Brute force isn't always the answer. After you."

Valex looked down the stairs into the murky blackness. "Me? What the hells, no way! That looks terrifying!"

Vel cocked an eyebrow at her friend. "What are you talking about, you big scaredy lizard? You've never had any trouble plunging headfirst into danger before."

Looking chagrined, Valex muttered, "Well…one: I'd always had a drink or two before, so of course I wasn't worried, and two: Something about this place freaks me out. Giant lady painting, fancy furniture, weird maids. I don't like it."

"It's alright to be frightened, my new friend." Johanne's voice was warm, but she spoke up from right behind him and he jumped anyway. "But trust in the Lord of Lights, and you too can be saved." She clutched her weapon, said a prayer, and a ball of light floated into view over their heads.

"Shall we?" she said and descended the stairs.

Valex tried to follow, but Vel attempted to slip in front of him to secure the safe, middle position. Their shoulders caught in the frame, and after a brief struggle Vel elbowed Valex in the stomach lightly and slipped after the exorcist. Valex gulped, and began to follow, looking over his shoulder every few steps.

They reached the bottom of the stairs and stepped onto a dirt floor. The small ball of light cast shadows around the room, which was encircled by a double row of wine casks, each with a small plaque and a shiny spigot to pour from. The centre of the room was dominated by some kind of oblong crate, which was a polished black and nearly seven feet long.

"Oh gods. Is that a coffin?!" Valex's voice cracked with shrillness.

Vel laughed, moved to the wall, and began to inspect the casks. "Fallow's Reed—four years aged. Next one is…. Grand Covus, ten years. There's one here that says Tizen Mill…but there's no date…" She trailed off, confused. These were clearly wine barrels, but none of these cities were particularly known for their vintages, and the years didn't make sense. A socialite like Godfrey should have been holding onto wine aged twice or three times as long. She turned the tap on the keg marked Grand Covus slightly, catching the flowing red on her hand. Then she touched her tongue to it, but she spat it out almost immediately. "This isn't wine. It's blood." She looked from the kegs to the coffin in the centre of the room.

"Yes, it does appear that Alison was wrong." Johanne opened the casket, found it empty, and poured a flask of clear liquid onto the crimson silk within, "But hopefully the creature is not very old, judging by the reserves. Vampires live a long time, and get exponentially more powerful with age. Come, I'll purify this space, and we'll rejoin the others to share what we've seen."

Johanne raised the hand clutching the knuckleduster over the coffin and began to chant rapidly. The aura of golden light returned to swathe her, and the cellar heated up. After a few verses, she lowered her hand into a loose boxer's stance, and drew her right hand back. The aura coalesced into the hand, creating the illusion of a massive, golden gauntlet, and she snapped a punch forward into the side of the casket.

Two things happened at once. The first was that the light that Johanne had cast was unceremoniously extinguished, and they all felt a terrible squeezing sensation in their guts as a feeling of perverse coldness flooded them. The second was that every barrel in the room exploded, showering them in cold, sticky blood. The coffin erupted into golden flames and was reduced to cinders in moments. They stood in the dark for a moment, the only sound the blood dripping from them, and then they heard a creak from the top of the stairs and a ghastly green light flooded the stairwell.

"The master...would like...a word." Silhouetted by the strange light from the kitchen, the maid stood at the top of the stairs, her bones popping and creaking unnaturally, a look of frenzy splashed across her distorted features.

As soon as Kaylessa and her allies crossed back into the laundry room, they knew something was wrong. Torches now flared with an unnatural green light, casting wild shadows all across the space, and as soon as Barakas stepped over the threshold, the door slammed shut with a noisy clang. He whirled to tug it open, but the door wouldn't move an inch. Brutus was whining from the other side, but Barakas turned to the group and shook his head grimly.

"Then we need to press on," said Alison. "First order of business is to find Johanne and the others—see if we can deal with the corruption." She went to move through the room, but Shenarah held an arm out to stop her and pointed upwards. The ceiling of the room was sagging down several feet, and in the ghastly light they could see a dark stain had spread from the source of the sag, spilling out across the room. Kaylessa touched the wet spot on her neck and looked at the pool of blood that coated the floor, accumulated from the dripping from above. She moved to wipe her hands off on a nearby garment and shuddered when she realised it was a child's dress, long scores torn through it.

"Come on." Alison's face was a mask of grim determination. "We're wasting time." She led them back into the main entry hall, which had undergone a similar transformation. The torches and fireplace here had altered to the strange, heatless green, and dissonant music spilled down the staircase from a clearly out-of-tune instrument.

Kaylessa looked at the portrait of the lady of the house and stopped in her tracks. The beautiful features had become a ruined wasteland. The cheekbones, once sharp and defined, were rotted away, showing flashes of bone, and her luscious dark hair had become wispy and grey. Worst of all were the eyes; the once demure blue had become completely black and they bulged from their sockets. As if in a trance, Kaylessa approached the painting with a hand outstretched. It seemed the eyes were keeping pace with her, coaxing her forward, and she had almost touched the canvas when a spectral blue arm reached out from the frame, clutching her wrist.

Barakas noticed first and with a shout, he snapped a branch from the enormous club on his back and threw it to the ground near Kaylessa's feet. There was a rumble and the rich wooden floors split open as roots shot out of the ground below, encircling the elf's feet. The arm from the painting gave a tug and Kaylessa cried out as the two forces pulled at her. The pull caused whatever was attached to the arm to stretch out from the painting, mouth unnaturally wide, seeking her own.

Alison's blade whistled through the air, but the spirit made no move to dodge it until it made contact with its forearm, the silvered edge shearing through the arm like butter. A cloud of noxious green smoke poured out, and a shriek reverberated through their heads like a war horn. "Shenarah, the painting!" The monster hunter called out, as the rest of the spectre freed itself from the painting and sailed towards her.

"Right!" Shenarah had already looped fabric around the end of one of her silver arrows and was pouring a thick syrup onto it. With a strike of a tinder, the end of the arrow erupted into blue flames, and she fired at the painting's centre. Both it, and the visage of the woman burst into similar blue flame. It burned for only a moment, and was gone just as suddenly, but the portrait reverted to its original form, and the ghost was nowhere to be seen.

"I…what was all that?!" Kaylessa shook her head, trying to clear the fog from her mind.

Alison sheathed her blades. "A curse. Something tells me that our host isn't very receptive to inquisitive guests, but an arrow soaked in sap from the great tree does the job. Now, where is Johanne?"

The wall to their right burst with a crash, and a form flew through the air towards the staircase, where it crashed to the floor. Johanne stepped through the hole in the wall, arms and shoulders enshrouded in golden light, her fists raised in a defensive stance. Valex and Vel followed closely behind. She knelt beside the body of the grotesque housekeeper, whose neck was tilted at an insane angle, but whose jaws were still snapping, and she said a quick prayer before hammering her palm into its forehead. The monster screamed, burst into a flash of light, and was gone by the time their vision had returned.

"These abominations are an affront to the creator, and must be dealt with as such." Johanne wiped the blood from her knuckles, and slipped the knuckleduster off her hand. "We burned a coffin in the basement and the house changed—shall we head upstairs?"

"I always thought the church was full of pacifists, touting the virtues of peace and love," Valex whispered to Vel. "But that was an ass-whooping of celestial proportions."

"Some churches, I suppose. Alexander's devout are typically zealous and judgemental, and they are able to call on their god's armaments. If they ever found their way into Hawkers Alley, where I'm from, the place would clear out in an instant. Come, they're headed upstairs."

The party climbed the stairs and reached a long hallway, which had a railing to overlook the entry hall and a door to their left and right. The horrid music was playing from the room on their left, but Kaylessa pointed to the other door. "That is the room that's right above the laundry room, we should be able to figure out—Oh gods! The stench!"

She recoiled as she opened the door, but Vel covered her face with a cloth and slipped past. The small room was fairly nondescript with a large writing desk to the right side and a bookcase on the left, but no sign of what was causing the smell. Vel looked at the bookcase and saw grooves scratched in a semicircle on the floor, as well as a singular book that carried none of the dust of the others. She rolled her eyes, *rich men and their secret rooms*, before pulling the book and gagging; the smell was much worse. Forcing the door open, she looked in and felt her stomach drop. The small room was packed, wall to wall, with bits and pieces of human remains. "I think we've found our missing villagers."

Alison cursed and ducked back into the hallway, but Johanne sighed, sliding the knuckleduster on and approached the pile, chanting. Vel retreated as well and approached Alison, who was leaning against the wall with a hand over her eyes. "You alright?" she queried.

"Yes. No. It's just… I still held out hope that we could save some of them. This is so much like what happened with Colin that I…I will see Godfrey's head adorn the spikes of his own mansion before dawn. I swear it."

"And we'll be right beside you when you do," Vel said, and Alison looked at her, astonished. "Our stakes may not be personal, but it's clear there is an evil at work here, and it needs to be dealt with. Now, I don't know about you, but I'm about ready to smash whatever's making that god-awful racket." She cocked a thumb at the other door, where the music continued to swell.

With a grateful smile, Alison wiped her eyes and approached the door, her allies in tow. She threw the door open, eyes darting around for threats, and finding none, allowed them access. The room appeared to be a library, with walls covered in dusty tomes, tables in the centre covered in official-looking papers, and what appeared to be an ancient harpsichord in the corner, which was, unsurprisingly, playing by itself.

Vel tapped Barakas on the shoulder, and gestured to his club. "May I borrow this?" He handed it over, and she clutched it two-handed, raised it over her head, and began to rain blows down on the instrument, which groaned musically as it was reduced to firewood.

Valex snickered, but his attention was caught by a stack of documents on the table, and he began to read. "These are transfer requests, of goods and properties, but…The first one is Alistair Godfrey, whose wealth was transferred to him by Albert Gotten…who received his wealth from Alphonse Grosmeman…My god, the handwriting is all the same. It's the same man, he's been moving things for centuries. It just keeps going back."

"And I'm willing to bet if we followed the trail we'd find a calamity like the one that befell Tizen Mill at the site of each transfer. Disgusting. Come on, let's end this." Alison gestured towards a staircase at the back of the room, next to a door with a small plaque that read "Barnelby's Room."

Valex, eager to prove his worth amongst such powerful allies, rushed to the door and opened it cautiously. The tiny man was seated at a desk with his back to him, silhouetted by a large picture window. *I'm not going to give him a chance to attack,* Valex thought smugly, and conjured a fireball in his hand. He threw it into the man's back, where it erupted, knocking Barnelby forward and through the picture window. He screamed briefly before falling to the ground below.

Valex frowned. From what he had seen, the creatures here should have been a sight more resilient than that…He walked to the shattered opening and looked down at the twitching remains of the man, but a letter on the desk caught his eye, and he began to read:

Dearest Tabitha,

I hope you and my new grandson are well. Things have been very hectic around the house, the Lord has been coming and going at all hours, but I know how busy he gets. Lady Godfrey is still bedridden, I'm afraid, but Bathilda, our maid, says her strength grows every day, and she'll be back on her feet in no time.

How is little Michael? Hard to believe he is already two years old. I can't wait to meet him, I've enclosed a little more money than I usually send so you can buy him a little some-thing extra, from his grandfather.

I love you, daughter

Barnelby

Valex's stomach plunged and with a grimace he understood that Barnelby was just a man, maybe under the creature's thrall. He hastily stowed the letter and the small pile of coins in a leather pouch on his belt, pasted a smile on his face, and turned to his allies. "Another abomination slain! Shall we continue upstairs?" His voice was a bit squeaky, and he hastily made his way to the stairs.

Barakas looked into the room with awe. "I'm impressed, son of dragon. To dispatch a ghoul with a single spell is no mean feat. You are much more powerful than I gave you credit for."

"Uh…Yep, that's right, surprisingly powerful." The guilt eating away at him, Valex scampered up the stairs before anyone else could speak and found himself in a master bedroom. This part of the house clearly had seen a woman's touch—artful furniture surrounded a large, four-poster bed in the centre. The bed's sheer curtains were drawn, and a figure was draped underneath the sheets. Alison stepped forward, tore the curtain down unceremoniously, and threw back the cover on the form resting beneath. Lying on the red-stained bedclothes was the subject of the painting downstairs, the details strikingly similar, save for the ruined chasm that was her throat.

Alison groaned and removed two silver coins from her pocket, placing one on each eyelid before turning to face her allies. "Clearly we're too late to save Tizen Mill, but it's not too late to keep this from happening somewhere else again. We've searched the entire house, and the only spot left…" she pointed to a wrought-iron, spiral staircase, which looked like it led up another floor, "is the roof. This creature may be old and powerful, but I mean to end it. I know this isn't your fight, so I won't be upset if you decide to flee, but I need all the help I can get." Her eyes scanned the group and seeing no doubt, she ascended the stairs.

They emerged from the shadowy parapet onto the flat roof of the manor. Rain fell down on them in a steady sheet, hurting the visibility, but the sound of clapping rang through the air and they turned towards the source. A lone man stood on the edge of their roof, perfectly dry in spite of the weather, and he turned to face them.

Godfrey had an arrogant face, albeit a very handsome one. Rich, dark hair swirled around his head, but his eyes glowed red through the haze of rain. He wore the silk suit of an aristocrat, accessorised by several glimmering bronze pieces of armour, and a large, grey wolf pelt was draped on his right shoulder, offset by the black cape that hung down from the left. He ceased his clapping, raised his left hand and snapped his fingers, and a golden goblet appeared in the free hand.

"Bravo! I must say, in the three hundred years I've been roaming the earth, no one has ever come this close to stopping me. Watching you scurry about my home like frightened mice made for a good show." He threw his head back and laughed, the sound rich and intoxicating. The smooth features of his face made judging his age impossible, but he stood almost as tall as Valex. "I was willing to let you take your shot at me, completely fair, but you had to go and break my favourite toy!" He waggled a finger at Valex, as one would to a naughty child, and continued, "Poor, sweet Barnelby. Ever diligent in his duties, I actually neglected to turn him. His devotion was so strong, and his mind so pure, that he couldn't imagine I was anything other than a saint. I had actually planned to bring him to the next town...and now he's gone."

"Oh Valex... did you know?" Kaylessa's big eyes sought Valex's metallic ones, and he dropped his head in shame.

"Regardless," Godfrey interjected, "turnabout is indeed fair play. You took one of mine, so I shall take one of yours. The question is... which one?...Hm..."

Suddenly he had vanished, and they heard his voice ring out from behind them. "Yes, you'll do."

They whirled around to see what had happened, but by the time they turned, Godfrey was nowhere to be seen and neither was Shenarah. The sound of a crack broke through the night, and they turned to see Godfrey standing in his original position, holding the lifeless body of the elf by the neck. A grievous wound from her throat poured blood into the outstretched goblet. Once the goblet was full to the brim, he carelessly tossed the elf's body from the edge of the roof and took a large swallow of the blood. "Ahhh yes. It's been ages since I've had elf blood, and I do enjoy a drink before brisk exercise."

"You monster!!" Barakas roared, charging across the roof, the lean muscles already rippling and shifting. His transformation to panther completed in midair, and he launched himself at the vampire.

"Bad kitty!" Godfrey taunted, laughing. "What you need is some training!"

Barakas' claws lanced outward, but Godfrey dropped the empty goblet into the air, where it vanished. He caught the panther by the throat, and raised a clawed hand to the air to strike Barakas' exposed stomach. As he flexed the hand and his nails grew into long, ghastly claws, a sound rang out—*thwack*—and an arrow fired by Kaylessa lodged itself into the centre of his palm. Godfrey looked at it as one might look at a mosquito and casually tossed Barakas from the roof. Using his free hand, he ripped the arrow from his palm, which began to stitch shut at once. Flexing the hand experimentally, he turned to face the rest of them, arms outstretched. "Come then! Show me what you're worth!"

"To arms!" Alison drew her silvered blades and sprang across the roof, running low to the ground, and Vel followed suit. The two women wove between each other and took positions on either side of Godfrey, striking and dodging. Vel's blades seemed to be little more than a hindrance, but Godfrey snarled as Alison's silver touched his pristine flesh, and the scores stayed.

Johanne put the knuckleduster on again and knelt in prayer, golden light soaring across the expanse to coat her allies. Godfrey riposted Alison's strike and slashed at an opening in her guard, but his claws caught in the golden light and bounced back. He snarled and turned towards Valex and Johanne.

Valex was flipped frantically through his tome for a spell that could help his allies, and as he stopped to look at the combat, his gaze caught that of the vampire, who was staring into his soul. A warm sensation flooded his belly and he heard a voice in his head: *My servant, these miscreants look to do harm to your master! You must deal with them for me, kill the one with the golden hair.*

What? Valex's thoughts felt muddy. *Who would dare attack my great and noble master, Alistair Godfrey?* He turned to look at Johanne, whose eyes were clenched shut in concentration, and fury bubbled up inside his belly. With a growl, he threw himself at her and gripped her throat in two hands, knocking her to the ground.

As the light vanished around Alison and Vel, Godfrey's snarl melted back into a smirk. He parried Alison's thrust and yanked her into the air by the throat. Startled, Alison tossed her dagger into the air, and Vel deftly snatched it and buried it into Godfrey's back. He turned to her and roared in her face, his features becoming more and more animalistic before he lashed out with a savage kick to her midsection. She flew through the air and screamed as her arm was pierced by one of the roof's spikes. "Wait your turn, vermin!" Godfrey shouted, returning his attention to Alison. "I'll attend to you shortly!"

Having expended all her arrows to no avail, Kaylessa rushed forward. The situation was hopeless: she could see Valex and Johanne, tumbling around on the ground; Vel whimpering as she tried to extract her skewered arm; and Alison, suspended in the air with Godfrey looking up at her balefully. Kaylessa scoured her memory, knowing that in her studies Sariel had briefly emphasised the threat of the vampires. Their presence in the deep wood was known, but they rarely left the darkness of their dens. She knew that silvered weapons could pierce his flesh, which didn't help her now, and that destroying his coffin would sever his eternal life until he could find a new one…but there was something else…

Her mind suddenly grasped what she was looking for, and she rushed forward, her plan in place. Dropping her swords, she removed her precious shortbow from her back. With a pang of regret, she brought it down over her knee, snapping the yew arms into jagged stakes. As she sang a song under her breath, her presence began to fade. Now, she stalked forward towards her enemy as fast as she could without making a sound.

Godfrey brought Alison's throat to his mouth and nuzzled the soft flesh almost reverently. "Oh…I can smell the agony and despair in your blood. I will savour this feast and cask the rest of your friends to satiate me on my travels." His lips drew back to reveal his jagged fangs, but before he could plunge them into her throat, a pressure in his spine intensified into a bolt of ragged pain, and he dropped the woman with a gasp.

His silk shirt was tented with a wooden spike that had been driven through his back. Staggering around, he saw Kaylessa crouched behind him, another piece of the bow clutched in her fist. "That...that was for the town," she said, "for the poor woman you called your wife, and...for Shenarah and Barakas."

Godfrey let out a howl that pierced the night and fell to his knees, acrid maroon smoke spilling out of his clothes. "Impossible! I've lived for so long, to be bested by a mere child!"

"I am an elf, monster, and I too have lived long. Long enough to know evil when I see it, and to strike it down."

She turned her back as Godfrey's skin melted away, revealing a skeletal visage. That began to erode as well, until all that was left of the once-powerful creature was a pile of clothes.

The clouds finally broke and allowed the first rays of dawn to hit the sodden rooftop. Valex suddenly stopped throttling Johanne and had time to say, "Wait, what...?" before the young exorcist hit him across the side of his face hard enough to send him sprawling. Kaylessa went to Vel, and after counting to three, tore her arm free from the iron spike. Vel howled like an animal and as she tended to her wounds, she looked over the edge of the wall. On the stones below, Shenarah's body lay, twisted and lifeless, next to the charred husk of Barnelby. She scanned the large tree beside the entrance and was relieved to see the battered form of a green panther, snarled in the branches, but breathing.

Alison rose to her feet shakily and looked at her companions in sorrow. "Come," she called out in a hoarse voice, "The monster is dead, and we need to take care of our own."

The sun had risen into the sky by the time they had finished burying Shenarah and Barnelby. They looked solemnly at the two mounds of dirt, and Barakas walked forward and dropped a handful of soil onto Shenarah's resting place. "Sleep well, old friend, in the arms of the Earth Mother." No one knew what to say, so they let the silence carry, until a familiar voice called out from behind them: "Alison!"

They turned to see a hooded man in plate mail dismounting his horse. As he approached, Wravien pulled his hood back, concern plastered across his craggy features. Alison hesitated for a moment, then began to walk towards him with her head down and her fists clenched. They had just reached each other when Alison's hand rocked out, whip-quick, and struck Wravien across the face.

Vel, Valex, and Kaylessa all watched, open mouthed, but Wravien took the blow, and turned his face to the younger woman, who glared up at him for a moment before dissolving into tears. "Oh, you stupid, stupid man!" she cried out, throwing her arms around him. He baulked for a moment, but wrapped his own arms around her as she sobbed into his neck, "What have you done? What's happened to you?"

"There, there. I promise there will be time enough to explain everything, I'm just glad you are alright." He petted her hair, then turned to face Vel, Valex, and Kaylessa. "You have my gratitude, as well as my praise. Had I known an elder vampire had taken roost, I would have joined you post-haste. You've done me proud. Let us make camp, I think it's time to explain some things to you."

CHAPTER 12
EVERYTHING'S EVENTUAL

Day 1450 – Somulous Experiment: I understand now. I am unstoppable and have ascended to the power of a god. The voice continues to whisper even as I cut up the remains of our king, whom I've been able to make disappear both from his castle and the thoughts of the people. All they know now is that they are, and always have been, ruled by me and me alone. The voice should be happy, but it tells me that across the ocean there is more to be done. GRIMHOWL

They made camp in relative silence, the strangeness of doing so during the daytime not lost on them. Against expectations, Wravien was as active and diligent as the rest, even directing Barakas to use his powers to help the forest grow around them and obscure their site from the road. Once the camp had been set up, Wravien drew the strange, curved sword from his back and approached the waiting firepit. He spoke a quiet word in a foreign language, and a small blue flame crawled the length of the one-sided blade, before spitting off the end and combusting the stack of wood into a merrily crackling fire.

Anxious as they were to hear what Wravien had to say, their eyelids were drooping from the exertions of the previous night, and he commanded them all to get some rest before he went on. Alison took his suggestion with a cool gaze, which Wravien avoided meeting, and the rest of them hunkered down to sleep.

Valex woke to the sounds of crickets and only the fire to light the clearing. He rubbed sleep from his eyes and looked towards the fire, where Kaylessa and Vel sat with Wravien. No one else was around. He stretched, then joined them and said, "What happened to our new companions?"

"I've explained what needed to be explained and sent them on ahead. They have their own work to do, and I've decided that the council we need to keep must stay between us. Have a seat, Valex."

The dragonborn did as told, and all sets of eyes were upon Wravien, who paid them no mind and stared into the fire. After an uncomfortable amount of time, he finally broke the silence, and quietly said, "I'm not sure where to begin…Or even how much you'll believe. I've never been one for leadership, and I'm not sure how to persuade you that what I'm saying is the truth, but I hope my actions over the last year have proved that I can be trusted. Can I ask you to hear what I have to tell you, and trust that it's the truth?"

His eyes searched the group, and he opened his mouth to speak, but the words failed him. His gaze dropped to his wringing hands, but Kaylessa reached over and took one of them in her own, "Sir, you've done well by us, and we haven't been given cause to doubt you yet. I can't speak for them, but I promise to give you an open mind." Kaylessa said.

Valex nodded and Vel made a grunting noise that could have been assent.

Wravien composed himself, and spoke without raising his head. "Tell me, what do you know of Xerka?"

Vel and Kaylessa shared a confused glance, then snapped their surprised attention to Valex when he spoke up. "The island nation to the south, right? I know that there are rumours that the people who live there have…strange powers, but when the wall appeared around the island ten years ago, we lost contact and very little has been heard from them since." He looked bashfully at the women. "Callum had a few books about it."

"So far, so good, Valex. What most people don't know is that the wall isn't some man-made structure, at least not conventionally, but something from a nightmare that rose from the ocean. I saw it once, in my youth, a wall of alabaster white, covered in protruding spikes and skulls. A wall of bones, protected by a mist that hangs over the south seas. Even the bravest of the Tempest soldiers won't come within ten leagues of it, as it does something strange to people...Their fears come to life, and most who enter, never return."

"While I appreciate a good ghost story around the campfire, Wravien," Vel said dryly, "I fail to see how this country's issues affect us. Are we supposed to save the people there?"

"Oh, no, the island is already lost." He said this as if it had no bearing on their conversation. "But the man responsible for the corruption won't stop there. He plans to bring an army across the sea, laying waste to Meridia and all who live here, until not a living soul remains. I've seen it happen."

"What do you mean, 'you've seen it happen?' Spouting off about some foreign king conquering the land, are you some kind of fortune teller now?" Vel laughed, a harsh bark.

But Wravien only looked at her stonily. "Not a king... a lich. More of a conqueror, I suppose, and I know because I've lived it once before." He took a deep breath, letting his words hang for a moment. "Remember, all I ask is for you to keep an open mind. I know how this all sounds. Five years from now, the madman begins his siege, and it happens faster than anyone can respond to. I was conscripted by a mercenary group to help repel the army, but by then it was far too late. The rulers of Meridia had been corrupted, and the army he brought was made entirely of the undead. A handful of sellswords never stood a chance, and on a beach a half-day's ride from here, I died for the first time."

"You...What? What in the hells are you talking about?" Valex couldn't hide his disbelief. "What do you mean, died? How are you here then?"

Wravien laid the red sword across his lap and ran a hand down the hilt absentmindedly before responding. "That is a long story, and one I'd prefer to tell you in the safety of Ravencroft. The only thing you need to know right now is that I was given a chance to change the course of history we're on, and I need your help to do it."

"Assuming all of that is true…" Kaylessa mused, "how can the three of us stop something like that? Who is this lich?"

"I dare not speak his name, not out in the open like this. His powers allow him to extend his presence into the minds of others, and I haven't spent the last thirty years preparing to have it undone now."

"Thirty years?" Valex asked, incredulously. "You, what, were sent back in time thirty years?"

"Yes, and I almost wish I had been given ten more, but we'll have to make do. I came out to meet you three here because, very soon, one of his experiments will succeed and give him a lasting edge in the fight to come. If we can intercept it, I think you'll be one step closer to believing me, and we'll be one step closer to stopping him. What do you say, will you join me for one last job before I reveal the rest to you?"

"With a hook like that, how could we resist?" Vel smiled at him wryly. "I assume we'll still get paid, even if we're saving the world?"

"Of course, I would never dream of making Vel Valdove work for free. Just know that the stakes are very high." Wravien said.

They rested until dawn, and when they awoke, they found that the vast majority of the tear down had been completed, save their bedrolls by the still-burning fire.

Wravien called them over to their horses once they had finished securing their packs, and he began to draw a crude map in the dirt with a stick. "Right, I don't have all the details, but from what I can remember, today's job will take us to Blackcombe Mountain. A great red dragon, Blazescale, makes his home there, and for the last century he has maintained a good relationship with the village at the base of the mountain. He provided his protection in exchange for various sacrifices, mostly gold and silver, the odd virgin… but something has changed. Their usual sacrifices go unheeded, his brood takes up residence in the village, and Blazescale goes on a rampage."

"You have reason to believe this…lich is responsible for the change in the dragon?" Valex asked.

"All signs point to yes. After the destruction of Blackcombe, Blazescale vanished entirely until the day of the siege, and I saw him flying overhead during the final days. I have to warn you, this will be the first time I attempt to directly stop something that the lich has put in motion, so I don't know what the repercussions will be, only that we're running out of time."

"So…how do we do this then?" Vel asked, arms crossed. "We follow your lead?"

"Actually, I was thinking the opposite—I'll be your extra muscle on this job. It will provide me a good chance to see how you conduct yourselves, and I'd prefer word gets out that you saved the village, rather than me. It might buy us more time."

They rode south, and the journey was devoid of small talk. Even the normally chatty Valex was lost in thought, and they all kept casting glances at their battle-clad benefactor. They only had a vague idea of what Wravien was capable of, and the responsibility of issuing commands to him weighed heavily. After a few hours, they saw the peaks of the Blackcombe Range on the horizon, and as it grew to fill the sky, Vel called their party to a halt.

"We need to be smart about this. We have no idea what we're walking into, but if Wravien is right, then we're waltzing into the lair of a mythical beast. Valex and Vel, follow my lead when I engage the village chief, and Wravien, you can…uhh…" She trailed off, and Wravien smiled at her expectantly. "Vel, relax. I spent most of my life as a sword for hire, I take orders fairly well."

"Right. Then I want you to hang back and make sure we don't get surprised."

"Rear guard. Roger." He stepped off his horse as the others did the same, and he took up a spot at their flank. "Let's get to it."

They smelled the fire before they saw it. The path to the village wound through the craggy mountain pass, but as they got closer, they heard voices crying out, as well as aggressive-sounding reptilian noises.

"Shit, we might be too late. Valex, you and Kaylessa approach from the front. How are you at sneaking, boss?" Vel asked.

She looked at Wravien's heavy gear dubiously, but he tugged at a leather strap that held his blades across his back. "I can hold my own. You want to double around through the trees, I take it?"

"...You read my mind," Vel said, clearly annoyed at having her thunder stolen. Wravien laughed lightly, and then shrugged. "Sorry, I'm pretty used to this strategy. Lead the way."

Vel and Wravien slipped into a thicket of woods on the side of the road, while Valex and Kaylessa followed the winding path. They rounded a corner, and Kaylessa threw an arm out in front of her companion, a finger drawn across her lips. They peeked out from behind an outcropping, looking into what remained of the town square. Most of the buildings in their immediate sightline were ablaze, and a small group of humans of all ages were bound and gagged, surrounded by strange, reptilian creatures.

The creatures' size and skin made them look almost dragonborn, but their heads sported wild frills, they had no horns and had a crazed, feral look in their eyes. The square held maybe ten of them, most eyeing their captives hungrily, but a few stragglers were sifting through the rubble, or snapping their razor-sharp teeth at the floating embers. They didn't look particularly intelligent, but their armour and weaponry said they were not here to make friends. The blades of their axes were a strange, shiny stone, and most of them were covered in bizarre war paint.

One of the creatures, clearly the leader judging by the way his companions skirted him, let out a screeching cry, and the rest of the lizard folk swivelled their heads in his direction. It was a massive creature, the frill on its head encompassing its face like a lion's mane and it stepped towards one of the blindfolded men and kicked at him in disdain.

"We surrender! We'll do whatever you want, but we don't underst–" The blindfolded man's words were cut short as the lizard man drew the blade of his axe clean through his neck, severing his head. A claw flicked out and grabbed a hank of the dirty hair, and he raised the man's head over his head like a trophy, letting out another ear-splitting cry that his companions returned with a vigour.

Kaylessa drew her blades. "Valex, we've got to do something! They're defenceless!"

But Valex pointed across the square where Vel was waving her arms trying to get their attention. "Can you make out what she's saying?" he said, squinting across the clearing.

Kaylessa frowned, and shook her head.

"Oh, for heaven's sake." He drew his tome, uttered the command word, and the spectral blue owl appeared on his shoulder. "Just speak into the owl, it will relay what you've said back to me," he said to the bird, then he tossed it into the air behind them, where it pinwheeled and soared high over the square.

Kaylessa began to ask what he was doing, but Valex silenced her with a gesture. They followed the owl's progress to where Vel had hidden itself, and only had to wait a few more minutes before it returned.

Its beak opened, and Vel's husky voice spilled out as if recorded. "Valex, this is weird. I hate it. Ugh. Anyway, distract these guys. Wravien and I will sneak in from behind and try to thin the herd. Buy us as much time as you can." The message delivered, the owl cocked its head at its master, who dismissed it with a curt nod of his head. It vanished in a swirl of blue smoke.

"A distraction? What should we do?" Kaylessa looked over the wall of their makeshift cover, hands still gripping her sword's hilts.

Valex whispered, "I have an idea...It might work, but it might also end disastrously. When I give you the signal, come out swinging...or singing, whichever you think will work better."

She was about to ask what the signal was supposed to be when Valex burst from their hiding place, calling out in a cry similar to the one the leader of the lizard men had made.

There was a moment of stunned silence, and all heads present in the square turned to face Valex. The leader shoved past one of the smaller lizard men and approached him, head tilted, and spit out a string of slithery-sounding syllables.

Valex baulked slightly, then began to produce single barks in the alien language. The large lizard man looked more thunderstruck with each word Valex said, the frill on his neck standing stark upright.

Befuddled, Kaylessa watched the scene unfold, Valex looking more and more uncomfortable. The entire troop of lizard men had drawn nearer to him and were letting out snaps and growls as Valex stammered his way through the exchange. She noticed movement in her peripheral, and the lizard folk at the rear of the pack began to disappear in ones and twos. Her mouth dropped open as she saw one of their chests burst open from the force of the longsword thrust through it, while a gauntleted hand protruding from the alley cupped its mouth. She blinked, and the spot where the lizard man had stood was now vacant.

There was a sharp hissing noise, and Kaylessa returned her attention to Valex. He was backing away from the leader, who was advancing on him, thumping his chest. Valex's right hand was doing a strange, flapping motion at waist height. *That's weird,* she thought, *is that a nervous tic? Maybe he can't reach his spellbook?*

"Kaylessa! Little help!" Valex called out, breaking her concentration, and she saw him turn to run towards her. He stumbled on the rocky ground, just in time to narrowly avoid a horizontal swipe of the brute's weapon and continued to careen towards her.

Oh. The signal. She drew her blades and rushed forward in time to parry an overhead strike from the lizard man's axe. Her blades were crossed overhead, but even with her stance braced, her boots slid in the dirt from the force of the blow. She flicked her eyes left and right, anticipating followup strikes from his companions, but when nothing came, she thrust her swords forward with all her might, sending the axe skyward.

Valex sidestepped her, tome drawn, shouted a command word. A galeforce wind emanated from his palm and struck the lizardman in the chest, sending him flying off his feet. With his bulk cleared, they looked at the astonishing sight of an empty courtyard, save for the bound captives. A glint of steel caught Valex's eye, as Vel sprang from an alley and stepped in a smooth semicircle in front of the leader, who had just regained his footing. She dragged her dagger through his stomach, spilling his entrails onto the ground in front of them. With her free hand, Vel reached out and gave the hulking form a gentle push, and it toppled to the ground in a puff of arid dirt.

Vel wiped her face with the back of her hand, leaving a slightly luminous smear of blood on her cheek, and rested her hands on her knees as she caught her breath. By contrast, the much-older Wravien looked relaxed as he cleaned the blood off his sword on a swatch of fabric tied to the lizard man's waist.

"Okay, we must have taken out, what, half of them?" Vel panted, accepting a canteen of water from Kaylessa. "Should be smooth sailing from here, right?"

Wravien shook his head "No, if my experiences with dragon's lairs are any indication, the weakest of Blazescale's children would have been sent down to the village, and the rest will guard his horde."

"Did you say horde?" Vel spoke quietly.

Kaylessa looked towards the captives, who continued to sit in silence. ""We should free these people. Shall we send them to Ravencroft? There isn't much left for them here…"

"Horde, you say? As in a treasure horde?" Vel spoke louder this time, the glint of treasure unclaimed shining in her eyes.

"Yes, Vel. A treasure horde." Wravien gave her a pitying glance, then explained as one might to a child. "Red dragons are notoriously greedy, and value gold over all else. With how long the village has been offering tribute, I'd be surprised if there isn't a second mountain inside the first, made entirely of plundered goods. Good thinking Kaylessa, it can never hurt to have more people to support us."

"What are we standing around for then?" All signs of her previous exhaustion banished, Vel hurried towards the path that led up the mountain, a spring in her step.

"I swear, if she found out my organs were made of gold," Valex sighed, "she wouldn't hesitate to split me open and take me to market." He began to trot after Vel, and once Kaylessa and Wravien had issued instructions to the freed villagers, they followed behind.

The way up was treacherous and slow going, and even Vel had to slow her pace. "We need to conserve our energy," Wravien counseled them. "We may have to fight a dragon at the top of this climb, and god knows how many more of his children."

They passed numerous burned-out husks of homes built along the ridge and stuck to the shadows anytime something slithered nearby. The sun blazed gaily overhead in a cloudless blue sky, and the heat quickly became unbearable. Valex, Vel, and Kaylessa had all doffed their cloaks and stowed them away, and even Wravien was showing signs of fatigue, sweat beading down his brow and dripping onto his heavy plate.

"How is it this hot?" Valex complained, as he tied his cloak around his head. "Shouldn't it be getting colder as we climb?"

"It's a dragon's lair, Valex. Red dragons are fiery in nature, and the landscape will shift to accommodate that. The mountain itself is going to throw off heat as if it's on fire," Wravien grunted. He motioned for the group to duck behind a large boulder, as a pack of many-legged drakes scuttled across the road. After watching for a moment, he was about to motion them forward, when a shadow fell over them.

Valex sighed in relief. "Finally, the gods are on our side! I've been praying for a cloud for hours...wait..." His eyes scanned the horizon, which remained a deep blue, and crystal clear...Which meant...

"Down!" Wravien's shout was thunderous, and for the second time since they had met him, he drew the red blade he wore on his back. A single edge ran the length of the curved blade, and he gripped the hilt in both hands before shouting, "Hi-no-tori! Bakuhatsu!" The words were strange, but at their utterance, the blade erupted into crimson flames, doubling in length. Wravien slashed upward into the sky, and the path of his sword cleaved the giant fireball that had been hurtling towards them in two. The force of the stroke drove him to his knees, but his wide eyes were glued skyward, and Vel, Valex, and Kaylessa followed his gaze.

Hovering thirty feet above them was the largest creature any of them had ever seen, by far. It was the dragon, Blazescale. The stories of dragons had described them as slender, serpentlike creatures, but this one defied that definition. Huge, sinuous wings flapped as it hovered in place, sending sand and dirt blasting through the air, its chunky torso hanging below, its tail nearly dragging against the ground. The monster was as large as a castle, and its massive bulk continued to obscure the sun. Its great head was crowned with many gnarled, golden horns, and its cavernous mouth, lined with row after row of sharp, serrated teeth, was opening again. The dragon began to draw breath in and a small ball of fire appeared in its mouth that was growing larger by the second.

"Run into that house! I'll lead it away! I'll meet you at the cave at the top of the mountain!" Wravien cried out over the vacuum of the beast's inhale. They turned and ran blindly, all logic forgotten in the face of something so monstrous. Kaylessa had never been so scared in her life. She sprinted and stumbled in the loose stones, and then the force of the second fireball making contact with Wravien's sword threw her from her feet. She struck her head against a rock, scrambled for purchase, and cast a single, terrified look behind her. Blazescale had made landfall, and it raised a monstrous talon skyward to strike at Wravien, who looked very small. Kaylessa's terrified mind noted something strange, a small purple object protruding from a nasty wound on the dragon's left side. The wound looked very painful, and strange purple lines of light pulsed under the dragon's red scales, but Kaylessa's attention was broken by the sound of metal clashing.

Wravien had drawn his other sword and somehow managed to parry the dragon's swipe, the effort causing him to go sliding through the dirt, sending a cloud of it billowing all around him. As the dragon stomped after Wravien, Kaylessa forgot to be curious and remembered to be afraid for her life, dashing after her companions into the ruin of a mine shaft.

Inside, Valex was sitting on the floor gasping, while Vel pried a board off of the shuttered window, twisting left and right to witness what was going on outside. Kaylessa caught her breath, then placed a hand on Valex's shoulder.

"Are...are you okay?" she asked, but she stepped back when Valex's haunted eyes met hers. "No. I don't know if I'll ever be okay. Are you? Are either of you?" he said.

"It's...disconcerting to be sure." Vel spoke without facing them, a small tremor in her normally confident voice. "To face something that large. It defies logic."

"And one of those is my ancestor? How the hells is that supposed to work?! Gods, what's going to happen to Wravien—he's going to be eaten for sure!"

"Don't be so certain," Kaylessa said. "He's got that magic sword, and he was able to deflect all the blows I saw the dragon throw at him. The question is, what do we do now?"

"You heard the man." Vel turned, her face pale, "We meet him up top."

After waiting an inordinate amount of time, they cautiously made their way out of the mine and began to proceed up the path. Night was beginning to fall, the air was getting thinner, and blessedly, colder, but the mountain continued to radiate an ungodly heat. The packs of reptiles that had been scattered all over the mountain path had all but vanished, but the party's pace was still considerably slowed due to the caution they were exercising. They inched their way along, until they finally rounded a corner, crested the apex of the mountain, and saw the gaping maw of what had to be Blazescale's lair. The mouth of the great cave was at least fifty feet high, and an ominous red light spilled out into the twilight that engulfed them.

Vel pushed her fear aside and approached the cave's mouth on one side, while Valex and Kaylessa maintained their cover. She chanced a look inside, snapping her head back when she saw the pulsing eggs that lined the entryway, but not before she had seen the awe-inspiring sight of Blazescale's treasure horde. A mountain had been an apt description; coins of every colour made up the bulk of the pile, but even with just the quick glance she was able to take, she saw bejewelled chests, finely wrought pieces of armour, and even what looked like a gilded statue of some long-dead king. Somewhere, between her fear and her avarice, the cold part of her noticed the impression in the mound of treasure that marked it as Blazescale's resting place.

As she heard the sound of thunderous wings behind her crashing through the air, her heart plummeted and her instincts took over. Deftly sidestepping the eggs, she rushed towards the mountain of treasure, and began to dig and scrape at it, concealing herself within its confines.

Valex and Kaylessa heard the sound as well and dove into a nearby fissure that had formed from the heat. They trembled in the dull red glow, the unspoken question of the fate of Vel and Wravien hanging between them. As they watched, the titanic form of the dragon glided to a stop at the cave's mouth, blasting a cloud of acrid dirt up in the air from the force, then trundled inside. There were deep gouges in the beast's hide, some bearing the telltale scorch marks of Wravien's magic sword. The way it was walking spoke to a deep level of fatigue, and as they held their breath, they heard a loud thump and the clatter of coins cascading down.

After a while, Valex let out a soft laugh. Kaylessa looked at him wide eyed, but he cocked his head towards the cave entrance, and she realised what had made him laugh. In the silence they heard a deep whistling inhale, followed by a whuddery exhale. The dragon was asleep.

"Looks like running around with Wravien tuckered the big fellow out," Valex chuckled, but jumped when a voice behind them spoke.

"Aye, him and me both."

They whirled in their cozy hiding place to see an out-of-breath and soot-stained Wravien. His armour had several deep scores where the claws had almost penetrated, and most of the gleaming metal had been torched to an ashy grey. Part of his right eyebrow and beard had been burned away, but he looked otherwise unharmed. Looking about, puzzled, he queried, "Where's Vel?"

Their surprise forgotten, the realisation of their friend's fate struck them both at the same time, and they turned towards the cave entrance, fear written on their faces. "She's inside." Valex uttered breathlessly. "She slipped in just before the dragon showed up."

"Don't panic just yet, this might work in our favour." Wravien poked his head out of the fissure and surveyed the cave. "We need to figure out how the dragon is being controlled, and judging from the snores, Vel is out of any immediate danger and is in the best position to solve the mystery."

"Wravien, I think I might know what's causing it." Kaylessa spoke softly from his elbow, her voice cracking slightly. "When I was running away, I saw something strange had been stabbed into his side. The wound looked…ghastly."

"Hm. A cursed artifact maybe? If that's the case, removing it should limit the effects of the curse, but if we're wrong, we're going to have a seriously angry dragon on our hands. This is your op." He looked at Kaylessa and Valex seriously. "How should we proceed?"

Valex's face was tight with determination. "If someone is controlling him, I want to help. As a dragon who has been made a slave, I won't stand for it to happen in front of me."

Kaylessa nodded. "I'm of the same opinion. Regardless of the future, the beast must be in great pain, and I want to alleviate that if possible."

"I think you're both right." Wravien stood up and stretched. "Let's head to the cave opening and see if we can signal Vel. But we'll need to be prepared. The effects of such a curse likely won't wear off immediately, and even then, dragons don't take kindly to intruders in their lairs. Most importantly, if he summons his brood, we'll have to be careful not to kill any of them. Curse or not, killing a dragon's young in front of them is a one-way ticket to the afterlife."

Vel adjusted the chest she had placed on top of her hiding place in the pile of treasure and watched Blazescale tromp through the cave opening. It stopped briefly to sniff the eggs at the front of the lair and without warning, blew a gentle flame over them. Whatever was inside wriggled happily. Her field of vision was obscured, but she saw that the dragon was limping slightly, and she held her breath as it walked directly towards her.

Luckily, it appeared fatigue won out over caution, and Blazescale climbed the pile of gold above her. Being this close to it, she could feel the overwhelming heat pouring off its body, making the coins around her heat up considerably. Just what had her plan been? She was now trapped in something straight out of a nightmare, but as she considered her options, she noticed the change in the dragon's breathing. Shifting her body ever so slightly, she looked through a crack in the metal of the chest to see the form of the dragon. She winced as the motion caused a few coins to cascade down the pile, but was relieved to hear the dragon snort, and adjust slightly, before continuing to snore.

Well, that's better than being awake and furious, she thought, *but it doesn't change my situation.* She looked around the immediate area for anything that could be of use and saw movement at the cave's mouth. Kaylessa's small white face poked around the corner, scanning the room. Vel removed a dagger from a holster at her shoulder, and tilted the blade left and right, trying to catch a glimmer of the iridescent red light that shone through the room. A flicker of recognition on her friend's face told her she had been successful, and she watched carefully as Kaylessa tentatively stepped into full view and raised her arms above her head. She reached down and patted a spot on her ribs, before pointing at the dragon above her.

Vel twisted and squirmed, trying to make as little noise as possible, until she found what Kaylessa was trying to show her; it looked like the handle of a dagger, protruding from an oozing, infected wound on the dragon's ribs. The purple striations that led away from the cut pulsed slightly, as if alive. She chanced a look back and saw that all three of her companions now stood at the cave mouth. Steeling herself, she gripped the handle of the strange blade and immediately felt a crawling sensation in her mind. But she also felt the dragon begin to stir. Throwing caution to the wind, she twisted her body to plant both feet on either side of the entry wound and pulled the handle with all her might.

Pulling the blade felt like trying to yank a tree out of the ground, roots and all, and she saw several purple tendrils rip from the dragon's flesh with the blade as it slid free. She was acutely aware of the feeling of being watched, and then aghast to see a single, mad eyeball spinning around on the hilt of the dagger. Before she could process it, however, Blazescale let out an ear-splitting roar and rose to his feet, the force throwing her against the wall of the cave in a shower of coins.

The roar rang through the valley outside the cave, and two large red drakes emerged from holes in the mountain's face, soaring through the air towards the entrance. Wravien drew his swords and turned to face them, placing himself between them and the dragon. The roar seemed to affect the eggs as well, which began to pulse and flex grotesque, claw-like shapes pushing on the sinewy membrane. Kaylessa quickly pulled out her harp and begun to play a soft, soothing melody, which seemed to halt the struggling of whatever was contained within.

With a shake of his head, Valex ran through the entryway towards the mountain of treasure, where Blazescale continued to bellow, roaring into the air and releasing a plume of fire, making the cave feel like the inside of an oven. Facing the elder dragon, Valex felt something primal wake up inside him, and when he called out, it was in the same tongue the lizard folk had spoken.

"Great one!" His voice thundered out of him, and he understood the strange words he was saying. "Calm your ire! We are here to aid you! Something is trying to control you!"

Even before he finished, he believed it was futile. Blazescale's eyes were clouded in fury, but then, even as Valex watched, he saw the haze in them began to disperse. He just needed to buy a little time. Welling up all the mana he possessed, he cast his thoughts to dark, heavy clouds, and cried out a command word in the foreign tongue. Another power welled up inside him, something ancient and draconic, and the cave shook as tendrils of lightning broke through the cave's ceiling and bound the dragon, wrapping its legs and wings in jaw-like manacles. Valex cursed as he felt Blazescale struggling to break its bonds, but he heard a voice in his head, rumbling like thunder: *Admirable, little one. Though he is not of my brood, I shall help you break him. Seek out Leviathan when you are ready, I would look upon you with my own eyes.*

Valex felt the lightning surge through him, and he clenched his fist. The restraints on Blazescale doubled their tightness and brought the dragon crashing into its own mountain of treasure, with coins and artefacts flying around the room, as it was driven through the horde and into the stone floor of the cave.

"Mortal! You dare to lay magic upon the mighty Blazescale?! You shall rue the day—Wait, where am I?" The voice shook the cavern, and somehow Valex was still able to understand it.

"My lord," Valex still tingled from the energy that coursed through him, his voice vibrating. "You have been corrupted and in your madness, attacked your followers! I was forced to contain you."

"Release me, whelp, or face my wrath!"

Through the fury, Valex could tell that whatever hold had been placed on the dragon had dissipated, but he couldn't release the bonds until he knew his companions were safe. "I implore you, great elder, call off your brood, so we may speak!"

Blazescale uttered a piercing roar. The drakes outside abandoned their assault on Wravien, and the eggs in the chamber ceased their twitching. It was not a moment too soon, because Valex felt whatever power he had tapped into begin to ebb from him, and he released his spell.

Blazescale flexed his wings in the air and rose to his feet, glowering down at Valex.

Wravien approached, undoing the clasp that held his sword on his back, and he knelt before the dragon, placing the blade across his knee. "With respect, we have come to free you from a terrible fate, my lord. Forces beyond our ken sought to incite war and had succeeded in turning you against your followers."

Blazescale growled but touched the spiked tip of his wing to the wound on his side, grimacing slightly. "I see. I imagine you wish for me to spare your lives for such assistance?"

Valex dropped to one knee beside Wravien, and followed suit with his reverential tone. ""Only if it pleases you, great one. But if not for my friend Vel, the control on you could have become permanent." Valex looked around to find her and gasped when he saw her standing at the side of the room, holding the wicked-looking dagger out in front of her. An eyeball on the dagger bore into him, and it's purple tendrils whipped around the air. Vel's vacant stare said something was wrong, but before they could attend to her, a horrible voice filled their heads, battering their thoughts aside like the teeth of a monster.

Well, well, well. My patron told me that the phoenix would find champions to oppose me, and here you are. Little worms, how did you escape my gaze for this long? The invasive feeling of the voice in their mind was very similar to being contacted by Valex's cursed book, but something about this felt even more ominous. The tentacles attached to the blade now found purchase on the side of Vel's neck, and with a squelching sound, broke the skin, and began to pulse. *I see...Ravencroft, is it? You seek to build a resistance to something that hasn't yet happened? Curious. You do not worry me, sellsword, but you've disrupted my experiment, and that won't stand.*

Wravien had paled when the voice began to speak but seemed to have regained himself. Throwing the scabbard of his sword to the side, he dashed across the room, shouting the words that caused the blade to erupt into flames again.

Perhaps a test—once I've located your...

The voice was cut short as Wravien plunged the tip of his sword into the bulging eyeball, puncturing it. The dagger's blade shattered like glass, and Wravien reached out a hand to grasp the writhing tentacles, pulling them from Vel's neck with a wet, ripping sound. Vel's eyes fluttered, and she collapsed into Wravien's outstretched arms.

Blazescale spoke to Valex, who was watching the events unfold in disbelief. "You face a powerful adversary, small one. To think there is something out there that could sway my will. You have done me a great service, child, and I would be remiss not to repay such loyalty. Something ails your spirit, and I shall grant you release."

The dragon breathed in and exhaled a soft white flame that enveloped Valex. He jumped, expecting to be burnt, but the flame washed over and through him, making him feel lighter than he had in months. Once again, he dropped to one knee, and faced the dragon reverently.

"And to your companion, I shall bestow this." The dragon's talon deftly plucked a shining amulet from the pile of gold. A masterfully-cut ruby shone between two outstretched golden wings, bound by a finely wrought chain. "Call my name, and I shall bestow a small piece of my power upon you. Be wary though, a dragon's flame is not easily mastered."

"Valex!" Kaylessa called from where she and Wravien were trying to rouse the unconscious Vel. "We need your help!"

Blazescale settled onto his haunches and flicked his head dismissively, and Valex scuttled over to his companions. Vel didn't look much worse for wear, but Wravien's face held a look Valex had never seen there before: panic. He was shaking Vel's unconscious body, his sword laying discarded at his side. Valex knelt beside him and removed a stick of incense from his bag, breaking it under Vel's nose. The sharp smell of pine filled the cave, and her eyes snapped open. She rolled to the side instinctively and then staggered to her feet.

"Vel, I need to know exactly what you saw or heard while you held the blade." Wravien's tone was gentle, but the undercurrent of urgency cut through.

"It was awful. It felt like my brain was covered in spiders, working their way into my thoughts." She shivered from the memory.

But Wravien was not to be deterred. "He said Ravencroft. Did he pull the location? Does he know where it is?!" Wravien grabbed the front of Vel's cloak, but she shook him off with a reproachful glance.

"I don't know."

"We need to go. Now." Wravien looked towards the resting dragon, who was watching them through one cracked eyelid. "Will you allow us to leave? We need to meet our enemy before he gains an advantage."

"I will allow it, provided the possessed one returns the treasures she has stolen." Blazescale didn't move, but Vel heard the malice in his tone, and emptied her pockets of the hastily stashed coins.

"Come, I'll explain the rest on the way," said Wravien. "We need to hurry. If Arcterus reaches Ravencroft before we do, all is lost."

CHAPTER 13
THE BEGINNING OF THE END

Day ??? — Somulous Experiment: I've encountered something strange in my experiments. I had intended to see if, using a conductor, my powers could influence something primal and ancient: an elder dragon. Everything was going as the voice said it would, until I felt a snap in my own mind and was suddenly flooded with the thoughts of a young woman. She resisted, of course, but after I subjected her, I was flooded with new information—a man...a town... and the concept of resistance? The arrogance is deplorable, but it provides a unique opportunity to attempt another method of corruption. I will enjoy this. GRIMHOWL

As soon as they were confident that Blazescale wasn't going to attack them the moment their backs were turned, Wravien was off like a shot, even in his bulky plate mail. Vel, Valex, and Kaylessa had to struggle to match his breakneck descent down the mountain. Every so often he would get too far ahead and stop, but his impatience was written in his posture.

"Please," he called back to them, "we need to make haste. The fate of the world depends on it."

Vel and Kaylessa's hair was plastered to their scalps with sweat, and Valex's laboured breathing sounded more like a dog's than a person's. "Wravien, I don't know what you're expecting, but having us die of heatstroke on this godforsaken mountain won't make the world any safer," Vel snarled, spitting the words between ragged breaths. "We need to rest...or at least walk."

A shadow fell over Wravien's features, almost causing Vel to step back, but he sighed, slowed to a trot, and then came to a stop. Valex plopped down onto the ground immediately and began rummaging in his pack for his nearly empty canteen.

Kaylessa approached Wravien, wiping a sweat-soaked lock of hair from her forehead. "I know you're anxious, but we're going to get there when we get there. Maybe now is the time to explain the rest of this mess."

Wravien looked into the sky. "Yes... Yes, you're right. Gather round."

Valex pivoted from his position on the ground to face him, and Vel sat on a nearby rock with her arms crossed. Kaylessa sat down beside her and looked at Wravien expectantly.

"So I told you about a madman from Xerka..." he began.

Valex interrupted. "This...Arcterus, right? I thought we couldn't say his name."

"It's too late for that now." Wravien had winced at the mention of the lich's name, but pressed on. "I don't even know if that's what he's calling himself yet, but in my time his name was Arcterus Grimhowl. Normally, a rogue lich would be manageable. Difficult, but no great threat. Arcterus, however, wielded power unlike anything anyone had ever seen. When his army walked out of the ocean, it must have numbered in the tens of thousands. All trained soldiers, all undead, and all perfectly in his thrall." He grimaced and paused for a moment before continuing, "Do you know why people lose wars? Fear. You face overwhelming odds, and suddenly you know you may not see your family again. Break an army's morale, and the day is yours. This army, however, had no such weakness. For every ghoul I cut down, two more took its place, unphased."

"So, if you had all this time in the past, why didn't you just go kill him before he amassed an army?" Vel asked nonchalantly.

Velax shot her an impressed glance. He hadn't thought of that.

"Believe me, I tried. She said it wouldn't work, but I still charted a crew and tried to sail to Xerka. We had a crew of forty-five soldiers, and forty-four men died that day." He looked pained at the memory, but Kaylessa had noticed something peculiar.

"She? Who said it wouldn't work?"

Wravien studied his battered knuckles and then looked up at them with wide, pleading eyes. "This is the part of my tale that's the most unbelievable, but once I tell you this, you'll know damn near everything I know. If you choose to walk away, I won't blame you…though it will mean our eventual demise."

Valex frowned at his benefactor. "We've come this far, haven't we? You were right before; seeing *is* believing, at least as far as this Arcterus is concerned. I have to say, though, I think it's high time you gave us a little more credit. If we haven't run from you screaming by now, it's safe to say you can count on us."

Wravien smiled and shook his head. "Of course… you are right, Valex. I haven't trusted anyone in a very, very long time, and after thirty years of caution it's a hard habit to break. But, if you're going to believe me, I have to start trusting you. Those many years ago, when I stood on that beach, watching my comrades get torn asunder, I felt something in me break. I walked into that wall of cold, dead flesh, ready to meet my maker. What came as a true surprise, however, was when I actually did.

"I felt intense pain, then cold, then nothing at all. I opened my eyes and I was floating in a void of black space, completely alone. My first thought was of disappointment—that this was all the afterlife held, but then I heard a voice. I heard her." Wravien stroked his beard and for a moment, in witnessing his wonder, they saw the man he might have been. "The voice asked me if I wanted another chance. I was furious…and dead, so of course I said yes. She asked what I would give up, and I said, 'Everything.' Then she revealed herself to me. It's hard to describe, but it was like a great bird, only much bigger. A thousand times larger than Blazescale, with wings that burned with cool, green flames, and eyes that knew only love and compassion. I faced the God of Life, Phoenix."

He paused, as if waiting for one of them to suggest, perhaps, that he needed an exorcism. When no one voiced dissent, he continued. "She told me many things. It's hard to remember it all; it was thirty years ago, but there were four things that I'll never forget. First: Arcterus' power was not his own; it was given to him by her elder brother, the God of Darkness, Terminus. Second: The purpose of my mission was to find four champions: a slave, an orphan, a sage, and a wanderer. Third: These champions would be the key to finding champions for her brothers and sisters, the other gods, and we would need their power to overcome Terminus, the strongest of them all."

"And fourth?" Kaylessa asked softly.

He spat the words out, bitterness in every syllable. "That if I chose this path I could never live a normal life, and I could never be the one to strike the final blow. Truthfully, this world never held much that I deemed worth saving. But Arcterus stole not only my life, but the lives of the few people I held dear, and I need to see him pay."

He let his declaration hang in the air, then seemed to remember himself and looked at his companions. "Well, there you have it. When I awoke, my wounds were gone, and I was lying on the same beach I'd died on, but it was deserted and calm. The only thing I had on me that said I hadn't imagined the whole thing were these blank tarot cards," He reached into his pouch and pulled out four cards. The first three were emblazoned with images that eerily depicted Kaylessa, Valex, and Vel, and the fourth was blank. "The cards became clear once I'd made contact with each of you. I don't have all the details, but I'm sure you can piece together the same things I did. You three are the champions, and the people you've recruited to join us in Ravencroft fulfil the third term of our contract, I hope. Does anyone want to walk away?"

Valex spoke as if Wravien hadn't posed the last question. He spun the blank card towards him and tapped the inscription at the bottom. "You said four champions, but there are only three of us. Who is the wanderer?"

"...I don't know. I've been searching for them this entire time, but to no avail. Phoenix hasn't spoken to me since that day, so I just have to trust that we'll find them when the time is right."

"Well, I don't know about you two," Valex addressed Vel and Kaylessa, "but I've seen and felt things since we've begun this journey that could only be described as divine intervention."

"Yes…and everything Wravien has told us has been true thus far—I see no reason for him to start lying now," Kaylessa said.

"I joined this merry little band to make sure I could provide for my brother," Vel said softly, "and I'll be damned if I let some crazy person across the world undo all my hard work. I assume we'll…"

"Yes Vel, you'll still get paid," Wravien interjected, smiling slightly.

"Well then, there you have it. We're with you, boss, till the bitter end. What now?" Valex asked.

"We get back to Ravencroft, and we stop whatever Arcterus has planned. I've got some ideas for after that, but those can wait." Wravien stood and patted dust off his greaves. "Looks like the sun has gone down some. If we hurry, we can make it back to town by nightfall."

He turned as they rose, then spoke with his back to them. "You know, that's the first time I've told anyone that. I'm glad it was you three."

And before they could respond, he jogged away down the road.

Once they'd retrieved their mounts, they rode hard and fast, their horses kicking up a veritable sandstorm on the dirt road. As they followed the setting sun, Vel, Valex, and Kaylessa thought about what Wravien had told them. Valex was curious, Kaylessa felt empowered, and Vel was indifferent, but they all had a similar thought coursing through their minds: *Why me?*

About an hour's ride from Ravencroft Wravien called a halt, standing in his stirrups and shielding his eyes as he looked out at the southern sea.

In the distance, Kaylessa made out noxious green storm clouds gathering on the horizon.

"Ride, like your lives depend on it." Wravien spurred his horse, which whinnied in protest after the already arduous ride, and Vel, Valex and Kaylessa followed.

They could just see the signpost for Ravencroft when they heard a cold, dead voice booming all around them. Kaylessa cried out in surprise, and Valex clapped his hands to his ears.

"Ah…There you are. Vermin always run back to their holes, even when they know it's hopeless. Your petty resistance doesn't concern me, but this is a good excuse for a test of my powers. Enjoy what's left of your lives, little fleas." The disembodied voice let out a mad cackle, then cut off as suddenly as it had begun.

Wravien rounded the corner into the town square, where the villagers were gathered in a mob in front of The Kraken. As soon as they saw him, though, they milled towards him, spouting questions.

"Oy, what's this about vermin?" Kornid asked in his Dwarven brogue.

"Some kind of test?!" Quebys called out.

"KHAN XARLUG IS NO FLEA!!" Khan roared.

Wravien tried to lead them towards the doors of the bar, but the crowd stopped and a lull fell over them as they all began to hear a distant, whistling noise.

"Say, what is that?" Valex asked, pointing to the sky.

Kaylessa followed his finger and her stomach plunged. "Everyone! Duck for cover!"

There was an ear-wrenching crash, and the fountain in the centre of the town square exploded. The force of the blast sent the townsfolk flying left and right, and chunks of stone rained down upon the square.

Her vision swimming and ears ringing, Vel shakily got to her feet and looked towards the small crater where the fountain had stood.

A humongous great-sword had fallen from the sky and embedded itself in the soil of the square. It was easily several times larger than any sword she had ever seen, and its jagged black edge pulsed with a sinister energy. Her eyes widened as she saw the monstrosity that was clutching the handle of the blade, a great mass of bone and flesh with glowing green eyes. It let out a dissonant roar, and the ground shook as rotting fists ripped and tore their way out of the earth, and dozens of shambling monstrosities took form in the square.

The chaos was absolute—voices cried out all over the courtyard, mothers tried to herd their blood-stained children together, and a wave of panic swept through those left standing.

Vel jumped up onto a nearby cart and cried out in a piercing shout, "Everyone, stay calm! We're not about to let something happen to our home! Those of you who cannot fight, seek cover! Those of you who can, to arms! For Ravencroft!" She thrust her rapier into the sky at the last decleration, and the spell was broken—a hearty cheer went up and the town sprang into action.

Vel jumped down from the crate to face Valex, Kaylessa, and Wravien, who were all looking at her admiringly.

"I couldn't have said it better myself. I'll handle the big one." Wravien pointed at the hulking undead, which had released its grip on the sword's handle and was shambling towards the front of The Kraken. "You three need to destroy the sword. If our previous encounter with one of his blades is any indication, the curse is emanating from there."

He turned towards the undead, drawing his twin blades. "Hey! You—the bag of bones! If you're looking for a fight, you've got one right here!"

The giant turned at the call, let out a roar, and rushed to meet him.

All around them, their friends faced foes of various levels of decomposition. Kornid had drawn his great-sword and was channelling lightning into the blade as Johanne waded into a crowd of animated skeletons, her knuckles glowing with holy radiance. Khan had a battle axe in each hand and was cleaving through wave after wave of zombies, a childlike look of delight on his face. Alison and Fingers herded injured villagers into the barracks, while Quebys rode atop the back of Barakas in his panther form. She cackled merrily and threw fireballs all around, while his powerful claws tore into the walking dead.

"We've got a job to do!" Valex shouted to Vel and Kaylessa over the din of the melee. "Any ideas?"

Vel studied the blade intently. There was another mad, pulsing eyeball in the centre of the cross guard, but it was protected by some kind of red jewel that covered it. Clearly Arcterus had learned something in their previous encounter. "Right. First things first, we need to get it out of the ground or we're going to be overrun by these things. Second, if we can do something about whatever is protecting the eye, I can puncture it and this will all be over."

"I'll get it out." Kaylessa drew out her harp and shot a brief glance at Barakas before gritting her teeth and stepping forward, her eyes closed.

"I think I can clear the way for you," Valex said, conjuring his mana into an open palm, where a small ball of ice appeared. "You'll have to trust me."

Kaylessa reached out with her senses, found the spirit of the great tree, and beseeched it for guidance. She started to sing an ancient song in Elvish, and gnarled roots burst from the ground, wrapping around the blade of the great-sword and slowly inching it from the soil. The sword pulsed a deep purple. Its resistance pushed against her and Kaylessa nearly faltered, but then she doubled the tempo of her song and the sword began to rise out of the earth again.

Valex pointed his palm towards the blade, consulted his tome and called out a command word, and a beam of frost shot across the courtyard, connecting with the blade where ice crystals began to form. He looked at Vel, who nodded and dashed towards the sword, nimbly sidestepping the debris that littered the ground. She reached the edge of the crater and jumped into the air—but the blade was too far away.

Valex called another command word and threw two concentrated discs of magical energy towards his companion. The discs floated in midair and she landed on the first one, bounced up onto the second, and then leapt into the air with her rapier drawn. She held it in both hands, blade pointed down, and Valex dropped the spells he was casting. He pooled his remaining energy and forced all his attention to the blade of Vel's sword.

A bolt of bright-blue lightning arced from his outstretched hand and connected with the blade, wreathing it in crackling electricity. The tip made contact with the layer of ice and as Valex clenched his fist, the ice shattered, smashing the layer of red crystal along with it. The rapier's blade punched smoothly through the bulbous eye, a horrible cry rang out in the air, and the handle of the giant sword exploded. A massive shockwave knocked Vel from the air and swept Valex and Kaylessa off their feet.

"Impressive." The cold voice boomed through the still air. "Perhaps I underestimated you. Still, I learn from my failures, and you won't be so lucky next time."

The voice sounded just as arrogant as before, but Valex thought he heard pain behind the hubris. *Good,* he thought savagely, *I hope that hurt.*

Bodies littered the square, some human, but mostly undead. Valex rose to his feet in time to see Wravien dismember the enormous corpse. Its arms fell to the ground with a wet plop. The sellsword let out a primal howl, crossed his blades, and severed the creature's ruined skull from its torso. The body slid to the ground, and Wravien smiled as he wiped blood from a wound on his scalp. "I don't believe it…We won. Maybe we can change things after all."

As the sun rose, they tended to their dead. The corpses summoned by Arcterus dissolved into the earth the moment the sun's rays touched them, but there were more than enough bodies of their fellow townsfolk to keep the villagers occupied. They had just about finished, when a very solemn Tim, his head wrapped in a blood-soaked bandage, bid them to come to The Kraken, where Wravien was seated alone at the large table at the back of the room.

"Valex. Vel. Kaylessa. I can't believe I'm saying this, but we did it. Seeing the three of you work together, I'm confident you are the champions I was sent to find. The world will one day be in your debt."

"Hey, boss, it's the job right? I'm just glad we were able to save as many as we did." Valex was smiling, but Wravien shook his head.

"I may have been in charge when we started this, but you no longer work for me. Starting today, we're comrades. We may have won a battle, but the war is just beginning. There will be much to do in the coming months, but I'd say today, we've earned this." Wravien gestured to four mugs of ale on the table. He raised his glass and said, "To you, to us. To Ravencroft." They echoed his toast and downed their ales.

Valex had never tasted something so sweet.

THE WANDERER

EPILOGUE

———

The well built woman with the tangle of red hair pushed back the flap of her yurt and winced as the sun reflected off the icy tundra into her eyes. She took a few steps out into the centre of camp, relishing the way her footsteps crunching in the snow broke the silence of the morning.

The stillness couldn't last forever; she knew that soon enough, the rest of her tribe would be awake and pestering about what they should do next. She sighed, running her hand down the thick braid of red hair that hung down to her waist, and firmed her resolve. They couldn't go back home, not anymore, and her father had been gone for two weeks too long. He was the advisor to the chief, and the tribe's decision making process had come to a standstill, which they couldn't maintain much longer. Their enemies were coming, and they couldn't be held off forever. . She was the best fighter her tribe had and the most likely to survive the search for him. Today was the day; she had to leave her tribe and find him.

Something soaring through the sky caught her attention. It was too late in the morning for an owl, and the bird certainly did not bear the telltale colouring of the eagles that frequented the area. As it flew through the sky towards her, she cocked her head, puzzled, and said, "What is a raven doing this far north?"

ACKNOWLEDGEMENTS

———

What an undertaking! Before settling down to write "Path of the Raven," I'd never done any creative writing outside of high school, but I'm glad I took the plunge at the request of friends and family. I was very lucky to meet a friend in Vancouver, Sunny, who introduced me to Dungeons and Dragons. I remember telling him, "Look, I'm a nerd, but THAT is some real nerd stuff," But I'd just gone through a bad break up, and thought, *what the hell, why not?* One session later, I was enraptured, and when I moved back to Edmonton, I knew I had to take a run at writing my own story.

This is the story that grew out of that thought, and I have to give credit to a lot of people for letting it get as far along as it has. First and foremost, to my Dad, Mom, and my brother, Tyler, I would never have gotten from manuscript to publishing if it wasn't for your faith in me, and my idea. That same brother, as well as my sisters, Kayla, Deanna, and (now) Dakota, you guys propelled me through the story writing, and helped to craft the delightful characters that are Vel, Valex, Kaylessa and our unnamed Wanderer, and I hope I've done them justice.

I need to thank all the family members and friends who read through my chapters, telling me that the story was good enough to keep going. I also need to thank my friend Luis, who let me stay with him and his girlfriend for 6 weeks in Mexico while I wrote this draft, as well as my friends Matt and Cecily, whose D&D store The Clumsy Dragon was a safe haven for me to continue to craft the world. Matt was the mastermind behind helping me morph my original map of Meridia (made in microsoft paint) to the beautiful work you'll find in this book.

Lastly, I want to thank you, whoever you are, for taking a chance. Picking up a book, looking at the cover and reading the back, is always a gamble, but If you enjoyed the story held within these pages, then the gamble paid off and there will be more to this tale, a story that will complete the tale of Wravien and his band of misfits, and I hope you'll come along for the ride.

ABOUT THE AUTHOR

Devon Manning is a Dungeons and Dragons enthusiast who enjoys creating his own campaigns and sharing them with friends and family. He is also a singer-songwriter with his own solo act called Lionhearted, which showcases songs about mental health. When he's not writing or playing music, Devon enjoys practicing archery, boxing, scuba diving, painting, and playing video games. He lives in Edmonton, Alberta.

9 781039 147041